JILL DOBSON

The Inheritors

Book 1 of The Survivor Covenant

Press release issued by the Western Space Alliance (Asia–Pacific Division) and the SRAE Corporation, 17 April 2050

RESTRICTED (Level X+)

Unmodified original document

Archives reference: WSA/SRAE-34956949-17042050

The NovaGaia Biodome Project, incorporating a prototype lunar base and Self-Regenerating Artificial Environment (SRAE) technologies, has entered the final testing phase. The project leader, Nobel laureate bio-engineer and visionary Professor Amelia Liu-Martinez, says the Biodome 'will be humanity's stepping-stone into space and its salvation'.

The perfection of the SRAE system and its potential adaptation to a multitude of hostile extra-terrestrial terrains will mark the beginning of human settlement of the cosmos, as the Earth's environment continues its projected decline.

The Biodome is the first attempt to establish an off-world base since the failed SkyCity project, the brainchild of trillionaire

Marius Chang.

The maximum population capacity of the Biodome is 60,000. If that number were exceeded, the life-support system would be severely strained and eventually collapse. The optimum is 45,000. The population will be strictly monitored and measures taken to keep it stable.

The semi-transparent geodesic Biodome, enabled by recent breakthroughs in thermoplastics and zero-gravity engineering, allows for a self-contained habitable environment on the otherwise uninhabitable lunar surface. The atmosphere, temperature and moisture levels will be regulated by an AI system developed in partnership with the housing, construction and agribusiness conglomerate DOMUS. Food will be produced hydroponically, utilising methods of water-minimal non-soil bio-regeneration successfully deployed in regions with endemic food shortages caused by the degradation of arable land, perma-drought and/or chaotic weather patterns. Energy will be provided by solar and nuclear means. All wastes—organic and nonorganic—will be recycled to 99% efficiency. The attainment of the long-elusive 99% rate was announced by Professor Liu-Martinez with great fanfare last year.

The Biodome, developed under a public–private partnership, will operate under the joint jurisdiction of the Western Space Alliance and the SRAE Corporation. It will be linked to Earth via shuttle connections from bases in Australia, the Free State of California (FSC) and Scotland. The Biodome is fully self-sufficient and can exist independently from Earth. While this situation is not envisaged in the foreseeable future, all personnel will be indoctrinated in the appropriate isolation protocols.

Setbacks in the developmental phase almost ended the project, but several key technological breakthroughs, including the achievement of 99% renewability, drew fresh interest from investors.

The current location of the Biodome prototype is highly classified, given the ongoing controversy around the project from environmental extremists and terrorist elements.

The successful completion of the NovaGaia Biodome Project will mark the beginning of the most significant phase in human history since the development of agriculture and the written word. As Professor Liu-Martinez stated, in a speech to the Singapore Human Futures forum last year, 'Our species has outgrown planet Earth. The Earth is our mother, but we all have to leave home sometime. The universe is our inheritance. By reaching out to claim it, we open up the way for a new and glorious future.'

Post-Event Settlement of the Dome

Executive Summary

RESTRICTED (Level X+)

The exact nature and final trigger of the Event is complex. The Second (Multipolar) Cold War that began in the 2020s–2030s led to a proliferation of nuclear and post-nuclear weapons systems unimagined in the years of disarmament, along with the rapid development of cold fusion nuclear energy technology following the geopolitical disruption of remaining fossil fuel supplies and several severe winters in which millions died.

In the chaos of the Aftermath, it was not possible to ascertain the sequence of events. What we do know is that at approximately 11.24 am on 26 September 2052, nuclear salvos from the twenty-five known nuclear-weapons nations and other sources (unofficial nuclear nations, terrorist organisations) eliminated major cities, while space-based weapons systems took out communications satellites. No warning was provided to the public. While the total megatonnage is a matter of conjecture, it is assumed that the barrage did not reach saturation levels. The total extent of damage is unknown. The total number of deaths and casualties is unknown but estimated to exceed six billion.

While accidental triggering was not impossible, responsibility is presumed to lie with eco-terrorists acting with the support of rogue states and techno-anarchists with the capacity to hack and override military systems. Various movements and regimes in the Global South, as well as eco-terrorist elements in the North, regarded survival strategies such as the Dome Project as a sign that wealthy nations had given up on the Earth and were preparing to evacuate a selected minority of their own citizens, leaving the bulk of humanity to die along with the planet.

The anger and unrest generated by this unwarranted belief had led to increasing violence, unrest and extreme actions in the years before the Event, forcing national authorities and international security bodies to take correspondingly strong responses.

In the immediate aftermath of the Event, nuclear winter effect briefly halted global warming, which led to unfounded speculation that certain elites had engineered the Event. Such speculation led, in certain parts of the world, to the overthrow of what governing structures remained and their replacement with a variety of extremist regimes or factions, although knowledge of this was very scant.

Some scientists warned that nuclear winter would soon be followed by nuclear summer. This would lead to renewed and accelerated global warming, destroying what life had survived the Event and the nuclear winter.

While scientists had very limited capacity to observe and measure the state of the Earth in the years following the Event, a consensus emerged that it was damaged beyond any hope of renewal and was rapidly becoming uninhabitable. In many key food-producing regions, the fertile topsoil had been burned or eroded away, leaving a barren desert landscape. Many areas and populations were subject to ongoing high levels of radiation that created endemic health problems and fatalities, along with critical shortages of food and water.

Very few people knew the location of the Dome. From the early days of the Aftermath, those who did know attempted to reach it for sanctuary, bringing with them other selected survivors. Many perished during the Exodus, a journey of thousands of kilometres across terrain that had been hostile even before the Event.

In order for a community to survive within the Dome, strict measures were necessary. If the Dome became overcrowded, its regenerative systems would fail, so only a limited number of people could be admitted. Not all those who came to the Dome were willing to submit to this level of governance, and difficult decisions had to be made for the greater good.

By winter 2055, the Dome was declared at capacity by the Survival Committee and the decision was made to seal up the entrance. It has remained sealed ever since.

In the exigent circumstances forced upon us by catastrophic climate collapse and nuclear disaster, collectively known as the Event, it is necessary, in the interests of all survivors, to exercise a complete and stringent control.

—Article One, Part One, 'On the Establishment of Post-Event Governance'
The Biodome Survivor Covenant
July 2055

One

The party was in full swing when Claudia and Ally arrived. Voices and laughter filtered into the gloomy fifth-floor hallway of G-Block, Building 4. At this time in the twenty-four-hour cycle, DOMUS turned the lighting low to save energy and mimic the old day–night pattern, although people were awake and productive at all hours.

Martin opened the door of res unit 38. A tall, athletic girl with very short hair loomed at his shoulder. The low beat of party music from the Senior Youth League channel was playing in the background.

'Are we late?' said Ally, who hated to miss out.

'Everyone else is already here,' said Martin.

'Arnie's nuked already,' Juanita, the tall girl, added. 'He's had four cannies in the last half-hour.'

'That's not much, for him,' said Claudia.

'Pierce brought some hardbrew from the Barracks,' said Martin. 'You'd think the Mentargh want junior citizens to get wasted. Come and get some before Arnie drinks the rest of it.'

They followed him into the kitchenette. It was exactly the same as the kitchenette in Claudia's res unit, the kind assigned to two-person family units, although Martin's mother hadn't lived there for a while and he was on his own.

The recycling bins were already overflowing with empty drink canisters. Several were rolling about on the floor. Martin kicked one out of the way, then changed his mind and picked it up.

'I'll have to requisition some drone-labour to get this lot down to the depot tomorrow,' he sighed.

'Martin! You know there's no such thing,' said Juanita. 'You should know better than to even joke about that kind of subversive crap. We'll all help you clean up.'

Martin pressed a fresh cannie into her hand. 'Please have some more hardbrew, Juanita. For the smooth and efficient functioning of my party. For the greater good.'

Synthanol came in red canisters, but the ones he gave them were silver. Only the Mentargh were permitted to produce real, high-strength alcohol. After the first mouthful, Claudia could feel a new warmth radiating from her solar plexus. Synthanol had a thin, metallic taste and went down like water, and you had to drink a lot of it to feel the effect. She took a second mouthful.

'Super-efficient, eh? It'd be worth joining the Mentargh just to drink this all the time,' said Martin. 'Given my minimal chances of recruitment, I need to stay friends with Pierce.'

'Is he wearing his greys?' said Ally. She peered into the crowded living area, a dim mass of bodies in standard blue citizen rig.

'No, the ungrateful freeder,' said Martin. 'I hold a promotion party, and he won't even turn up in his sexy Mentargh cadet-trooper uniform. Which I know you were just gagging to see, Ally. Seeing Juanita with a new armband isn't the same, I know.'

Claudia had already noted the black band around Juanita's left arm, signifying probationary recruitment to the Mentargh. It was very unusual for promotions to be announced before the Senior Youth League Trials, which weren't due for several months.

Ally's face dropped.

'You know Pierce, he's a bit funny about the Mentargh,' said Martin. 'Brother issues.'

'If I had my greys, I'd be wearing them,' said Juanita.

'Weeding out antisocial elements will be just your style,' said Martin. 'Zooming around on a powerbike and crashing parties with your troops in black. Your very own glorious future.'

Juanita took this as a compliment. 'I was told in my interview that individualism and subversion are becoming more common,' she said gravely. 'The Mentargh are taking special measures. I can't tell you any more than that, but it's a bigger problem than you think.'

'I'll have to stop being such a weirdo, then,' said Claudia.

Juanita looked at her sharply. From behind, Martin pulled a face at Claudia and mouthed at her to shut up. Juanita's zeal had always been a harmless joke among her friends but being recruited into the Mentargh was no joke.

Claudia grinned innocently and took another slug of the hardbrew. Not only was it potent, but it also tasted good.

Inwardly, she was kicking herself. It was stupid to tease Juanita like that, now that she was as good as in the Mentargh. Even though Claudia was an obedient citizen, a good student and a diligent if not always fully enthused Youth League member, she'd never quite fitted in and Juanita had always sensed that. Only her Ideology rank—Level V, like Pierce—

put her above suspicion. Most people in their cohort were Level III and likely to remain there.

'I can't see Pierce,' said Ally wistfully. 'Who's that weird-looking girl? The one in deadclothes.'

'Ah,' said Martin. 'That's Davina. Arnie's new friend.'

'Where did Arnie say he'd met her?' said Juanita.

'Juanita thinks Davina has free-spirit tendencies,' Martin told the other two.

'I don't like her attitude. And those ridiculous clothes,' said Juanita.

'Please don't start your Mentargh act, not at my party,' said Martin. 'Not unless you have more hardbrew, anyway.'

'Is there more? That was yummy,' said Ally and sat down, rather suddenly, on one of the two kitchen stools.

'Freed, Ally, have you chugged yours already? I'll have to send Pierce back to the Barracks for a special requisition, just for you,' said Martin. 'Here, have a red. That's more your speed.'

At that moment, a person Claudia had never seen before pushed her way towards the kitchenette. She was solidly built and almost as tall as Juanita, but what caught Claudia's attention was the way she was dressed. Instead of the blue citizen rig, she wore a three-piece outfit: trousers, jacket and what seemed to be an inner jacket, made of a bristly green and brown material Claudia did not recognise, with strange round fastenings down the front. Even stranger was her headgear: what seemed to be a flattened bag of similar bristly material with a soft ball-shaped object, also textile, at the top. Both the garment and hat were very worn and grubby and gave off a distinctive organic smell of dirt and decay, like a hydroponics tray gone bad.

When people had first come to live in the Dome, they'd worn whatever they still had, all sorts of Old World rags, but that was a long time ago and everyone now wore the same minimum-impact clothes. It was rare to see deadclothes, especially on someone their own age. Claudia was wary but also intrigued.

'And here she is, Davina the free spirit,' said Martin. 'Every party should have one. Davina, this is Claudia and that is Ally, who nuked herself in five minutes on one silver.'

'Hi,' said Davina, looking Claudia up and down. She'd written off Ally with a glance. 'Claudia, the Ideology genius. Arnie told me about you. You're Mentargh Boy's special friend.'

Claudia felt a hot flush spread up her neck and right up to her hairline.

'I didn't know you were going with Pierce,' Ally said to Claudia, sounding hurt.

'I'm not,' Claudia insisted. She and Pierce had been friends since Basic Ed, and they'd been in the same Ideo class, until Pierce had gone into the Mentargh stream.

'I heard what I heard,' said Davina. 'Level V, eh? You must know all sorts of exciting secret shit. Stuff the average citizen isn't trusted to know.'

'Everyone is told what they need to know,' said Juanita. 'Information overload leads to confusion and inefficiency. It used to be a massive problem in the Old World.'

'Among all its other massive, terminal problems,' said Davina. 'I know, I should be grateful that my life's knowledge has been pre-decided for me, saving me the stress of finding out anything myself or asking questions, but sometimes Level III seems a bit … low.'

'You don't have a right to know things just because you're curious,' said Juanita. 'There has to be a social purpose.'

Unwarranted curiosity was a sign of individualism, and Claudia was aware of her own guilt. Being a conscientious student was a social positive, but sometimes she asked too many questions.

'Where did you get those deadclothes?' Claudia asked Davina. She'd never seen any close up.

'They used to be my grandfather's, before he died of multi-cancer,' replied Davina. 'Dad wanted to put them in the recycler right away but Mum wouldn't let him. Before she died, she told me where she'd hidden them.'

Claudia reached out to touch Davina's jacket. The material felt rough and thick, the opposite of the thermally adaptive, lightweight fabric used for all clothes in the Dome. Up close, the smell was even stronger.

'Did people actually wear clothes like that in the 2050s?' said Ally, screwing up her face as if this would help her see Davina's outfit better. 'It looks like it was made out of sheep.'

'Wool,' said Claudia.

Davina gave Ally a look of contempt. 'My grandfather was an *individual*.' She pronounced the word with slow insolence. 'Back then, it was allowed.'

'You shouldn't be wearing them,' said Juanita.

'Why not?' said Davina. 'I don't like the blue rig. It doesn't suit my personal aesthetic. Show me a quote in the Ideo that says I can't wear what I want, and I might reconsider.'

Juanita couldn't think of a relevant article, despite her Level IV Ideology rank.

Claudia could. 'Standard clothing ensures material and social equality. All necessary indications of rank and status will be bestowed upon the individual by the Dome authorities. This is also a practical consideration, as the limited productive resources of the Dome would not support the production of clothing for individual taste. The rampant individualism and cult of self-expression in the twentieth and twenty-first centuries up to the Event led to an extremely wasteful clothing industry, called "fashion", which contributed to environmental degradation and collapse. Such misuse of resources is not permitted in the Dome. Article 394, Subsection 42.'

Claudia had hoped to impress Davina, but the girl looked at her as if she'd just pulled off her head and tossed it in the air.

'Is this your party trick? Quoting reams of Ideo? I can't believe you even remember the article and subsection. You're a freak.'

'Everyone should wear the same rig,' said Juanita. 'Why would you even want to stand out like that? And why would you want to smell like that?'

She glared at Davina and shouldered her way into the living area.

'Don't mind her,' said Martin. 'She's always been a bit too keen for comfort, but we've all known her since Basic and she's a softie, really.'

'Yeah, right,' said Davina. 'The Mentargh doesn't recruit softies.'

'What sector are you from?' said Claudia, still smarting. 'Arnie's never mentioned you before.'

'D-Sector. Dad works in Energy. I'm in the same Science Ed stream as Arnie.' She said this casually, but Claudia immediately sensed an evasion. Not an omission—if Davina had been wearing a uniform, her science tech trainee insignia would've been clear enough—or even a distortion, but it was clear to Claudia that as well as being classmates, Arnie and Davina had something else in common and that Davina wasn't going to say.

'Dodgy D-Sector,' said Martin. 'You're such a cliché, junior citizen. You could've brought us your local brew, so we could compare it with the MT stuff.'

'I've only just met you lot,' said Davina. 'I haven't decided if I want to poison you yet.'

She laughed in a way that seemed almost unfriendly to Claudia. D-Sector had a free-spirit reputation, but people didn't usually joke about it so openly.

'What League grade do you play?' Claudia asked. She had no memory of seeing Davina at any Youth League matches or events, although of course Davina would've been in standard active rig, which made everyone look the same in a crowd.

'Third,' Davina replied. This was the lowest. 'I can't wait for the Selection Trials to be over so I'm shot of the whole thing.'

Even Martin was taken aback. 'I know the training sessions can be a pain, especially with our coach, literally, because he's a sadistic beast, but everyone has to do it.'

The six friends had all acquitted themselves with merit over their ten compulsory years of Youth League, junior and then senior. A large part of this was participation in the Game. Before the Event, there used to be hundreds of different sports, which was very wasteful and individualistic. In the Dome, everyone played the Game. Each of the friends had been assigned a position within the Game according to their strengths. As Senior Youth League officers, they each supervised a squad of juniors.

'Uh, where to start?' said Davina. 'Trying to control hordes of screaming little freeders and get them to run or march in the right direction. Having to chase a ball up and down a playing field while being smashed into by people like your mate Mentargh Girl who really, *really* care about who has the freeding ball. I'd freeding *give* it to them, with a kiss, but that's not the rules, and I try to keep my demerits and warnings below alert level. Let me tell you, from hard-won experience, because I can see that none of you runts play attack or defence, that the combined mass and velocity of someone the size of Mentargh Girl produces an impact force that requires serious pain meds. I am not going to miss that one little bit.'

'But you'll still have to play in a citizen division,' said Ally. 'Everyone has to play.'

'Trust me, I have calibrated my performance to the lowest credible level. After the Trials, I'll be out on the field with a bunch of lightweights and Oldies who will bounce off me like pillows.'

Claudia didn't particularly like the Game either, but she could see the point of it and Davina's cynicism grated.

'The Game is designed to maximise community spirit, cooperation and inclusion. Everyone can play the Game,' she said. 'If you get hurt, it means your technique is wrong or that the other person isn't playing fair.'

'Nobody freeding plays fair. And don't quote that Ideo crap at me. The Game's fine if you like that kind of thing, but if you don't it's a freeding bore.' Davina took a swig of her drink, as if it was perfectly normal to have such opinions.

Ideo wasn't crap. It was the nearest Claudia could get to having her questions answered. And that was her problem: she had so many questions, and answers only generated more questions, like cancer cells that kept dividing and growing.

Naturally, she discussed all her deviant thoughts and

chronic curiosity with Kate, her Youth Mentor. Her desire to know more about Before and how people had lived back then was a defect in an otherwise healthy intelligence.

'What position do you play?' Martin asked Davina, a discernible reserve in his voice.

'Forward two. For obvious reasons.'

So did Juanita. Claudia had a sudden, satisfying vision of Davina being tackled by Juanita.

'Come on, share!' said Martin, nudging her. 'You can't smirk like that in my face and not tell.'

'Nothing! Honestly.' Claudia blushed.

'I know, you're scheming to get Ally drunk so you can have Pierce all to yourself,' said Martin.

'I think Ally is achieving her maximum capacity without team assistance,' said Davina.

'What? Are you talking about me?' Ally's head jerked up.

A storm of cheering and laughter erupted from the living area.

'Arnie, you freeding chemo-brain!' someone shouted.

'What's going on?' Martin jostled his way towards the noise. 'This is my party, you're not allowed to have fun without me.'

Claudia and Davina followed him. The others were gathered around a boy who was downing a silver cannie. His round, cheerful face was flushed, but he kept his balance with practised ease. The boy facing him could barely stand up.

'Benny challenged Arnie to a skoll battle,' someone told them. 'They're on to round five.'

'This is all Pierce's fault, bringing so much hardbrew,' Martin muttered. 'He can freeding well help clean up the mess afterwards. Benny's going to recycle in a big way, I just know.'

Davina laughed. 'Citizen Arnie, status update!'

'Radioactive!' he called back. 'This is my natural state.'

'Don't encourage him, for freed's sake,' said Martin. 'What a waste of good hardbrew.'

'Thanks to Mentargh Boy, we'll probably get resupplied soon enough,' said Davina. 'That's how it usually works, isn't it? They look after their own.'

Claudia wondered if Davina had been in some trouble with the Mentargh before. Her attitude was negative but also puzzlingly dismissive.

'Are the Mentargh coming soon? When are they coming?' Ally's breath was hot and sour in Claudia's face. She leaned heavily against her friend, clutching her arm. 'Pierce will know. Look, there he is.'

Claudia picked out the familiar head of black hair among the crowd. Pierce was wearing blues like everyone else. Like Juanita, he wore a black armband. Below it was another armband stamped with a Roman V. Claudia wore a matching band on her own arm.

Seeing her, Pierce made his way over. 'Have you just got here? You look way too sober.'

'Are we going to get any more hardbrew? Benny and Arnie have drunk the lot.' Ally leaned against Pierce and fluttered her eyelashes. She was so obvious around him that it was embarrassing for everyone else. Claudia found her behaviour extremely annoying.

'I'm sure I can find some, if you need a top-up.' Pierce's tone suggested that she may not need one.

'Isn't that the main perk of being a Mentargh cadet? Not having to drink that wastewater?' said Davina.

Pierce looked at her, sizing her up in the way that Mentargh always sized people up, and Claudia wished that Davina could tone it down, just a bit.

'It's one of them,' he said evenly. 'But you can keep drinking the wastewater if you don't want to owe the Mentargh any favours.'

'Since they're both technically illegal, I'll go for the one that tastes better,' said Davina.

'Is synth really illegal? But everyone drinks it,' said Ally.

Davina snorted. 'The Mentargh would have to arrest everyone in the Dome, including themselves.'

'True enough,' said Pierce.

He opened a silver cannie and passed it to Claudia. 'Let's test your social skills, junior citizen. Skoll!'

'I can't!' Claudia protested.

'It's easy. I'll show you.' Pierce grabbed a cannie of synthanol for himself. 'Ready?'

'Mentargh Boy's trying to get you nuked,' said Davina, and she laughed again. Claudia realised that Davina was drunker than she seemed. 'Bad Mentargh Boy!'

'Me? I'm a responsible cadet-trooper,' said Pierce. 'It's my duty to help parties along, build the communal spirit that enables our survival.'

'By melting our brains with hardbrew!' said Davina.

Ally looked confused, then pouted, because she felt ignored.

Claudia eyed the cannie. She could still feel the effects of the first one.

'Come on. One big swallow,' said Pierce. He held his own cannie up to his mouth.

'That's an order,' said Davina. 'You'd better do what Mentargh Boy says.'

She seemed curious about what Claudia would do.

'I'll drink it!' said Ally.

She reached out, but before she could grab the cannie, Claudia tipped her head back and drank. It took several swallows, and she spluttered when some went up her nose, but she got most of it down in the end, with some coughing and spillage. Davina banged her on the back, very hard. Claudia felt that she might have understated her ability as a Game forward.

'Bravo, Claudia!' Martin appeared, clapping. 'You've been indoctrinated into the protocols of partying at last. About freeding time.'

As Claudia straightened up, still coughing, the cramped unit seemed to tilt and sway. She felt someone grab her by the arms, and she thought it was Davina, but it was Pierce. His grip was very strong. Without it she might have fallen over.

'Thanks,' she whispered, embarrassed.

He nodded and let her go, as if suddenly ashamed.

'I think you should have another,' said Martin.

'Are you both trying to get her drunk?' said Davina.

'Everyone else is, so why not? I've still got some cannies of synth left unless we're due a visit.' Martin gave Pierce a meaningful look.

'Yeah, when are they coming?' said Ally, her face eager.

'I don't know. They might not come at all. Anyway, this party has already peaked,' said Pierce. He seemed to resent the question.

'Whose fault is that?' demanded Martin. 'People can't handle hardbrew. Look, my unit's like the Aftermath, freeding bodies everywhere. Everyone's totally slaughtered.'

'Isn't that a sign of a good party?' said Davina. She looked at Pierce. 'Isn't that your job, to make sure we all have a good time?'

'Aren't you having a good time?' he said, pretending to be hurt.

'I could do with another freeding drink,' she replied.

Martin fetched some more cannies of synth. As some people left, others arrived with their own supplies, and the party picked up again.

The accumulated effect of alcohol and synthanol gave Claudia a vague, detached feeling. It was much easier to socialise when she'd been drinking; she laughed easily for no particular reason and smiled a lot, like Ally, although she didn't flutter her eyelashes at anyone.

At the same time, while she was chatting and laughing, one part of her mind remained clear and the drabness of the surroundings came sharply into focus. The monotone grey of the room; the low lighting; her friends' blue rig, worn from repeated reconditioning; the bare, grubby walls.

She had always lived like this and knew no different. They were all so lucky to be living in the Dome.

Through a half-open door, she could see Martin's bunk, now occupied by two people. They seemed to have fallen asleep before making any progress. Someone was throwing up in the toilet.

Davina suddenly started to sing the Youth League anthem, waving her cannie in time.

We are the children of Armageddon

She sang discordantly, making the words ridiculous.

We are the inheritors of a golden future

Humanity will arise once more

She fell flat on her back and stuck her feet straight in the air. Martin and Arnie collapsed together, laughing helplessly.

Claudia was shocked.

So was Juanita. 'That Davina is a bad influence. If the Mentargh show up, she'll be in big trouble.'

Afraid for Davina, Claudia edged over and shook Davina's arm.

'Stop it! Juanita's watching.'

Davina shook her arm free. 'Freed Juanita!' she said loudly. 'She's a freeding pain. I wish she'd get lost.'

There was a hush, then people began to snicker. Juanita said nothing, but her face went red.

'She heard that.' Ally appeared behind Claudia, looking rather dishevelled. 'Oh, Clau, I've got such a freeding headache.'

'That's what happens when you drink too much. Lie down somewhere or go home.' Claudia had no intention of going home herself, not yet.

'Have some water,' added Pierce.

As Ally tottered towards the kitchen, she lurched into him and almost fell.

'Hey, be careful!' he exclaimed, grabbing her arm.

She smiled gratefully at his concern.

Two

Eventually those still present and conscious realised they were hungry and gravitated to the kitchen. People had brought along their snack rations, but not much was left.

Martin went through his foodstore and pulled out a couple of small pizzas.

'You're lucky I went to the distro yesterday,' he said. 'This is my entire quota of pizza, so you all owe me.'

Personal quotas weren't transferrable, but there were ways around it, and as long as food wasn't being wasted, it was rare for action to be taken.

'That's all you freeding eat,' said Arnie. 'We're doing you a favour by forcing you to diversify your diet. You can have my green goo-stew.'

Citizen Meal No. 34, despite being highly nutritious on all counts and very easy to produce, was unpopular for reasons food engineers had been unable to resolve.

'I don't know why everyone complains about No. 34,' said Juanita. 'It tastes fine to me.'

Pizzas were the most popular light meal item, especially among teenagers. They came in a variety of flavours that referenced foodstuffs that had gone out of fashion even before the Event, such as dairy cheese and processed meat. Eating a slice of pizza topped with red circles of spiced protein and soft white circles of lab-cheese, Claudia had no idea how it compared to its long-ago original, but it was much better than No. 34.

'What time do the Mentargh usually call in this sector?' Davina asked Pierce.

'Around now if they're going to come,' he replied, unwillingly.

'I hope they bring some more hardbrew,' said Martin. 'Synth tastes foul after the real thing.'

'Yeah, I could see how you forced it down,' said Arnie.

'They might, or they might not,' said Pierce. 'They usually only bring synthanol to Senior Youth League parties. And the Party Machine, and the jennies.'

Davina scowled. 'If we didn't have to report parties, would they even know who was having one?'

'The Sanitation Officers always know when I've had one,' said Martin. 'Even if I manage to unblock the toilet.'

'You mean, when I unblock the toilet,' said Arnie. His practical skills made him an asset to all private gatherings.

'Imagine having a party they didn't crash,' Davina went on. Claudia wondered if she was always this outspoken or if the hardbrew was making her careless. 'Bashing through the door like they own the place, handing out booze and drugs and checking up on everyone: who's sleeping with who, who's acting strangely, who's drunk and who's not, because not getting with the collective vibe is antisocial.'

'You mean, a private party? Off the record? Do people actually do that?' Ally's mouth hung open.

Davina ignored her. 'I mean, don't the Mentargh trust us to have fun without them? Why do they have to be monitoring us all the time?'

Claudia saw Martin widen his eyes, very briefly, at Arnie.

'Because they care about us, and they want us to have a maximum amount of socially useful fun to build and strengthen community bonds,' he said.

'The Mentargh exists for the good of society,' quoted Juanita sternly.

'The Mentargh exists to control society,' said Davina.

The atmosphere froze. There was always banter at Martin's parties, but Davina made no pretence of joking.

She and Juanita glared at each other over the remains of a pizza topped with pink salty lumps and round fungal shapes.

'Isn't that the same thing?' said Claudia, and Davina looked at her sharply. 'Society has to be monitored to ensure its correct functioning. A disharmony not taken care of causes an imbalance in the Dome, which could jeopardise society as a whole. Chaos leads to death. Order is survival.'

'You're quoting Ideology again,' said Davina. 'It's boring. Stop it.'

'But I'm agreeing with you,' said Claudia. 'The Mentargh controls society—for its own good.'

'So, you're both right, and we really need some more booze,' said Martin. 'Pierce, can we send out a distress call? Party malfunction?'

Arnie folded another piece of pizza into his mouth. 'Claudia, you've just raised my expectations. I want to go to a party so freeding good that it threatens to overturn social order and bring on chaos. Sorry, Martin, you haven't quite managed it this time around.'

'Even if the Mentargh do exist for our own good, it doesn't mean we have to like it,' muttered Davina. 'Arnie, for freed's sake, leave some pizza for the rest of us.'

'We're lucky to live in the Dome,' ventured Ally. 'Nobody's alive Outside. We should be grateful and not complain.'

Her uncharacteristic outspokenness made her redden and look quickly to Claudia for support. Claudia avoided her gaze.

'I'm glad someone's got some sense around here,' said Juanita.

'If you went Outside, you'd either bake to death within an hour or die slowly of radiation,' said Martin.

Every junior citizen learned this fact in Basic Education.

'Thanks for the reminder,' said Davina.

'Yeah. So if you don't like the Mentargh, you don't have much of a choice,' said Pierce.

'Don't we?' said Davina.

The very idea of choice, although ridiculous, sent a strange frisson through Claudia. What did Davina mean?

'Whatever anyone thinks of the Mentargh, they should have a healthy respect for it,' said Pierce quietly.

He often seemed ambivalent about the Mentargh himself, despite growing up with his brother in the Barracks, but to hear him admit that other people might also resent it was new and unsettling for Claudia.

'You have my total respect, Pierce, old friend, and not just because I can never beat you in an arm wrestle, but is it wrong just to imagine things being different?' said Arnie. His tone was as casual as ever, but Claudia felt that he was testing them, as he already had by bringing a free spirit like Davina to Martin's party. 'I mean, we have no choice about living in the Dome, and we're always told how awful things were before, because the Old World basically destroyed itself, and we're lucky to live in 2085, in an orderly and efficient society and have all our needs met—food, shelter, healthcare, education, occupation, identity, community—but ...'

'But what?' said Juanita.

Arnie shrugged. 'It's way past my bedtime and Citizen Benny has incited me to drink far more hardbrew than I should, and the fungal protein on that pizza might have hijacked my brain, so don't take any of this seriously. We live in a perfectly functioning and optimised society, and all our needs are met, and the Mentargh looks after us so nicely, thank you, Pierce ... I'm not arguing with any of this, so no more Ideo quotes, please, Clau, it worries me when you do that ... it's just that, sometimes I wonder, is this all? Is something missing? Am I a total weirdo?'

While he said this, he picked at the various scraps of food on the pizza trays, not meeting anyone's gaze. Nobody looked at anyone else.

Claudia understood exactly what he meant. It was the unnameable, unspoken sense of dissatisfaction, a feeling of chronic emptiness, a longing without an object. She had never heard anyone say it aloud before. She almost held her breath, waiting for the others to respond.

'We have everything necessary for survival,' said Juanita sternly.

'He's not talking about survival,' said Davina. 'What he's saying is maybe we can do better than just surviving.'

'This is exactly how people sink into individualism,' said Juanita. 'It just creeps up on you. Discontent, dissatisfaction, constant doubts. Arnie, you need to discuss this with your mentor before it gets any worse. Seriously.'

Davina rolled her eyes and was about to say something

when the door buzzer went.

Ally spun around. 'They're here!'

'Sit tight, citizen, it's not the Mentargh,' said Martin. 'They usually just bash a few times and then barge right in. It's probably old Jemima.'

He went to the door, and they heard his voice through the thin partition, intermingled with a weaker female tone.

Davina, who was nearest, leaned back and looked around the corner.

'Who is it?' said Ally.

'An Oldie,' Davina replied. 'An old woman.'

Martin reappeared. 'Typical. She's run out of milk again. Whenever her cat goes missing, she leaves a bowl of milk by the door to lure it back.'

'No way! She doesn't keep an animal, does she?' exclaimed Juanita. This seemed to outrage her even more than Davina and Arnie combined.

'Shh! She's ancient, but she's not deaf!' said Martin. 'Of course she doesn't have a cat. The Sannies would've killed the thing years ago. Old Jemima's gaga. Thinks it's still alive.'

'Or maybe she just chugs more than her tiny quota of milk and she's exploiting your good nature,' said Arnie. He put on a squeaky voice. 'Such a nice young man, wasting his milk resource on me!'

'And you're not a nice young man.' Martin punched Arnie in the arm before he opened the coldstore. 'I'll have to take it over for her. She needs someone else to pick up the bowl and put it down again. Honestly, I don't know how she even makes it to my door.'

The thought of such decrepitude was appalling, and every-one felt a bit shocked and disgusted.

'I'll go,' said Claudia.

'Really? Well, if you insist.' Martin passed her a small white cannie. 'I'm warning you, she likes to talk. She's outlived everyone in her age cohort by about a hundred years and she needs the company. We'll see you in the morning.'

A small, shrunken figure was waiting in the doorway.

'Citizen Jemima?' said Claudia.

The Oldie's face creased up like a piece of lab-leather ready for recycling. 'Are you one of Martin's friends? I don't see many young people these days.'

'I'm Claudia,' the girl replied, trying not to stare.

The Oldie was even shorter than Claudia and very frail, with wispy white hair and rheumy eyes. She wore a green overall, which signified that her status was inactive. Inactives were on lower rations than active citizens. The overall hung loosely from her bony frame, the stick-like legs terminating in a pair of slip-on shoes that had once been pink and fluffy. Oldies often wore deadclothes along with their standard rig. For inactives, it didn't matter what they wore: the less drain on common resources, the better.

'Has Martin delegated the milk run to you?' Jemima was inspecting Claudia as closely as Claudia had inspected her.

'I offered. I don't mind.'

'I'm only a few doors down,' said Jemima. 'But at my age, it's a fucking marathon.'

Only Oldies used archaic swear words. Claudia had no idea what Jemima meant by a marathon.

The old woman shuffled off and Claudia had to shuffle not to overtake her. Lots of female Oldies had advanced osteoporosis, among other chronic geriatric conditions. Claudia had learned this as a trainee medical technician. Jemima's back was hunched over almost ninety degrees.

'Martin's a good kid. A good citizen. He's the only person in the block who talks to me,' said the Oldie.

'What about the Senior Citizens' Circle?'

Jemima snorted. 'I'm the oldest one there and they're all idiots. No, I keep myself to myself. I have nothing to contribute to the smooth and efficient functioning of society and nobody cares what I do.'

Claudia thought that must be very lonely.

'I don't get lonely,' said Jemima. 'All the people I wanted to be with died a long time ago.'

The corridor was lined with identical numbered doors. Jemima stopped in front of G4-5-41. An upturned food tray lay in a pool of congealed milk.

'It gets kicked over by everyone who comes along,' said Jemima.

Claudia picked up the tray with a guilty pang: it was probably one of them who had kicked the tray and not even noticed.

'Martin's very kind to share his milk quota,' Jemima continued. 'But if Lucky comes looking for me and there's no milk by the door, she might just move on and live somewhere else. That's what cats are like. Although I don't suppose you'd know.'

She glanced at Claudia, and the girl had the sudden sensation of being assessed by an acute, searching intelligence. It was like having a high-powered light shone in her eyes. Just as suddenly, it was turned off.

'Well, come on in.' Jemima swiped the door open.

The unit was exactly the same as Martin's, with the standard furniture and fixtures. Claudia's attention was immediately drawn to the shelves. Where Martin's were mostly empty, Jemima's held printed material, actual books. There were even a few photographs propped up in front of them.

Claudia had never seen printed books or pictures. At the time of the Event, most text and image files were stored digitally, and the servers had been destroyed. Some people had brought hard copies with them to the Dome. These were now stored securely in the Archives, and only a few people, with very high Ideology rank, were allowed access.

'My own personal archive,' said Jemima. 'I'm just an Oldie, what does it matter?'

Claudia put the milk cannie on the table and went over to the shelf. The titles were printed vertically on the spines and she had to turn her head to read them.

Post-humanity: A Philosophical Enquiry

Hive Mind: The End of the Individual and the Death of Liberal Society?

Chemical Consensus: Soft Control and Social Order

The Limited Society: Choosing Survival over Freedom

The Coming War with China

After Democracy

On the Governance of Survival Societies

Regeneration: The GAIA Solution

'Print books were going out of fashion way before the Event,' said Jemima, watching her. 'A niche product. I used to have quite a collection.'

The titles made no sense to Claudia. She looked at the photographs. The colour was faded and the shiny paper creased in places, but the images were very clear. In one, a man and a woman, obviously a much younger Jemima, were standing against what seemed to be a wall of vegetation, except there was no wall holding up the green. Green walls were integral to the Dome's environment, helping to regulate the moisture and air temperature.

In another photograph, the young Jemima and another young woman, in what looked like very colourful underwear, were standing in front of a large body of water with no apparent boundaries. Above them was another stretch of blue. The Dome was always grey, sometimes darker or lighter. Claudia had learned that the sky used to be blue, but she hadn't imagined it would be so … garish.

'Who are these people?' she asked.

'The man is my husband, Jorge,' said Jemima. 'I met him at university. We were both studying climate science. He died in the Event. The woman is Hetty, my sister. We went travelling together back in the 2020s. That was taken on some island, I can't remember which one. She was in Europe when the Event happened. I have to assume that she died.'

She said this matter-of-factly. The Event had happened almost thirty years ago; nobody grieved anymore.

'All my relations died,' Claudia said. 'Except my mother, and my father, of course, although I never knew him, or any of my other relatives. I was born afterwards,' she added, unnecessarily.

'Of course you were,' said Jemima. 'This is all you've ever known.'

Claudia's picture of life before the Event, formed by Ideology, was vague and negative. She always saw it in black and white; a bleak, joyless world of poverty and famine, war and terrorism, political, a vast anarchy in which individuals struggled for survival against a backdrop of escalating global disintegration and chaos. By comparison, the Dome was a haven of security: a familiar, ordered world in which everyone had their appointed place and responsibilities. Some younger children were even growing up with the idea that the Event had been somehow engineered by the Survival Committee to save humanity from itself.

Her mother never spoke about Before. Most Survivors didn't. It was too painful and traumatic. Also, Survivors were usually very careful about what they said in front of younger people who'd grown up in the Dome.

'Things were really awful before, weren't they?' said Claudia. She knew the answer; there was no reason for her to ask such a question, but it popped out before she was aware of thinking it.

'It depends on what you mean by awful,' said Jemima, and waited.

'I mean, the planet was dying, there was the Second Cold War, people were starving, the sea level was rising, society was collapsing. The Event was just the final blow. I mean, it was inevitable. If society had been functioning correctly, it wouldn't have destroyed itself, right?'

Claudia had drunk a lot and her words came out in a jumble.

'Functioning correctly!' Jemima pronounced this with scorn. 'And I suppose that's how we live now. Although my functioning is pretty creaky these days.'

'The Dome is a perfectly regulated and efficiently function-ing society,' said Claudia. It was safer to quote Ideo than to try to use her own words.

Shockingly, Jemima laughed. Half her teeth were missing. 'Oh yes, the corporate line. You have to learn it all by heart, don't you? But what do you and your friends think? Are you really happy with how we live now?'

Arnie had only just asked the same question.

'We're grateful to be alive,' said Claudia, and she was responding to Arnie and her own doubts as much as to the strange Oldie. 'We're the lucky ones. How else could we live? There's nothing else left.'

'You honestly can't imagine anything better? No, I don't suppose you can. How sad.' Jemima's eyes, set deep within soft folds of skin, were like slivers of blue glass. 'The world was certainly in a bad way before the Event, but things were far from hopeless. In some ways, they even seemed to be getting better. The Event itself was catastrophic bad luck. An unexpected set of circumstances that all converged at once. But you won't learn that in the Ideology.'

'It was inevitable,' Claudia insisted, feeling herself in danger. She edged towards the door. 'Society was falling into chaos and people were dying all over the place. Civilisation was destroying itself.'

She had been warned about Oldies and their peculiar, corrupting ideas. The horror of the Event and the Aftermath had sent many people mad. Yet, Jemima didn't seem crazy, apart from thinking her cat was alive. In fact, quite the opposite.

'I should be going,' said Claudia abruptly. 'I should really be discussing this with my mentor. I have this problem, you see—'

'Life used to be so interesting. So rich and varied,' Jemima was saying. 'You've only been taught half the story. Even in the worst of situations, there was always hope; the possibility that things might change. The way we live now is so limited and sterile, joyless, *boring*. Humanity is going to die out from boredom, not radiation or global warming.'

Claudia had already buzzed Martin's door when she realised that she'd left his milk behind.

28

Three

'I hope the cat said thank you,' said Martin as he let her in.

She clutched his arm. 'Martin, those books! The pictures! She's got her own freeding Archive in there!'

He glanced all around before replying, in a whisper, 'I know! I pretend not to see anything. She says some weird stuff as well. I don't think about it. She's just an Oldie, it doesn't matter. Nobody checks up on them.'

This was true. Unlike active citizens, Oldies did not report to anyone and were generally left alone until they died. Medical resources were not wasted on them. Claudia had already learned the criteria for intervention, and Jemima was far too old for anything more than a painkiller or a minor wound dressing. Oldies who were suffering badly or could no longer look after themselves were given a humane 'final dose'. Many requested it. Only fully qualified med techs could approve finals.

'Forget you saw anything,' said Martin. 'She's just a crazy old woman.'

She wanted to ask more—what had Jemima said to him?—but he pulled away.

The party had gone quiet. Lots of people had left, and the music from the Youth League channel had become mellow, as it always did at this time of the cycle. Arnie and Pierce were trying to lift a comatose Benny off the floor and out of the way. Juanita was collecting cannies and lining them up, very neatly, along the wall, a sign that even she'd gone past her usual limit.

There was a thump from the corridor, and an outraged cry, followed by laughter.

'Sorry, Ben. You're too heavy,' said Arnie.

The indistinct reply was followed by violent retching.

'Benny puked,' said Arnie, as he and Pierce made a speedy retreat into the living area.

'Oh, freed!' said Martin. 'You could have dragged him as far as the toilet. Just as well, I suppose,' he added, philosophically. 'We've already used up enough water, with everyone puking in there and flushing it every five minutes. I got a warning from the Sanitation Officers the last time I had a party.'

The encounter with Jemima had left Claudia feeling unsettled. It was a relief to be back among her friends and their usual antics. Martin was right: she had to forget about Jemima.

They all converged around the low table in the living area. Martin, Arnie and Davina had a very shouty conversation that made no sense, and Ally had a fit of giggles. Juanita was giving Pierce a play-by-play description of her last Game match. Claudia curled up at one end of the divan. A night of drinking and noise always had this effect on her. Her head buzzed, and when she shut her eyes to block it all out, she saw, very clearly, the picture of a young Jemima and her sister Hetty beneath the glaring blue of the sky.

She surfaced to the jarring discord of new voices. Hulking figures in black, some wearing crash helmets, loomed overhead and filled the unit with their presence.

Someone shook her, not gently, by the shoulder. It was Juanita.

'Wake up, Claudia, it's the Mentargh!'

'God, what a stink,' said someone.

'Check the kid in the hallway,' said another.

'Freed, he hasn't choked, has he? One of those a night is plenty.'

One of the newcomers removed his helmet and shook out his thick black hair. It was Luke, Pierce's older brother, a commander in the Mentargh.

'Looks like you've all had enough to drink,' he said.

His silver emblem of rank glittered coldly under the light shaft, and when his gaze fell on Claudia, he seemed to be reading her mind. She looked away quickly. Aside from his authority and menace as a Mentargh officer, Luke had a special, unnerving quality all of his own.

She glanced at Pierce. All vestiges of party spirit had vanished and his face had a sullen, closed-off look.

'Just as well we didn't bother bringing any more booze,' said Elliot, Luke's second. He was taller than Luke and heavyset, yet somehow less threatening.

'Time to take a trip,' said Luke. He tossed a plastic container onto the table.

'Yeah, it must be drug o'clock,' drawled Davina, but Claudia sensed an apprehension under her bravado.

'The synthanol doesn't get you very far,' said Elliot. 'This will.'

'How far?' muttered Davina.

'How far do you want to go, citizen?' said Luke. He spoke mildly, but the warning was unmistakable.

Claudia wished Davina would shut up.

'I've never had a complaint about Mentargh drugs,' said Arnie. He picked up the container and tipped its contents, some pink capsules, into his palm. 'Your jennies are always first-rate, and this junior citizen is always grateful.'

'Listen to this kid!' Elliot laughed. He clapped Arnie on the back, and the boy almost toppled forwards. 'I like your attitude.'

Luke wasn't fooled. This was clear enough to Claudia, although his face barely moved, and then she felt a shock as he looked back at her, as if reacting to her thoughts. She quickly dropped her eyes.

The others were gathering around the table as Elliot unfolded the Party Machine.

'We busted a party a few nights ago,' he was saying. 'Big scene, totally chaotic. Nobody had reported it, but we found it easily enough. People laid out all over the floor, wasted on homebrew and pirate jennies, and some joker was even vaping, can you believe? Anyway, half the bodies had to go to the clinic, after all the bogus shit they'd taken. We arrested all the others.'

'Why do people take the fake stuff when they can get the real stuff?' Juanita asked. 'I don't understand.'

'Some people don't like the Mentargh coming to their parties,' said Pierce. He didn't look at Davina.

Luke's gaze settled on his brother. Claudia felt a flare of hostility from Pierce. From Luke, nothing. He seemed to absorb it like a black hole swallowing light.

'They're the sort of parties we most need to attend,' he said evenly. 'Has everyone swallowed?'

He touched the Machine, bringing it to life. The flat screen suddenly acquired depth, as if an abyss had opened up in the table. Colours eddied and coalesced, bathing the assembled faces in an eerie radiance.

Claudia tried to stifle her panic as everyone placed their hands on the screen. She always found the trips unnerving, but she'd never felt so reluctant before. Her heart was racing, and it took all her willpower to raise her own hands. A sour backwash of synthanol and pizza rose in her throat.

Across the table, she recognised a kindred resistance in Davina's face, the brashness leached from her. Arnie, too, seemed hesitant, for all his cockiness. Ally and Martin put out their hands without hesitation, as usual, and Juanita offered hers as if she didn't ever need them back.

Claudia was the last to hold out her hands. Luke was watching her. What would he do if she refused?

This had never occurred to her before, and she could sense his curiosity.

When she pressed her hands to the screen, a light surged up from the depths, sending green and blue tendrils around everyone's fingers. The room began to blur around them, the walls and ceiling running together in a grey blur and receding. Their outstretched hands glowed, as if the Machine had ignited their blood. The energy of the Machine flowed out and engulfed them. Claudia felt herself dissolve into the maelstrom of colour and light along with the others. It was as if the Machine had meshed all their nerves together and made them into one. At the same time, she was acutely aware of her physical body, her legs going slightly numb as she kneeled on the floor around the table.

The vision cleared and solid shapes began to crystallise out of the murk. Claudia saw the Dome as if from above, rising bravely from the red earth. It was undefinably altered: enhanced, a gleaming, beautiful metropolis of sheer glass and smooth white surfaces, softened by walls and overspilling tiers of greenery. The Machine grew warm under Claudia's hands. Love and pride pulsed up through her arms as she gazed at the panorama. Around her, she could sense the others feeling the same.

Yet, in her mind's eye, Claudia saw another Dome, the real Dome: drab and grey. She knew she was fighting the correct response, but she couldn't reconcile the image in the Machine with its tired, shabby counterpart in the real world.

The neuro-animation moved in closer, skimming over the clean clinical buildings, the wide recreation grounds, the shining steel funnels of the Air Purifying Plant and the concave stumps of the Power Station with its blinking red lights; the Hydroponics ziggurat with its rows and levels of tanks and culture vats and sun-lamps. And the Central Zone itself, the severe, uniform buildings joined by networks of walkways, the transparent tubes of the Transit system curving overhead, and the crowds of smiling, busy people, anonymous in their blue citizen rig, radiating health and happiness.

Immersed in this scene, it was impossible to have any doubts or to feel anything other than gratitude.

At this stage, Claudia usually submitted and joined everyone else in the flow, but this time, something seemed to block her. She was still aware of herself as an individual entity watching rather than merging with the experience. The emotions generated by the Machine seemed fake and tinny, a manipulation of brain chemistry. It was like being force-fed a mouthful of artificial sweetener.

Revolted, Claudia pushed back. Without the emotional

music, the Dome now looked like a badly done animation, the kind she'd made as a child in Basic. The people all had the same face, the same blank expression, and made the same jerky, unnatural movements. The cityscape seemed desolate and soulless, even sinister, something out of a nightmare.

Claudia had a lot of nightmares.

The vision suddenly folded in on itself and Claudia was completely alone. She had no sense of the others around her or even her own body. She'd heard that sometimes people died during drug trips if they resisted or slipped into some bottomless in-between state in which the mind was permanently unmoored from the body. It was even rumoured that the Mentargh used it to read people's thoughts, and that they'd slip a bad pill to individualists who threatened social harmony.

It was important not to fight the Machine, to go with the flow.

Had Luke given her the jenny? She couldn't remember.

The first thing she saw was the startling blue of the sky. Its intensity made her eyes ache. She blinked, marvelling at the colour and at the warmth against her skin, like a heat lamp on full beam.

And then a noise, a vast rhythmic breathing. Cold water rushed up around her bare feet and pulled away. Beneath the sky was another expanse, a different blue, in constant motion. The air was salty against her lips.

Ahead of her, waist deep in the water, were Jemima and Hetty, as they had appeared in the photograph. They were laughing and splashing each other. Seeing Claudia, the young Jemima held out her hand.

'Come on in, Claudia! Don't be scared.'

Claudia took one step forwards and felt her feet sink into something very fine and granular. A white-tipped line of water surged towards them and the two girls threw themselves into it, shrieking. As the wave approached Claudia it diminished, curling around and under her toes and sucking the sand from beneath them. She had a sense of the vast power behind it, inhuman yet alive and brimming with both enormous vitality and danger.

She was filled with an alien euphoria, like a charge of electricity.

Jemima and Hetty disappeared briefly and then reappeared, just their heads, bobbing on the surface, their hair plastered against their necks and shoulders.

'Wait for me!' she called and tried to wade towards them, feeling the full force of the water against her. The more she tried to push her way forwards, the more it resisted her, until it swept her up and hurled her away.

She landed on the floor with a thud and lay on her back, dazed. Directly above her was the pale luminous tube embedded in the low ceiling of Martin's unit. The warm, stuffy atmosphere of the unit, with its whiff of synthanol, pizza and vomit, closed in around her.

'Claudia! Are you alright?' Ally was shaking her.

She tried to sit up, and the room tilted.

'Are you going to puke? If you're going to puke, I'll get one of the bins. I'll get one anyway,' said Martin.

'Get some water,' said Luke. Squatting beside her, he held her chin in one hand and looked right into her eyes, turning her head slightly.

'I'm not going to puke,' said Claudia. Being face to face with Luke was intensely awkward.

'I haven't seen her react like that before,' said Pierce. He was directly behind his brother, looking over his shoulder, and for a moment, she couldn't tell them apart.

'Do we need to call a med tech?' said Juanita.

'No. That's not necessary,' replied Luke curtly.

Martin handed her a cup of water and she drank it down, suddenly very thirsty.

'I thought only pirate pills sent people on bad trips,' said Davina. 'Not the proper MT-issue jennies.'

'The Machine actually repulsed you,' said Arnie. 'It flared up and knocked you right off. You're a model citizen. What the freed were you thinking to make it do that?'

He looked at her with a new curiosity.

'I lost track of you,' said Juanita. 'We were all there together, and suddenly you were gone.'

'I got that feeling too,' said Martin. 'As if you'd just disappeared.'

'If that happens again, you'll need to be checked out,' said Luke. He stood up, looming suddenly very tall over Claudia. 'A bad reaction can mean all sorts of things. The Machine isn't usually wrong twice.'

'Yeah, the Machine's smarter than you are. No point trying to hide.'

Elliot's added warning lacked the chilly menace of Luke's. He recalled the other troopers, who had been waiting around, looking bored, and winked at the friends before putting on his helmet. 'There's another party in the next building that needs attention. No rest for the weary. We do our bit for the Dome's youth. See you lot around.'

As Elliot led the troop out, Luke stood for a moment, his eyes lingering on Claudia. She met his stare with what she hoped was blank innocence, but she felt herself to be transparent.

'Party on, kids. The night shift's not over yet.'

The baton hanging from his belt glinted dully as he turned to leave.

Four

'Well, what are we going to do now?' said Martin. 'They didn't even bring us any more booze. A serious dereliction of duty.'

He was leaning against the kitchen counter, spinning an empty cannie.

'I don't want to go home yet,' said Ally. Her older sister had moved in with her current boyfriend, and Ally hated being alone in the unit.

Claudia didn't want to go home either, but for the opposite reason. She preferred being alone in the unit she shared with her mother.

'Sorry I killed your party, Martin,' she said.

'I think celebrations might have reached a natural end point anyway,' he said.

'I need to go,' said Juanita. 'I've got an extra training session in a few hours, so I should get some sleep. I'll take some of these empties to the recycler for you, Martin.'

'Thanks, you're a star citizen.'

As the door closed behind her, everyone relaxed.

'I was hoping she'd go earlier,' said Martin. 'To be honest, she's getting on my nerves.'

'I know.' Arnie pulled one of his faces. 'You'd think she was running the freeding Mentargh already.'

'If you can't stand her, why invite her?' said Davina.

'We've been in the same cohort since Basic,' said Martin. 'There's always one like Juanita. That's just how it is.'

'She's our friend,' said Ally.

'Don't you have someone like her in your cohort?' asked Claudia.

Cohort loyalty was very important and people were rarely excluded.

'Maybe I'm the difficult personality that people don't invite places,' said Davina. She laughed, although this didn't seem funny to Claudia.

Synthanol and the party drugs often left people feeling gloomy, and the whiff of vomit didn't help. Martin had turned the ventilation on full, but the smell was persistent.

'I hate the freeding Machine,' said Davina. 'I always feel like my brain has been violated. All those fake feelings. I need to get myself back.'

'It's still too early. We can't give up,' said Arnie. 'We need to snap out of this antisocial funk. Now Juanita's gone, let's do something totally bad.'

'Like what?' said Pierce.

'If you don't want to play, Mentargh Boy, you can go home,' said Davina.

'Don't go,' said Ally and hung onto Pierce's arm. He seemed not to notice.

'I'm in,' he said. 'Someone has to make sure that you lot don't do anything totally stupid.'

'Let's get some vapes and have a cloud party,' said Martin, glancing at Arnie.

Ally wrinkled her nose. 'Yuck, that's no fun. And everything will smell funny for days afterwards, and the Sanitation

Officers always find out.'

'OK, so why don't we follow Luke's troop to the next block and go for a joyride on their bikes while they're inside?' said Arnie.

The very thought set off convulsions of laughter.

'When exactly did you learn to ride, citizen?' said Davina.

The use of powerbikes was reserved for the Mentargh.

'I think Luke would take extreme offence,' said Pierce. 'Let's keep him out of this. Davina, you're the representative free spirit here. You must have all sorts of hyper-bad ideas.'

'Direct challenge by the Mentargh!' Arnie whooped. 'Go on, D, shock him.'

Davina seemed suddenly reluctant, although it was obvious to Claudia that she'd already thought of something.

'Junior citizen, you are required to contribute to the common good,' said Martin.

Davina looked at Arnie and an understanding seemed to pass between them.

'You really want to be bad? Really bad?' she said coolly.

Next to her, Claudia could feel Ally shrinking.

'Surprise me,' said Pierce.

Davina looked them all over as if deciding whether they were worthy.

'Let's go for a walk in the Underground,' she said at last.

Most of the Dome's deep subterranean levels were closed off, except for the sections connected to the Power Station and other utilities. Access to it was classified as highly restricted.

Arnie grinned widely at the rest of them, taking in their reaction.

'Hyper-freed! How do you even get down there?' said Martin.

'There are ways in,' said Davina. 'You don't have to swipe. Once you're down there, it's free-range.'

'Wouldn't we get into lots of trouble?' said Ally.

'Only if they found us, and the idea is that they don't,' said Davina. 'Obviously.'

'If we did bump into someone, it'd be a maintenance worker or someone like that,' said Arnie. 'The Mentargh don't patrol the Underground, do they, Pierce?'

Pierce had kept quiet, gauging everyone else's response and shielding his own. His silent vigilance reminded Claudia of Luke.

'Not regularly, as far as I know,' he replied. 'It's too large, and nobody's meant to be down there, anyway.'

'See? We'll be fine,' said Arnie. He began to drum on the kitchen counter and jig about on the spot, as if dancing to music only he could hear. 'Let's go.'

'That's not to say the Mentargh don't go down there at all,' Pierce went on. 'Being in the Underground without authorisation is associated with a certain kind of activity. If the Mentargh find you, they don't stop to ask questions before they arrest you.'

'We're just going for a walk. Why would they arrest us?' said Davina. Her gaze was defiant.

'I'm in,' said Martin. 'I'm only Level III, I don't know any better. That'll be my excuse. What about you, Claudia? Mentargh Girl?'

He said this jokingly, not like Davina, but Claudia felt she was being forced to choose sides. Being Level V didn't mean she was Mentargh-track.

'Of course I'm coming.'

Perhaps her strange trip had warped her judgement. Usually

she stuck to the rules, but she felt an unfamiliar thrill of excitement. Also, she was still quite drunk. They all were.

'Me too,' added Ally, with an obvious lack of enthusiasm.

'Pierce?' said Arnie. 'Come on, you're not in your grey uniform tonight.'

'Oh, sure, I'm in.' He seemed provoked by Arnie's challenge. 'We can keep each other company in the Re-Education Facility. It'll be just like starting out in Basic together.'

'Yeah, great times, big laughs!' Arnie smacked him on the back. 'What are we waiting for?'

'I really don't think we should do this,' Ally whispered to Claudia as they headed out.

'Go home, then,' said Claudia. 'Nobody's making you.'

Ally seemed to hesitate. 'If Pierce is coming, it must be OK,' she reasoned, and hurried to keep up with Claudia.

Five

Outside Martin's building, the common courtyard was completely silent. The green walls between the residential blocks made the air cool and fresh, and the lights embedded in the walkway formed pale pools beneath their feet. One sputtered off and on. DOMUS regulated the lighting, but a human was still needed to physically fix or replace a malfunctioning light tube.

Davina led them past the Transit station and behind the blocks that backed directly onto the Ring. The Ring was a wide, empty stretch of land between the Central Zone and the four sectors, dominating almost a third of the Dome's area. In the original design it was a green zone, but at the time of the Event, it hadn't been cultivated. There was no need to go out on the Ring and nobody did, although it wasn't actually forbidden.

Leading them to the edge of the Ring, Davina took a small tech light from one of her strange outfit's many pockets and turned it on.

'Anyone else got some light? It's going to be pretty dark where we're headed.'

Pierce detached a small device from his belt. A strong shaft of light suddenly illuminated a swathe of hard-packed reddish earth.

'Ooh, fancy Mentargh gear. I'm jealous,' said Davina, and Pierce flashed it briefly in her face, forcing her to blink and look away.

The light of the two torches showed a distinct path across the Ring, marked with single tyre tracks.

'That's the Mentargh expressway,' said Davina.

'Do we follow it?' Ally asked.

'We avoid it,' said Davina acidly.

'I don't like her,' Ally muttered in Claudia's ear.

Claudia didn't reply.

They followed Davina onto the Ring, leaving the lights of the residential blocks behind them. Claudia shivered slightly, whether from fear or cold or exhaustion, she didn't know. It felt very exposed, being away from any buildings and on open ground, enclosed by darkness. Above and all around her soared the Dome's dome, the sole barrier that protected them from the Outside. The vast, semi-opaque shield wall was said to encompass an area as large as an old city.

Across the Ring from C-Sector rose the towers and blocks of the Central Zone. All the administration, higher education and medical facilities were quartered there, along with the Mentargh Barracks and the Youth League stadium and training ground. At this time of the cycle, with all its lights on, the Central Zone appeared in a nimbus, rising from the utter darkness of the Ring.

Very briefly, it was as if Claudia were seeing the Dome for the first time. She was aware of its stark geometric beauty, one of harsh concrete planes and pitiless glass, quite different from how the Machine had shown it. Awe was followed by a rush of relief and gratitude, a sense of safety, all the emotions she was supposed to feel, more or less, as a citizen of the Dome, but these feelings were sharp and fresh and real, not drug-induced, unless the jenny was still in her system.

Yet, at the same time, she realised how brutal it was, a machine for survival. But what was she comparing it to? Where were all these thoughts and feelings coming from?

'Claudia?' That was Martin. 'Are you OK?'

Without realising, she had stopped.

'I'm fine, I just felt a bit weird for a minute.'

'Yeah, that hardbrew is still kicking my brain around too. I can't believe Arnie is still walking, after all he drank. Come on, don't get left behind out here.'

Claudia wasn't feeling that drunk anymore, but that was the easier explanation. She hurried to catch up with her friends and the two small beams of light.

'Do you know where she's taking us?' Pierce asked Arnie.

'It's all new to me, Cadet-Trooper,' he said.

Claudia didn't think Arnie was being fully honest, and it was likely Pierce felt this too.

Davina suddenly stopped and swept her light across the ground. Her torch picked up a metal hatch with two handles.

'Here we are, citizens. Last chance to turn back.'

A shock ran through the group. After the Party Machine, there was often a lingering connection. Claudia could feel the adrenalin rising off Arnie, who was standing just in front of her. She felt a fierce curiosity herself, like hunger. She knew what they were about to do was deeply wrong, but she also knew she'd always regret turning back.

Later, she wondered why they had followed Davina so easily. Apart from Arnie, the anointed bad boy of their cohort, they'd all been model junior citizens. Had the hardbrew brought by

Pierce numbed their sense of responsibility? Had the desire to do something forbidden, with huge risks, been lurking in them all along, even in Pierce, the Mentargh cadet-trooper?

As Jemima had said, life in the Dome was boring.

Claudia had never thought this before, but Jemima's scornful words were now lodged in her brain like the automated voice that announced the closing of doors on the Transit or reminded citizens to dispose of their food waste in the correct receptacles for maximum recycling efficiency on the way out of the Youth League canteen.

Davina squatted by the hatch, grabbed the two handles and shifted the lid aside. The grating noise seemed very loud. Claudia glanced back at the distant residential blocks, wondering if people could hear.

'Down you go,' said Davina. 'I'll go last and close the lid.'

Arnie was the first, almost leaping down the narrow metal ladder. The air that came up through the shaft was stale and noticeably chillier.

Martin followed him. Claudia looked at Pierce. He shrugged, put his torch between his teeth and went down himself, as if he did this every day.

Ally quickly followed him. She giggled nervously, setting up a high-pitched echo that set Claudia's nerves on edge.

The rungs were icy against her fingers. When Davina shut the hatch overhead, the jiggling light of the torches barely scraped the dense blackness that surrounded them.

Claudia's feet eventually hit a grille-metal floor and she joined Martin, Arnie, Pierce and Ally in a tunnel. Thick skeins of wires and pipes ran along the sides and overhead. Claudia began to feel cold in her lightweight clothes, which were optimised for the Dome's steady and narrow temperature range. Maybe Davina's deadclothes would keep her warm down here.

Davina's feet, appearing on the ladder, were in the same utility shoes as everyone else.

'Welcome to Sub-Level One, junior citizens,' she said.

'How many levels are there?' asked Martin.

'I'm not sure, but it goes way down,' Davina replied. 'It's like a whole other mirror city. We stick to the higher levels. There's no power in the lower levels, so the air isn't recycled.'

Who was *we*?

Claudia glanced at Pierce. His expression did not change, but he couldn't have missed it. How far could they trust him? She'd never really thought of him as a Mentargh before, even though he'd grown up in the Barracks, but for someone like Davina, that was the main fact about him. Was Davina always this reckless, or had the hardbrew made her careless?

'That is so freeding spooky,' said Arnie. He sounded excited rather than scared. 'A whole other upside-down Dome.'

'Where are you taking us?' said Pierce.

'Just for a stroll, citizen,' said Davina. 'Follow me.'

Their long shadows on the cylindrical walls made Claudia think about the people who came to the Dome after the Event, seeking refuge. All those years ago, they had entered through tunnels like this, scared and starving and desperate to escape the chaos outside. Her generation was lucky to live in the Dome, whatever Jemima said.

'How often do you come down here?' Ally asked. 'I mean, you're not going to get us lost, are you?'

'I have no intention of getting lost,' said Davina. 'But you're welcome to get lost at any time.'

Claudia thought this was a bit harsh, but Ally was being

very irritating.

The tunnel sloped down. They passed hundreds of numbered doorways and then a vast hall filled with nameless machinery, vehicles with swollen tyres and bristling antennae, steel dishes metres across, what seemed to be scientific equipment under clear plastic sheets, and stacks and rows of metal containers the size of a residential unit.

'There's crazy amounts of stuff down here,' said Davina. 'A lot of it wasn't even connected to the NovaGaia Project.'

'What's that?' said Martin.

'It was really big before the Event,' she replied. 'The planet was dying, and there were plans to set up colonies on the moon. What they called the Biodome was a shared experiment, with the space people developing a lunar base and the Biodome people trying to hit total self-sufficiency. The Self-Regenerating Artificial Environment. That's what we live in now.'

'This stuff isn't covered in Level III,' said Pierce.

'I used to talk a lot with my granddad,' said Davina. 'I was curious, and I didn't get any answers in Basic. Is this the kind of thing you learn in Level V?'

'Some of it,' said Pierce, looking at Claudia. 'But not in much detail.'

'People did live here before us, you know, from 2046 to 2047,' said Davina. 'It was a psychological experiment as well as a physical one. They weren't supposed to quit, but more than half pulled out. Couldn't stand it. I bet you didn't learn that in Level V, Mentargh Boy.'

'What was their problem?' said Martin.

'That's so freaky, people living here before the Event,' said Arnie. 'I've always wondered about those dirty underpants under my bunk.'

'You filthy old man!' said Martin.

Arnie grabbed him around the neck and Martin tried to punch him, his arms flailing, and they both laughed, setting up an echo.

'Freeding idiots,' said Davina, but she was grinning.

After walking for what seemed like ages through another tunnel, they emerged into another large chamber. The air was immediately less stuffy, and Claudia could sense open space above and all around her.

Pierce played his torch around, picking out stacks of large crates and a vehicle with two metal arms, apparently designed to lift and transport the crates. The beam did not reach the far wall, giving the impression that they were standing on the brink of a dark abyss.

To one side was a double stack of what looked like modular cabins, very basic ones, in two rows. Each had the same logo in one corner: MNT Group.

'Is that something to do with the Mentargh?' said Claudia.

'No idea,' said Pierce. 'I'm just a cadet-trooper, I don't know much more than you.'

He seemed to resent the question.

'Where are we now?' said Martin.

'Just a storage vault,' said Davina. 'From here we can keep going down. We can't use the lifts. DOMUS would pick up any power usage.'

Davina was pointing out a door at the far corner when Claudia noticed a faint glow off to one side, between the cabins.

'Pierce, did you see that?' she whispered, pointing.

He turned off his torch. The other light immediately

disappeared.

'Is that the Mentargh?' Claudia felt cold all over, even though she was already chilled through.

'No,' said Pierce. 'They would have seen us long before this, especially with all the noise we're making, and they wouldn't hang back. Could be a maintenance team, but there's no reason for them to be down here. There are no working facilities, it's just storage.'

The others had started towards the door, unaware of the light. Pierce took Claudia's arm.

'We shouldn't have come,' he said. 'You know what goes on down here, don't you?'

'I'm not in the Mentargh. You'll have to tell me.'

He paused briefly before replying. 'Groups of people meet down here sometimes, to avoid surveillance. People with certain kinds of ideas.'

'Subversives?' Claudia's heart began to pound. 'Are there really such people? How do they avoid getting caught? The Mentargh know everything about everyone.'

'The system isn't quite as efficient as we're led to believe,' said Pierce. 'People who reject Ideology can cheat the system. Don't ask me how, it's way above my level. It's usually older people, but they infect younger people with their ideas. Obviously Davina's granddad got to her when she was very young.'

'But what do they actually do? We couldn't survive without Ideo.'

'These people don't believe in Ideo. They think it's evil, a form of mind control, and they want to undermine it.'

'But what's the alternative? Individualistic chaos? We'd all die,' said Claudia.

The two were suddenly caught in the glare of a torch and stood dazzled.

'Freeding hyper-freed! Is that you, Jim?' called Davina from ahead, and the torch released them.

An Oldie, a man, stepped out of the darkness to meet Davina. His gaunt face was framed by a gingery beard. The insignia on his blues indicated that he worked in the Department of Energy. Like many Oldies, he didn't wear any Ideo rank.

'I thought I recognised your voice.' The torch beam moved to light up the others. It was a powerful torch, the kind used by high-ranking technical workers or the Mentargh, and they had to shut their eyes and turn away. 'What the hell, Davina? Who are all these kids? You mentioned one friend you might bring along, not a whole bloody gang of them.'

'I told you I was going to a party,' said Davina. She sounded a little defiant, as if she was being told off, although Oldies had no automatic authority over junior citizens. 'We ran out of booze, and we got bored, so we came out for a walk. That's all. I didn't think you'd be down here tonight.'

'Davina, who is this old guy and what's he doing here?' said Martin. 'Energy is Sector D, and we haven't walked that far.'

'Junior citizens, this is Jim, one of my granddad's old mates,' said Davina. 'He used to do a lot of walking before the Event, bushwalking. It was like a sport, but not really, and you could do it on your own.'

'Wow, total antisocial individualism,' said Arnie.

'It sounds really boring,' said Ally.

Another voice, a woman this time, came out of the darkness.

'Jim, is that Davina? We're all having heart attacks back here. What's going on?'

Both Jim and Davina grimaced. Claudia glanced at Pierce.

His face was unreadable.

'Freed, Davina, is this what Oldies do for fun?' said Martin. 'Hang about in the Underground, freezing their ancient bones and burdening the system with their pneumonia?'

Another Oldie appeared next to Jim. She was wearing what looked like a pair of eye-shields, but with a thick patterned frame in pink and red. Both arms had been glued back on, and the eye-shields sat crookedly across her face.

'Hi, Davina. We weren't expecting to see you tonight.'

'Hi, Lisa,' said Davina.

'Davina, thank God for that.' The third Oldie, also a woman, had long grey hair and wore a baggy fleece jacket over her blues. The fleece was a non-standard colour and much too large for her small frame. Claudia couldn't work out the logo at chest level. It seemed to be some sort of animal.

'Hi, Lily,' Davina muttered.

'Does Jim bring all his girlfriends down here?' said Arnie. 'Doesn't he have room in his unit to entertain them? This guy is a boss, he should be in the Mentargh.'

The idea of Oldies in the Mentargh was pretty funny and even Pierce cracked a grin.

'I thought you were on shift tonight,' said Davina to Jim.

'They changed the schedule, again,' he said. 'One of the systems is offline and another one is barely working. I've done three double shifts this week.'

'Why don't they meet above ground, like normal citizens?' Martin asked Davina. 'The heating in community nodes is turned up especially for Oldies.'

Jim gave him a hard stare. 'I spent three years living underground after the Event. I feel safer down here.'

'That's intense,' said Arnie. 'My parents never talked about the Event at all. I have no idea how they survived.'

'Are they still alive?' Jim asked.

'No, they died years ago.'

'What were their names?'

'Jessie and Roy,' said Arnie. 'I never remember their ID numbers. I was only in Basic when they died.'

'I knew a Jessie, but not a Roy.' Jim shone his torch briefly in Arnie's face.

'I don't like Oldies,' Ally whispered to Claudia. 'They're creepy, and they smell funny.'

'Hey, Davina! I thought you were off partying with the inheritors tonight, living up your golden future.'

Another man appeared behind Jim. He wasn't quite an Oldie but not far off. It was hard for Claudia to put an age to anyone over thirty. People who'd lived through the Aftermath usually looked rough; they had permanent health problems as well as the high risk of cancer. The criteria for deciding who was worth sustaining and at what level of resource input were very detailed and a key part of medical training.

'Hi, Neil. The party died,' said Davina.

The Oldie called Neil was wearing a very tatty t-shirt, printed with a baffling image: a fluffy figure with two googly eyes, standing on stick legs on some sort of board that was propelled by a squiggly line that may have represented water. Beneath the picture were the faded words, MAKE THE SHEEPLE THINK! BYRON BAY ANARCHIST FESTIVAL 2045.

'When a party dies, you have to move on, seek out new flow and action, find fresh energy,' said Neil. 'There's plenty of room down here for everyone. Friends of Davina are friends of ours.'

'Is this your new crew, Davina?'

A girl their own age squeezed past the four Oldies and looked them all over.

'Hi, Luma. You know me, I make friends wherever I go.'

From Davina's tone, Claudia could tell that Luma wasn't a friend.

Luma glared at Claudia and Pierce. 'Level V, what the freed?'

'I keep an open mind,' said Davina.

'Level V, that's Ideology, isn't it?' said Lisa. 'My granddaughter is always quoting it at me, when I'm allowed to see her. It's like she's been brainwashed at some sort of strange Bible camp.'

'My grandparents were evangelicals,' said Neil. 'I used to know chunks of the Bible by heart. The King James version. At least it was better written than the Ideology.'

'Well, we know who wrote the Ideology, and it sure as hell wasn't God,' said Jim, and the others chuckled and rolled their eyes, except for Luma, who was still glaring at Claudia and Pierce.

'You know who wrote the Ideology?' said Martin, goggling.

'It's a bit more recent than the Bible, kiddo,' said Neil.

'What's the Bible?' Ally asked.

Jim shook his head, as if this obscure reference should be obvious.

'See, this is why we need to reach out to more young people,' he said to the other Oldies. 'They have no bloody idea about anything. Once we're gone and composted, nobody will know what life was like before. All they'll know is what the Survival Committee decided they should know thirty years ago.'

'Aren't you two supposed to be setting an example of citizenship and responsibility?' said Luma to Pierce and

Claudia. 'The Underground is out of bounds. You could get into some serious trouble.'

Oddly, she reminded Claudia of Juanita.

'So could you all,' said Pierce.

'The kids I work with think I'm a silly old fart, rabbiting on with all sorts of nonsense, and all the time I'm quietly subverting them,' Jim was saying.

'That's what you think,' said Lily. 'I think they just ignore us because we're old, and they're taught to believe we're daft.'

'I ignore his rabbiting half the time too,' said Lisa. She put her arm around Jim and kissed him on the cheek.

Claudia was shocked. It had never occurred to her that Oldies might still have urges. She could see from their expressions that her friends had the same reaction.

'I don't think we should trust them,' said Luma.

'If we don't trust people, nothing is going to change,' said Neil. 'You have to take risks to achieve anything, kiddo.'

There was a silence, and even friendly Lisa looked worried. Claudia could feel a prickle of doubt and fear pass through her friends. Except for Pierce. It was as if he'd expected something like this to happen.

Ally was the first to speak.

'I think we should be getting back to Martin's. People will be wondering where we've gone.'

'I think you probably should,' said Jim, looking at Davina, who nodded.

'See you around, kids. Party on!' Neil waved and stepped back into the darkness with the others.

'Neil's a free spirit,' said Davina. 'You shouldn't take him too seriously. People who lived through the Aftermath are often pretty weird.'

'What the freeding freed was on his t-shirt?' said Arnie.

'I know, I was trying to work it out the whole time,' said Martin, and they both laughed.

'What did he mean about changing things?' said Ally.

'Oldies sometimes miss how things were before,' said Davina.

'But things were really bad before.'

'Maybe not everything,' said Davina, very carefully. 'Maybe there were some good things that we're not told about because we can't have them now, and that would just make people unhappy and our survival depends on harmony.'

'So that's why we're told not to listen to Oldies or take anything they say seriously,' said Ally.

'That's right,' said Pierce.

'It's not actually forbidden to talk to them,' said Claudia. 'At least, there's nothing in Level V. But the Aftermath traumatised everyone who survived it. Some Oldies have antisocial tendencies and reject the core values that we need to keep surviving in the Dome. So you have to be on your guard against any negative influences.'

Like your grandfather, she wanted to say to Davina, but didn't.

'Double affirmation from the Mentargh and Level V, thanks,' said Davina. 'Which is why, junior citizens, you shouldn't tell anyone that we've been down here, fraternising with Oldies. Absolutely freeding nobody.'

'Don't stress,' said Martin. 'This is the most excitement I've had since Arnie fell in a mycelium tank because he was hungover and almost got done for sabotage as a subversive element.'

'I wasn't hungover, you tripped me up,' said Arnie.

Ally yawned hugely. 'It's freezing down here and I need the toilet. Can we go now?'

Six

When they emerged from the Underground, through the same hatch, there was a thin cover of dew on the hard-packed ground, visible as a silvery sheen. DOMUS lowered the temperature during designated hours to allow the warm air accumulated at zenith level to condense and precipitate, an imitation of the natural moisture cycle of Earth.

The sun blurred across the eastern perimeter of the Dome, a milky smudge against the massive shield barrier. To the left, Claudia saw the tiered glass of the Hydroponics Plant in B-Sector glittering, as it always did, briefly, this time of the cycle, as did the clear, sinuous tube of the Transit, mounted high on its pylons. To the right, the Moisture Regeneration Plant was still encased in darkness behind the residential blocks of C-Sector.

Claudia and Pierce walked slightly behind the others, just out of earshot. She was deliberately lagging, and she could tell he was doing the same.

The first C-Sector residential block loomed ahead, and there wasn't much time to talk.

'Just as well Juanita went home,' she said.

'I wish she'd stayed, and then none of this would've happened,' he said curtly. 'Davina's obviously reckless, but she wouldn't have taken the risk of trusting Juanita, even with all the hardbrew she knocked back.'

'So you think we shouldn't have gone?'

'For freed's sake, Claudia! Of course we shouldn't have gone into the Underground, which is totally off-limits, and met a bunch of Oldies who want to change things. Whatever the freed that's supposed to mean.'

'You could've stopped us,' said Claudia. 'Isn't it your duty now, to set an example and stop your friends doing stupid things and falling into individualistic ways?'

'Actually, it's my job to monitor people,' he said.

'What the freed does that mean?' Claudia didn't think it was possible to feel any colder. 'Are you going to report us?'

They were almost at the C-Sector perimeter. Pierce stopped and took her arm.

'No. It was a dumb party stunt, and you'd get off with a warning just for going into the Underground. Davina and her wrinkly mates, that's a whole other matter.'

'They're just free spirits,' said Claudia. 'It's not against code to wear deadclothes.'

Technically, wearing deadclothes was a form of recycling and therefore in accordance with the Dome's fundamental principles.

'Oh, come on, Claudia! I can see you're totally fascinated by Davina, with her punky attitude and those weird clothes and all the unregulated knowledge she's picked up from her granddad. There's a reason we learn stuff through Ideo: so we don't get the wrong idea about things. She's trouble.'

'If she's trouble, why aren't the Mentargh dealing with her? Is there something you're not telling me?' Claudia was suddenly so tired that she could hardly think. All she wanted was her bunk.

'Just be careful, Claudia. And promise me you won't go back down there. Please, just promise me.'

'Is that an official warning, Cadet-Trooper?'

His face closed off, and he dropped her arm. They resumed walking without another word, to where the others were waiting by the Transit station.

The overhead platform was busy with predawn workers as the shifts changed over. Nobody paid any attention to a group of haggard and yawning teenagers.

'Consider your promotion duly celebrated, Cadet-Trooper,' said Martin to Pierce. 'I'm off to my bunk. See you all at training.'

As usual after a big night, Arnie would crash at Martin's, and they headed off together.

The others swiped themselves into the Transit station. Ally and Pierce went to catch the cross-line, Pierce to the Central Zone and Ally to A-Sector on the other side. Davina and Claudia walked together through the glassed-in overpass to the circle platforms. They could see Ally and Pierce on the platform below. Ally was talking and waving her hands; Pierce was shrugging and nodding and mostly seemed to be ignoring her.

'Freed, she doesn't give up,' said Davina, yawning. 'He doesn't seem interested, not at this time of morning, anyway. I honestly thought you two were an item.'

'No, we're just friends,' said Claudia, yawning herself.

'We can trust him, can't we?' said Davina. This was her first real admission of what she'd led them into.

'I think so,' said Claudia. Discussing Pierce with Davina felt like a betrayal. 'He's been our friend since Basic. But now he's in the Mentargh, I honestly don't know anymore. You should probably tone it down around him.'

'I don't usually hang out with Mentargh,' said Davina. 'Arnie could've freeding warned me.'

At that moment, Pierce looked up and saw them standing there. Again, Claudia was reminded of Luke.

Ally looked up too and waved.

'Not being mean or anything, but she's a waste of resources,' said Davina.

Claudia had nothing ready to say in Ally's defence, so said nothing, and they went their separate ways, Claudia to the outer line and Davina to the inner.

Services were regular at this time of the cycle, and Claudia didn't have to wait long for a shuttle. The Transit coiled through the C-Sector residential zone. The brief beauty of sunrise had passed, and the Dome assumed its everyday appearance, not the one the Party Machine had shown them, nor the shining vision of safety Claudia had seen out on the Ring.

Which Dome did other people normally see, the shining vision conjured up by the Machine and the jennies, or the unfiltered, run-down version that Claudia saw now? Which one did Davina see? And Pierce? He was her closest friend, and she'd always been open with him.

The thought that perhaps she could no longer trust him made her feel unbearably lonely.

As the Transit perimeter line approached the Hydroponics Plant, it swung towards the Barrier Zone. Certain points of the outer line of the Transit were the closest any unauthorised person could come to the Dome wall itself. At ground level, it was blocked off by several security barriers. Access was restricted to workers with special clearance.

As always, Claudia strained for a better view. *Four metres thick, printed from semi-transparent thermoplastic, designed to provide protection against solar and background radiation as encountered on the lunar surface.* Every student learned that in Basic. The Dome recreated the protection provided by the Earth's atmosphere before it had been irreversibly damaged. The geodesic shield filtered out the main force of the sun, giving the Dome its perpetual greyness. People spoke of the sun with a sense of detachment. It travelled across their pseudo-sky every day, the only visible manifestation of the outside world, creating light differentials in the twenty-four-hour cycle but otherwise inconsequential to their well-being.

From the opposite window, Claudia could see the gleaming glass tiers of the Hydroponics Plant. She could just make out the blue-suited workers moving about the trays and tanks, and condensation trickling down the panes to the sill-troughs as the temperature was raised. Claudia wondered if her mother was there. Faye was rostered for the dawn shift, but that was no guarantee that she'd be out of bed, much less working.

The Transit stopped briefly at the Hydroponics Plant station and then turned away from the Barrier Zone and into B-Sector, passing between identical res blocks. On either side, the rows and columns of small windows were like a multitude of eyes.

Looking down into the long canyons created by the buildings, Claudia saw a man standing alone on one of the mid-level open walkways. He wasn't doing anything, just leaning on the rail and looking out and down. He was wearing blue overalls, signalling active status, so he should've been at work, at rest or at his designated non-productive activities. Nobody spent their down-time standing alone on an overpass. Like wearing deadclothes, it wasn't forbidden, but any unusual behaviour could raise questions.

As the shuttle passed overhead, the man looked up and their eyes met for a fleeting moment. He seemed startled, as if he'd expected not to be seen, and she had the feeling that she'd almost interrupted something.

Then the shuttle shot free of the res blocks and glided to a halt at the B-Sector station.

Seven

In the common entryway of Claudia's building was a large banner, heralding the approach of the 30th Anniversary Thanksgiving and the Selection Trials. Bold letters exhorted citizens to give their utmost to the glorious occasion, and underneath there was a smiling tableau of Youth League, Mentargh, citizen-workers and even a token Oldie.

Claudia swiped herself into res unit E8-6-12. Inside, it was completely silent, and for a blissful moment she thought Faye was out, but when she switched on the light and saw the debris, her hopes plummeted. The table and floor were littered with dented cannies, and a strong reek of roughbrew permeated the unit. The mess of several days had accumulated through the kitchen and living area, and a rancid smell drifted up from the waste unit.

It was a long time since the pizza at Martin's place, and Claudia was starving. She looked in the coldstore but all she found was a half-eaten tray of pea-protein balls and vegetables, obviously several days old, and a cannie of kefir.

A familiar depression closed over Claudia as she surveyed the chaos. Despair reflected a failure of individual resilience and Claudia did her best to be strong, but it was hard, especially when she was tired.

'You can't be bothered to pick up our rations from the distro, but you can be bothered to hunt down roughbrew,' she muttered.

Roughbrew was an illegal by-product of certain food production processes. It was much stronger than synthanol and even hardbrew and had addictive qualities. People who made it were severely punished on the grounds of social and productive sabotage. The stuff was dark brown and whiffed like a backed-up drain.

Claudia threw out the abandoned ready meal and made do with the kefir. She was too tired to go out again for food, even though the distro would be open now. She'd go later, on the way home from training that afternoon.

'Claudia, is that you?' A querulous voice came from the direction of Faye's cabin.

'Who do you think?' snapped Claudia. 'The Mentargh? They should arrest you for drinking that bilge.'

'Don't be like that,' said Faye.

She walked unsteadily across the living area and leaned against the kitchen partition. Her face was sunken and blotchy, signs of long-term roughbrew addiction, and her blue rig was stained in several places. Claudia could smell her coming; she badly needed a shower.

'Do we have any painkillers?' Faye asked.

'You haven't been to the distro, so we don't have anything.'

'Look in the top hatch. I put some there.'

Claudia found a pack with three pills left in it and tossed it at her mother. Faye made a feeble grab and missed. The pack skittered across the floor and disappeared under the table in the main room.

'You little bitch.'

Faye got down on her hands and knees, with difficulty, and groped for the pills.

Claudia watched from the kitchenette as she drank the kefir, draining the entire canister. Faye finally got hold of the pills and swallowed all three of them.

Still on the floor, leaning back against the divan, she glared at her daughter.

'You're a trainee med tech, you can get hold of decent pills, not the shit they give us at the distro.'

'I don't have access to the strong stuff. If you want stronger pills, you can go for a medical appraisal.'

'Bloody hell,' said Faye. 'You know I'm on my last warning. Do you want me chucked on the compost heap?'

'It'd be a better use of resources,' said Claudia. She left the empty kefir cannie on the kitchen bench, because the recycling bin was full. 'I'll pick up our rations after training this afternoon. Now I really need to get some sleep.'

She went into her cabin and snibbed the door shut. A small window let in the feeble light and looked out over the Central Zone. Building 8, E-Block, was the last in the row and backed directly onto the Ring. An inward-looking view of the green spaces between the blocks was considered more conducive to mental health than staring onto emptiness, and people with the right connections in the Citizens' Brigade sometimes managed to get themselves moved across. Nobody in their residential committee wanted anything to do with Faye, certainly not to live next to her.

After setting an alarm on the small screen by her bunk, Claudia crawled under the thin thermal quilt. Her head was spinning with exhaustion. As she fell asleep, a succession of images flickered across her mind: Luke's face in close-up,

Davina and her strange headgear, Neil's tatty t-shirt and its bewildering logo, the hulking shapes of storage containers in the Underground, and the photograph of the young Jemima and Hetty swimming in what must have been, she realised now, the sea.

Eight

The smell from the Med Block dining hall at lunchtime reached all the way down the corridor.

Claudia had once overheard one of the senior trainers, an Oldie, describe the smell to another Oldie as 'mushrooms, mould, rotting seaweed and wet boots'. Seeing that Claudia was listening, the senior trainer had immediately added, 'We're very lucky to have all our nutritional requirements met so efficiently.' The other Oldie had nodded. 'Yes, absolutely, we never had such delicious and efficient food in the bad old days.'

Claudia had the impression that they were making some kind of joke at her expense, but what they said was quite true, so how could this be?

The clatter of voices and trays was overwhelming. Behind Claudia in the service queue was a girl called Emma, known in med tech circles as Enema. She was in the level above Claudia and liked to consider herself a mentor.

'How's your Ed? Learning your stuff?' she shouted wetly in Claudia's ear.

'All good,' said Claudia, serving herself a dollop of kimchi to go with the day's stew. It was brown and lumpy and contained all the necessary amino acids and a good proportion of the vitamins and minerals required for the average person.

Enema took a large scoop of stew, Citizen Meal No. 23, and followed Claudia to a table.

'You wouldn't think it was fungus or plankton or some bacterial culture, would you?' she said, shovelling it into her mouth. 'I remember visiting the Hydro Plant with my class in Basic, and some of the stuff they grow there is really gross. I mean, the brown algae they make protein out of looked like shit, no joke. But really, we're much better off eating all this optimised lab stuff. People used to eat red meat and highly processed, nutritionally zero-value food products loaded with sugar and fat. So many kids were being born with severe allergies they had to go to special schools and wear masks and carry EpiPens everywhere. People in rich countries were eating themselves sick. Did you know that heart attacks were actually called "the disease of civilisation"?'

Claudia wished Enema wouldn't chew and talk at the same time.

A low tone sounded overhead, signalling the start of the anthem. With a massed scraping of stools, the trainees stood to attention. A moment of silence, then the familiar words of 'The Inheritors' poured out of the speakers.

Claudia had heard it so often she hardly registered the words, but the opening and the slow, triumphant crescendo always triggered the same response. By the song's final, exhilarating moments, Claudia always felt completely at one with everyone else who had survived the end of history and inherited a glorious future in the Dome, even Enema.

This time, the memory of Davina's mocking rendition blocked the music's usual effect. When the last refrain faded out and Claudia sat down to face the tray of congealing stew, it did look like something that had originated from wastewater management.

Announcements blared overhead, mostly concerning the coming Selection Trials, Youth League activities and the 30th Anniversary celebrations. Then the screens at each end of the hall and those suspended from the ceiling in the middle lit up. The hall fell silent as the familiar face of Commodore Melita, the Directorate spokesperson, appeared. She was dressed in the full black of the Mentargh. Beneath her insignia of rank was the Roman number of her Ideo level: XIV.

'Junior citizens,' she began gravely. 'I regret to inform you that the pernicious influence of subversives has caused a fall in the recycling rate in the last few months. Certain workers in the Materials Recycling Facility were influenced by the ideas and attitudes of a few, which resulted in neglect, laxity, absenteeism, outbreaks of individualism and discontent, and ultimately to a general decline in the efficiency and output of recycling and repurposing services. The protagonists have been identified by the Mentargh and will suffer the full consequences of their antisocial behaviour. All facility technicians are undergoing screening and counselling sessions to ensure that any remaining attitude contamination is exposed and dealt with. As a result of this unfortunate affair, the renewal period for non-essential items will be extended for the next six months.'

A collective groan arose from the seated diners. Enema booed.

'It is tragic, citizens, that the malicious actions of an antisocial minority can endanger the lives of the majority,' said the Commodore. 'This incident demonstrates to everyone the insidious, pervasive nature of subversion, and the pitfalls it holds for the citizen who is not on their guard at all times. I ask you, for the sake of our community's well-being, indeed, our survival, to give your wholehearted support in rooting out and crushing the contagion of subversion and individualism in all their subtle and destructive manifestations.'

There were angry murmurs of assent as the screens went blank. Claudia took a sip from her water cannie, eyes carefully averted. Did any of Davina's Underground friends work in recycling? She tried to remember the codes on their clothes, but apart from Jim and Luma, who were both Energy Sector, the Oldies hadn't worn any insignia.

Arnie was a materials tech trainee. What did he know? Had he been affected? Arnie had always been a free spirit, although his friends only ever said this as a joke, the same way they joked about Juanita arresting them one day, because it was impossible to take such things seriously, even if they could be true.

Next to her Enema was loudly abusing the subversives.

'They'll be wiped, no doubt about it, and good riddance! Wipe their brains and make them useful in the sewage works.'

'How do you know what happens in Re-Education?' said a boy on the other side of the bench, who was the same cohort as Enema. 'Have you been for a brain-retune yourself?'

The others sitting nearby all laughed. Enema did not have the gift of making people like her.

'What do you think happens to them?' she countered.

'I heard that the really bad ones are ejected,' said one girl. 'The ones who can't be recycled.'

'That's crap,' said Enema. 'The Dome is sealed up. Where did you hear that?'

'Can't remember,' said the girl and poked at the remains of

her stew, not looking at Enema.

'Unauthorised information is dangerous,' said Enema. 'You should report it.'

'I said, I don't remember,' said the girl. She picked up her tray and walked off.

Claudia kept her eyes on her tray. How responsible were Davina and her friends for what had happened in the recycling facility? As Commodore Melita had said, subversion was an attitude. Even if it wasn't acted on, this attitude could infect other people and lead to subversive action. If Jim, Lisa and the others had influenced, even indirectly, the workers at the Recycling Depot, they were as guilty of subversion as the workers themselves.

Davina certainly had an attitude. Claudia had to admit, she'd been attracted by Davina's in-your-face individualism and had agreed, against her better sense, to trespass in a forbidden zone. Level V Ideo hadn't been enough to protect her. Davina had infected them all that night, even Pierce.

Unless Pierce had gone along for other reasons. *It's my job to monitor you.*

He was their friend. They trusted him. Unlike Juanita, he still seemed like one of them, even though he'd grown up in the Barracks.

Did following Davina into the Underground mean that she, Martin and Arnie all had subversive tendencies? Claudia didn't count Ally. The idea of Ally as a subversive was a joke, a real one.

Claudia had not intended any harm, but she felt radioactive with guilt. Surely Enema could sense the hot waves coming off her? But Enema was now going on about the Selection Trials, chewing and talking at the same time. Tiny brown particles of food landed on the communal table around her tray.

The daily Civil Ed came over the screens, competing against the usual lunchtime hubbub. It was the clip on birth control, which Claudia had seen many times.

'The Dome is a finite area,' began the sugary female voice. 'Therefore it is vital that the population is kept at a constant. A stable population means enough food, housing, basic commodities, jobs and medical care for everyone. The maximum capacity of the Dome is 60,000. The optimum level is 45,000, roughly the number we are maintaining now.'

The presenter pointed to two animated graphs. 'To hold this constant, vigorous birth control is necessary. If we ever exceeded the 60,000 mark, conditions would become very unpleasant for us all. The Dome's capacity to recycle air and moisture would deteriorate and the temperature would begin to rise. Food would become scarce, and overcrowding would occur. The delicate ecological equilibrium would eventually fail, and we would all die. So you see, junior citizens,' she continued cheerily, 'we must all strive for zero population growth. This means learning to exercise effective birth control before the commencement of sexual activity.'

The dynamic display switched to an outline of the female body, showing the reproductive system in various unnatural colours.

'Not while we're eating!' one boy called out, and his friends laughed and pulled faces.

In the same bland tones, the presenter described the intricacies of fertilisation, the female cycle and the odds of becoming pregnant in tedious detail.

'Remember, young women, it is your responsibility to make

an appointment with your Area Health Officer before becoming sexually active. At the age of sixteen, it is compulsory for all females to be fitted with a contraceptive intrauterine implant.'

'I got mine done when I was thirteen,' said Enema, and someone sniggered loudly behind her back.

Claudia knew that Enema's implant was unlikely to ever be removed. She had a tendency to obesity, even with their controlled diet in the Dome, and a chronic respiratory condition that had once required a stay in the Med Centre ICU. She was sufficiently functional and totally loyal, a proper Ideo-brain, but her genetic material contained too many liabilities. As a trainee med tech, Enema surely knew this, so it was strange to Claudia that she would draw attention to herself by boasting about having her implant.

Claudia hadn't had her implant fitted yet. Ally said it hurt so much that she'd screamed and the med tech, a man, had told her she was a waste of resources and sent her away. Juanita said it didn't hurt that much, and you just had to get it over with for the greater good.

'Prospective parents may apply for a child licence, subject to genetic screening and other requirements. To remove a contraceptive device without authorisation and to become pregnant without a licence are crimes against the community. Such extreme individualism is severely punished. Remember, birth control is your duty to the Dome and to your fellow citizens. Our lives depend upon it.'

The screen blanked again.

'What were you doing in Gynie this morning?' said Enema. 'I thought your study unit were doing minor injuries.'

'We went to see a sterilisation,' said Claudia. 'The subject had removed her implant and was trying to get pregnant without authorisation.'

'Her gene screen had some serious issues,' added one of Claudia's classmates, who was sitting across from them. 'Like, no way was she ever going to get a licence. But she was desperate to get pregnant. They had to strap her down to sedate her. It was hard to watch, actually.'

'People are so selfish,' said Enema. 'They just want to breed for individualistic reasons, and they don't care about creating a burden for society.'

Claudia's classmate glanced across at her. They'd stood next to each other at the viewing window, watching the woman thrash about and scream as she was forced onto the gurney and her hands and feet were cuffed. Once the sedation had been administered, she'd gone limp very quickly. The process itself only took several minutes and was shown on an overhead screen. Once or twice, the woman had moaned.

'Is she fully sedated?' one of the students had asked their trainer.

'She should be,' said the trainer, frowning. It was the same Oldie who'd made the comment about the food smelling like wet boots.

'She's a criminal. She's lucky to be sedated at all,' said another student.

'That's enough,' said the trainer sharply. 'The Dome is a humane society. As doctors—as med techs—it's our duty to minimise pain and suffering, not add to it. God knows, there was enough of that in the Aftermath.'

Claudia liked this trainer and sometimes worried for her, especially when she stood up to younger trainers with harsher attitudes. When she was qualified to do sterilisations, Claudia would make sure that the subject was properly sedated.

The last class of the day, before PE, drill and Game, was Ideo. Unlike most people her age, who were bored by Ideology, Claudia enjoyed it, especially the parts about the Old World and what had gone so wrong. In the early years of the Dome, historians had recorded extensive interviews with Survivors. It was important to have a record, although access to the Archives was restricted. At Level V, students were judged ideologically mature enough to be exposed to selected extracts.

Claudia's study unit was currently studying the topic, 'Money, work and social dysfunction, 2000–2052'. The interviews were presented in audio-only or visual format and were always accompanied by an annotated transcript. A typical interview went like this:

Interviewer: Tell me, how did you live before the Event?

Subject: I lived in a shared house [=free-standing residential unit with private green zone] with five other people.

Interviewer: Was this a normal arrangement?

Subject: It used to be something only young people did, before they coupled up [pair-bonded] or bought their own place [individual ownership of residence], but housing was so expensive that people ended up sharing their entire lives. I was still sharing in my forties.

Interviewer: Is this how everyone lived?

Subject: Some people had money from their parents, so they could afford to buy, and then they could pass it all on to their own kids [see: inherited wealth].

Interviewer: But your parents didn't help you in this way.

Subject: My parents lived in a caravan [=small mobile

residential unit, originally for leisure use] on the coast. They gave up on the city and went bush [=semi-self-sufficient rural lifestyle, increasingly adopted by the economically marginalised]. Cities were for rich people.

Interviewer: So you chose to go to the city, knowing that it would be difficult?

Subject: That's where the jobs [see: work/income] were. And all the excitement. When I was young, I wanted my bit of that. I thought I could make a better go of it than my parents. Don't all kids think that? I was creative, I wanted to get a job in content production, and I didn't want to do it remotely [see: the internet]. All the big names were in the city. I got an internship [=unpaid work, often a necessary precursor to finding paid work] with a big company, and they put me up for six months in a pod [=basic modular accommodation provided for low-paid workers by large corporate and government entities]. After that, I was on my own. I found a communal house about 80km from the city centre.

Interviewer: You lived 80km from your place of work?

Subject: That was normal for most people. The public transport system had gone solar, when the government went through a green phase [=a period of prioritising environmental concerns and sustainability], but after that it wasn't maintained very well, and it wasn't very reliable. Rich people didn't like paying taxes [see: work/income], and they didn't use public transport, no bloody way.

Interviewer: But didn't they also benefit from a public transport system? Fossil-fuel-powered vehicles had been banned from the early 2030s. Most city centres by the 2040s had strict limits on any kind of private vehicles.

Subject: Rich people could afford the PV [=private vehicle] permit and always found some reason why they needed one. [Expletive], rich people were still flying around in private jets [=air transportation] in the 2020s.

At the end of each section, there was the summary and longer explanations of all the unfamiliar terms.

Work in the twenty-first century

The purpose of work was to earn enough money [=unit of exchange] to meet essential needs as well as to accumulate personal status and individual luxuries. However, there existed great inequality in pay and opportunities. Many people could barely meet essential needs, while a much smaller number could engage in almost unlimited consumption. From the 1990s onwards, following the end of the First Cold War, economic inequalities had increased steadily. By the 2040s, society was divided into a tiny super-rich elite, a larger rich stratum and the majority, the working poor. What used to be called the 'middle class' [see: social/occupational categories] no longer existed. The period from the end of the Second World War (1939–1945) to the end of communism (1989), when people in the so-called 'working class' [=technical/manual] stratum were materially comfortable and had opportunities for social and economic advancement, was a historical aberration.

In the Dome, every occupation is recognised as equally worthy and vital to the efficient functioning of society. Citizens are assigned to occupational training after Basic Education, at age thirteen, in accordance with their capacities and the needs of the Dome. Everyone contributes to the best of their ability, and there is no wastage of human resources.

Reading this, Claudia thought guiltily of her mother. Faye made minimal contribution and was a net burden. What did Ideology say about such people? She'd always asked questions in Ideo class, but now she was afraid of her own curiosity and what it said about her.

Claudia thought of Davina's Oldie friends and how freely they'd spoken. There were so many questions she'd wanted to ask. She'd sneaked a look in the reference list in her tablet: *Bible, daft, sheeple, anarchist.* There was nothing for *daft* or *sheeple*. The Bible was 'the main ideological book of Christianity, the dominant religion of Europe for two millennia, which spread to the Americas, Africa, parts of Asia, Australia and New Zealand [see: European colonial expansion] until the development of scientific thinking led naturally to its decline'. *Anarchist* was a sealed topic, requiring top-level clearance and supervised access: 'Person who rejects all form of organisation and advocates chaos, extremely dangerous.' Claudia had quickly blanked her screen, her heart beating a little faster.

Was Neil extremely dangerous? He seemed so friendly and open, if a bit weird—that t-shirt!—but subversion could be very subtle.

Jemima was far too old to be dangerous, but Claudia couldn't stop thinking about the photograph of the two sisters. It did not portray a world on the brink of destruction. They all knew how the planet had been ravaged in pre-Event days: the global warming that decades of meetings, treaties and promises had failed to halt; the rising sea levels that had wiped out several island states and ravaged low-lying littoral nations; the shrinking forests and expanding deserts; the endless wars; the firestorms and ice storms and freak weather; the loss of biodiversity and the destruction of the natural world; the death of vast tracts of the ocean, reduced to gyres of plastic waste; the immense, sprawling cities where poor people sweated to death in summer heat traps; the industrial and air pollution in developing countries as they struggled to catch up; rivers that foamed or glowed in the dark and poisoned the people who lived nearby.

But amid all this, Jemima and Hetty had gone swimming in the sea, and they had laughed and looked happy, if only in that one moment when the photograph was taken.

Nine

It was late when Claudia returned to the unit after training. She'd detoured to the local Distribution Office to collect their overdue rations, standing in a queue with other citizens grumbling about the new delay in recycling durables.

'Freeding subversives,' said one man, who lived down the corridor, and Claudia had frowned and nodded.

She was overdue for a new pair of trainers herself. Her old ones had been reconditioned the maximum number of times and the material was beginning to degrade. The team at the Fixer Centre had told her to get a new pair last time, but they were also very good at finding creative solutions. Perhaps they'd see her trainers as a challenge. Claudia's friend Benny was a trainee recycling tech, and he said the fixits were always nosing around the depot, asking for bits and pieces and sometimes just taking things 'for the greater good'. The rumour was that fixits could make you all kinds of off-quota items. The ones who'd survived the Aftermath were especially ingenious. It was important that their skills were passed on to the next generation, although their mindset was considered high risk.

As Claudia unpacked the rations and tidied the unit, collecting up the empty cannies, she thought, yet again, about everything that had happened the night of Martin's party. The Commodore's words from the lunchtime announcement kept playing through her head.

If thoughts counted as much as action, then Claudia was a subversive. Even if she'd never met Davina, there was the problem of her curiosity about the world before the Event. Even in the official history, Claudia sometimes glimpsed something other than what she was taught. The recent interview series, about the survivor who had run away from the city to go bush, had raised a question that Claudia knew better than to ask in class: didn't they have to ask permission to leave the city? Were people allowed to live anywhere?

Claudia and Faye had been assigned their res unit on the basis of Faye's occupational status. The residential committee decided where everyone would live, maximising efficiencies. Sometimes people moved without permission, like Ally's sister, and sometimes they would be called up on it, but with continual monitoring by DOMUS, the authorities knew, in theory, where people were at all times.

Except when they didn't swipe. The night of the party, Davina had taken them into the Underground without swiping. The controls on the hatch had been deactivated.

For the determinedly individualistic and free-spirited, there were ways of getting around the Dome without being tracked. People avoided swiping, using special routes and 'free' entry/exit points. It was called 'free-moving'. Claudia didn't even know how she knew this. Free-moving wasn't illegal, but it was a sign of other, more serious, inclinations. There was even a rumour that the no-swipe exits were kept that way because they provided useful information about antisocial elements.

All Davina's friends, the ones they'd seen and the others (how many?) who'd remained out of sight, must have knowingly used free-move routes to get into the Underground. Was the deliberate avoidance of surveillance a crime or just a sign that you might intend to commit one?

Minor infractions were a sign of deeper attitude problems and invariably led to more serious crimes. Attempting to hide such infractions was itself a warning sign, but the instinct of the average citizen was self-protection, a basic individualism that existed in all humans. Petty betrayals of the community happened all the time, like the fixits and their so-called 'creative side projects', and the Dome continued to exist without plunging into irreversible chaos.

This meant that, in reality, a certain level of subversion was survivable and actually tolerated. Nobody had stopped Davina from wearing her granddad's deadclothes, although obviously this free-spirit tendency was noted. The fact that Pierce was not going to report them, not this time, meant that he was aware, even as a very junior Mentargh trooper, that there was some invisible, unacknowledged margin.

The notion that there was actually a safe and allowable level of subversion ran counter to everything Claudia had learned, raising questions way beyond her Level V knowledge, and there was nobody she could ask, certainly not her Youth League mentor, Kate.

And maybe Davina and her friends weren't subversives, just free spirits who felt safer underground, as Jim had said.

Claudia felt reprieved, for the tiniest moment.

Changing things. Neil's words clanged through her mind every time she tried to minimise what they'd done.

She thought again of Jemima's photographs. The only

visuals she'd seen of Before were stills and selected clips from ancient news reports: out-of-control fires, war zones, starving people in desert landscapes, gigantic mounds of toxic rubbish sent from rich countries to poor ones, dead bodies in huge trenches, nuclear disaster zones and the smoking aftermath of terrorist attacks. She knew visuals were easily faked, but why would Jemima fake such pictures, which she'd saved in the Aftermath and kept with her, illegally, all these years in the safety of the Dome?

But Jemima was just a crazy old woman, as Martin had said. It was safer to believe this, even if she had to pretend to herself.

The unit was very quiet. After her last episode, either Faye had been taken to Rehab, again, or one of her co-workers had taken her in, to protect her. They often did that, to keep her Rehab count down. Claudia didn't understand why her mother's friends were willing to take such risks on her behalf. Faye was a net burden on the system, and Claudia preferred being on her own. She didn't like chaos.

A low but insistent summons sounded from the comms unit. Claudia gave the voice command, and the cheery face of Kate appeared on screen.

'Oh. Hi,' said Claudia. 'Were we scheduled today?'

'No, but I thought I'd check in. Just as well I did. You look a bit down in the dumps.'

'I do?' Claudia forced her face into a smile.

'That's more like it! Did you have a good time at Martin's party? I heard it was quite a blast.'

These routine questions took Claudia by surprise. She hadn't considered what she'd tell Kate, and she'd never held anything back. Kate had always patiently disentangled her thoughts, guiding her away from the danger zone of individualism, unwarranted curiosity and socially unproductive doubts, with appropriate Ideo quotes and reassuring logic.

Wayward thoughts were treatable, but actions were another matter. Claudia had no doubts as to Kate's ultimate loyalty. She wore the bright red uniform of a human resources technician, but her black armband, marked with a Roman VIII, signified her status in the Mentargh.

So Claudia lied. 'Yeah, it was apocalyptic. Pierce brought along some hardbrew, so things got pretty wild. Most of us were totally nuked.'

Kate flashed her a quick, penetrating smile, and Claudia smiled back. Counsellors were trained in close observation and lie detection, but Kate gave no sign of noticing anything unusual.

'The real stuff takes some getting used to. How about our Mentargh cadet and prospective cadet?'

'Juanita doesn't usually drink that much, but I think she was feeling it. She started lining up all the empties,' said Claudia. 'Pierce didn't seem that drunk.'

'Luke never shows it either.' Kate spoke as someone with personal, even intimate, knowledge, a disturbing thought. 'The best MTs never get blasted, anyway. It's too much of a liability.'

'Just as well the rest of us aren't up for promotion!' said Claudia, rolling her eyes.

She'd never faked it with Kate before. Surely Kate could tell? But Kate just smiled indulgently.

Claudia's deception pained her. She was also scared. If she moved beyond Kate's protective influence, who would deal with her doubts? She'd slide unchecked into the murky depths of subversion.

She was overcome by a brief, terrifying premonition of loneliness. Perhaps it would be better to confess everything to Kate right now.

'What's wrong?' said Kate, her face a picture of concern.

'Nothing. I'm just really tired. I've been doing extra training for the Selection Trials.'

'Yes, I know.' As Claudia's mentor, Kate had full access to her records. 'I'd expect nothing less of you.'

Claudia relaxed, and then Kate continued, 'But there's something I need to ask you about. Something quite worrying.'

Her tone was suddenly serious. Claudia's heart began to thump.

'Luke's troop came around, didn't they? With the Party Machine, as usual.'

'Yes.'

'He said you had a bad trip.'

Kate's tone was still casual, but she was watching Claudia intently.

'Oh, that. Maybe it was the hardbrew. Pierce made me skoll a whole bottle just before they turned up.'

'Hardbrew shouldn't have that effect.' Kate could be very persistent. 'To be frank, Luke says the Machine actually repelled you, threw you onto the floor. That's a very disturbing reaction.'

'Yeah, it gave me a big fright,' said Claudia. 'But I got over it quickly, and we kept on partying.'

Kate seemed to be fiddling with an unseen object beyond the screen. 'Claudia, there isn't anything you haven't been telling me, is there?' she asked at length.

Claudia's stomach tightened, but she managed to look

bewildered. 'No. Why?'

'Resisting the Machine is a sign of profound ambivalence.' Kate's eyes did not stray from Claudia's face as she spoke.

'I wasn't resisting,' said Claudia. Her mouth went dry.

'Claudia, you're not stupid. In fact, you're highly intelligent, and that could be your downfall.' Kate's voice was sharper now, and Claudia squirmed. 'Look, I know you have a strong tendency to individualism, and this problem with curiosity. The way you're going, you could easily end up a borderline subversive. I know you have that susceptibility, that weakness in your character.'

'That's not true!'

Kate softened a little. 'Claudia, it's quite a common danger when an intelligent person reaches the higher grades, especially during a certain rebellious period of adolescence, and you have a long history of divergent thinking. But this can be overcome. With proper guidance, it can be navigated carefully, and bypassed. That's why it's so vital that you tell me everything. Absolutely everything.' Kate looked at Claudia, emanating concern.

'But there's nothing to tell,' muttered Claudia. Her fists clenched savagely on her lap, where Kate couldn't see them.

Ten

After Martin's party, life went on as if nothing out of the ordinary had happened. Claudia and the others attended classes and Youth League drill and PE, played the Game according to the never-ending match cycle and trained for the Selection Trials: the usual routine, the usual banter and gossip. And they were always around other people, or at least Juanita or others from their cohort who'd gone home from the party earlier or, like Benny, had passed out on the floor. There was never any opportunity to talk about their adventure in the Underground. Perhaps that was for the best: to carry on as if it had never happened, a one-off divergence from the rules that had no meaning or consequences, as long as they never acknowledged it.

Claudia couldn't stop thinking about it. The secret expanded inside her, and sometimes she thought she'd explode. Surely Martin and Arnie felt the same? But they were always joking, never serious, and they never looked her in the eye.

Obviously, she couldn't talk to Pierce.

Ally didn't count.

After a long day of classes, Claudia stayed in the Central Zone to eat in the student canteen. Her training squad was scheduled a rest day, and she had no further programmed activity that cycle. She'd heard from Faye's friend Roz that her mother was 'doing well' and would be home soon. Roz had said this as if Claudia should be pleased. The dread of Faye's return hung over Claudia constantly.

She sat alone, although some of her study team were eating together at another table. Sometimes Claudia simply had no energy for people, especially after spending a whole day with them. After a few weeks of prac in res sector and workplace medbays, dealing with minor injuries, her team had come together that afternoon for some intensive group revision, feedback and self-assessment. Claudia had been criticised for administering more painkiller than necessary, a waste of resources. But she couldn't forget the moans of the woman in Gynie, strapped down and semi-conscious as she was sterilised. She could tell that some of her team felt the same way, but nobody had said anything in her defence. Her personalised daily revision now included the dose per bodyweight for all types of painkillers, and the criteria for using or withholding analgesia.

Someone from her team saw her by the recycling unit on her way out and called her over to join them, but she just waved and went on her way. Claudia had a reputation for being solitary, but she contributed fully to all teamwork and communal activity and was socially integrated to the minimum expected standard. Those who felt, all the same, that something wasn't quite right about her had a hard time finding anything to criticise formally.

What did Davina's study team and cohort overall make of her deadclothes? There were no such obvious free spirits in Claudia's circle. Did people just accept Davina's oddity and include her? Or did she reject them and stay aloof, preferring the company of Oldies?

Claudia left the building, feeling strangely restless. Usually she went home and sat on her bunk with her tablet, revising her Ed or playing games generated by AI to provide tailored stimulation or relaxation, depending on her needs and the time of the cycle. If Faye was home, she kept the door snibbed.

The E-Block Citizens' Brigade was having one of its many regular meetings, but these were not obligatory for junior residents, and as Faye's daughter, Claudia preferred not to remind her neighbours of their existence. Faye had been thrown out of the last meeting she'd attended for extreme antisocial behaviour, including inebriation, shouting and profanity.

At this time in the cycle, the Central Zone was almost empty. The space between the buildings had been designed to resemble an old city, with squares, walkways and benches. The four Ed blocks faced into a square. At its centre rose a narrow tower, as high as the surrounding buildings and covered in foliage. The foliage had been genetically designed to maximise air purity and help regulate the temperature. People called these structures 'tower trees', although in Claudia's understanding, they were nothing like trees.

Across the square, a lone figure came out of the Science Block, which was directly opposite. It was Martin. Claudia hadn't seen him by himself since the night of the party.

She waved and he came over.

'Claudia! What are you doing, hanging around Central on a rest day? Not extra study, I hope?'

'No, I've just come from the canteen. What about you?'

'It was my turn to clean up after a prac. You know what I'm like, unstoppable social contribution,' said Martin. 'My study partner's out with an injury, so I was on my own.'

'Nobody else stayed to help?'

'Everyone's really stressed about the Trials. Team spirit has taken a hit. It's every citizen for themselves.' Martin glanced at the surveillance device nestled in the leaves of the tower tree.

The devices were everywhere, and Claudia, like most people, was hardly aware of them. DOMUS was constantly monitoring everything that happened in the Dome, adjusting its systems for maximum efficiency and picking up any malfunction, mechanical or human, very quickly.

Would a junior citizen's sarcastic comment get its attention? It was unlike Martin to be concerned.

Claudia had her back to the tower tree. 'Have you seen Davina since your party?' she asked, lowering her voice.

'A few times. She's in the Science Block, but in a different cohort.'

'Do they all wear deadclothes too?' Claudia said this in a joking way, but Martin looked cagey. She could tell he was trying not to look up again.

'Actually, she wears blues at school. But with that … hat.'

'Really?' Picturing the combination, Claudia broke out in a grin, even though she'd been feeling tired and flat before.

'Yeah, it looks freeding weird, but her cohort seem to be used to it, and her trainer doesn't say anything.'

'She's an interesting person,' said Claudia.

'Yeah, she is.'

A group of students walked across from the Engineering Block towards the Transit station. The two friends fell silent as they passed. Claudia had never been conscious of taking such precautions, but this shared silence came naturally, as if they'd been doing it all their lives without thinking.

'Were you just heading home, then?' said Martin.

'I guess. Faye's back, so I'm not in any rush.'

Martin took a moment before replying. 'I'm actually on my way to meet Arnie and Davina now.' He seemed to be speaking to a point somewhere over Claudia's left shoulder. 'At the D-Sector node.'

Each res sector had a Youth League community centre, a node, where junior citizens could socialise outside of programmed activity and avoid the psychological pitfalls of social isolation. Claudia occasionally went to the local B-Sector node, to get away from Faye, but it was noisy and she preferred the privacy of her bunk.

'Why don't you come?' said Martin. 'Even you need a break from studying, Clau.'

'Yeah. Sure.' Claudia had never been to the D-Sector node and it was very out of character for her, but something inside her resisted the very thought of heading back to B-Sector.

Without any further talk, they caught the Transit across the Ring to the Moisture Regeneration Plant and changed to an inner shuttle for D-Sector.

The D-Sector YL node was even noisier and more crowded than she'd expected. Claudia swiped herself in after Martin and looked around, a little nervously. She knew Arnie often came to the D-Sector node, even though he lived in A-Sector.

'Is it usually this rammed?' she asked Martin.

'It's more popular than B-Sector node, that's for sure. You need to get out more,' he said. 'Not everyone studies all the time like you.'

She felt like she'd arrived too late for a party. Around them, other Senior Youth League officers were obviously getting drunk, and the background music on the YL channel reflected the mood. Although synthanol consumption was controlled by the Mentargh, Claudia knew that people often drank it from water cannies when they hung out at the nodes, and that the Mentargh didn't come down too heavily, especially at times like this, when everyone was stressing about the upcoming Selection Trials.

On the far side of the common room, Davina and Arnie were hunched over a table game, entirely absorbed by the screen. This time, Davina was wearing a long-sleeved garment with holes in the elbows over the standard t-shirt. Claudia could smell it several paces off.

Martin went to stand behind Arnie. As he looked over Arnie's shoulder at the game, he picked up the cannie sitting on the table by Arnie's hand and took a swig.

'Freed! Who brewed this?' he said, grimacing and shaking his head. 'Or did they just bottle this straight from the labriculture run-off tanks?'

'We don't all have access to Mentargh hardbrew, citizen,' said Davina, staring intently at the game screen. 'Yes! Arnie, you've just been nuked. Game over.'

'You noxious antisocial element,' said Arnie.

How long had they been friends? Their banter seemed very familiar.

The two looked up and saw her at the same time. Arnie seemed taken aback but pleased, unlike Davina.

'Mentargh Girl. I haven't seen you in D-Sector before,' she said, immediately wary and not altogether friendly.

'I found her in Central Zone, suffering from social isolation, and I thought it was my civic duty to bring her along,' said Martin. 'Unlike my freeding prac team, I'm always looking out for my fellow citizens.'

'Why are you always left doing clean-up?' said Arnie to Martin. 'You're too freeding soft on those social parasites.'

Claudia was already in defensive mode from the feedback session earlier. She stared back at Davina. 'It's rest day. I've got nothing else to do.'

'No special Ideo sessions?' said Davina.

'She knows it off by heart,' said Arnie. 'As you've already experienced.'

'Freak,' said Davina, but she seemed to relent. 'Sit down and play a round with me.'

Arnie got up to make way for Claudia. 'I'll get some drinks, for people who don't mind the local brew,' he said.

Claudia didn't feel like drinking but, as with Davina's command to sit down and play, she didn't feel she could refuse. By accepting Martin's invitation to D-Sector, she'd agreed to step out of her usual routine and behaviour and go along with the others or risk being rejected. Like the Survivors who'd been ejected from the Dome in the early days, except that officially this had never happened.

Davina chose a familiar program, based on the Game, and cranked up the level.

'I didn't think you liked the Game,' said Claudia.

'Oh, I don't mind it if I can play sitting down, and drink at the same time. Not having to take pain meds afterwards is also good. Don't bother trying to swipe in, just use Arnie's avatar.'

The game started, fast and hard. Almost immediately, Arnie's avatar was smashed into the ground.

'That's against the rules!'

'D-Sector rules,' said Davina. 'You need to be creative.'

Table games were programmed by AI and strictly regulated to meet standards of community cohesion, skills development and values indoctrination, with carefully paced dopamine bursts and reward intervals.

'How—?'

The game kicked off again and Claudia had to move Arnie's avatar quickly to avoid another smash. The screen showed that it had sustained some injuries and was only operating at 78%.

'Freed's sake, this is violent.'

Arnie's avatar kicked Davina's in the knee and brought it down. A red flashing light indicated a high level of pain.

'Nasty!' said Martin.

'That's more like it,' said Davina. 'You're getting the hang of this, Mentargh Girl.'

By the time Arnie came back with the drinks, the two avatars were bloody lumps. Davina's was 19% capacity and Arnie's was dead.

'That was freeding quick!' he said.

'Sorry about your avatar, Arnie,' said Claudia. 'Have I destroyed your record?'

The results of table games and additional information—a player's moves, what games were played, and with whom—all went on a junior citizen's datafile and were used to generate individual games and training exercises for private study.

'Don't worry. In D-Sector, it's all off the record.'

'How—?'

'Don't ask,' said Martin.

He and Arnie played a game while Davina and Claudia watched.

'All ready for the Selection Trials?' Even as these words

came out, the same question that everyone was asking everyone else, Claudia could sense Davina's impatience and boredom.

'As ready as I'll ever be. Nothing I do will make a difference, so why bother? They've already decided what to do with me,' she said. 'I suppose you're heading for a golden future in the Mentargh, along with Pierce and Juanita.'

Claudia was used to being seen as a unit with Pierce, the two Level V students, but being lumped in with Juanita as well was deeply wrong.

'I'm not like them.'

'That's what Martin and Arnie keep telling me, but I'm not so sure.'

'We've known each other since Basic. You've only just met me.'

'Which means I see things they don't.'

'Like what?'

'Someone who thinks she's a bit different'—Davina put a sarcastic emphasis on these words—'but is actually part of the system and benefits from it by sticking to the rules.'

'The system keeps us alive,' said Claudia, stung. 'Even people who don't like it.'

'Yeah, we covered that already. Don't bother repeating the quote.'

'It doesn't mean I don't have questions. You have some interesting friends. I liked talking to them. There are a lot of things I'd like to ask them, actually.'

The two boys had been apparently absorbed in their game, but Claudia felt their attention sharpen.

'What sort of questions?' said Davina.

'About Before. Stuff that's not in the Ideo. Oldies are dying all over the place. Soon there'll be nobody left who remembers what it was really like.'

'What it was *really* like? Do you mean, they're *lying* to us?' Davina's tone was mock-horror.

'You know what I mean,' said Claudia. 'They don't tell us everything.'

'I'm only Level III, a regular citizen-idiot, what do I know? I thought they started to teach you real stuff once you hit Level V.'

'No, they don't,' said Claudia, staring back.

The game bleeped and played a tinny rendition of 'The Inheritors' that segued into the sound of a flushing toilet. This did not happen in any of the official games.

Martin groaned. Arnie raised both arms in a victory salute. 'You lost focus, citizen. Fatal error, especially when you're playing with me.'

Claudia took a sip of her drink. It was homebrew, the kind made by civilians, off the record, stronger than the official brew but with a bitter taste.

The other three were looking at each other as if having a conversation without words. In the time it took Claudia to swallow one mouthful of the local brew and put down the cannie, she knew.

'You've been back, haven't you?' she said.

Martin looked sheepish. Arnie looked away.

'Why didn't you tell me?' She felt betrayed.

'Freed's sake, Claudia, you're Level V,' said Martin.

'So are you two free spirits now?' She didn't use the more serious word.

'Are you saying my clothes stink?' said Arnie.

He meant this as a joke, but Davina frowned. Was it possible she couldn't smell herself?

'What about you, Claudia? What happened on the Machine?' said Martin.

'Maybe Claudia has free-spirit tendencies that are so deep only the Machine can pick them up,' said Arnie. This was only half a joke.

'Yeah, that was pretty weird,' said Davina. 'I've never seen that before.'

She looked at Claudia as if reconsidering.

When Claudia opened her mouth to try to explain, nothing came out. It wasn't something she could share, or even explain.

'I've been having nightmares,' she said instead. 'Maybe the Machine picked up on that and kicked me off to protect the rest of you.'

'Really? I haven't heard that one before,' said Arnie. 'Maybe you have too many questions backed up in that Level V brain.'

They turned to Davina and waited.

She stood up, and Claudia saw that she was wearing a pair of baggy trousers. They were held up by a narrow brown strip around the waist, fastened at the front with a metallic device, and the legs were rolled up. Davina was quite tall, but her grandfather had evidently been even taller.

'Well, as long as we're on our guard against the pernicious influence of old people, I guess we're in the clear, ideologically speaking, if Mentargh Girl says so. Let's go for a walk, then,' she said.

Eleven

'See you in a minute.'

Instead of going out the main door, Davina headed towards the amenities corridor.

Martin and Arnie waited a few beats, then got up.

'Give us another minute. Make like you're just going to the toilet. You're not with us,' said Arnie.

Anxious not to lose sight of them, Claudia only waited a few seconds. She passed two cadet-troopers going the other way, talking and laughing as they came out of the toilets. They headed back to the main community area without turning around.

Beyond the toilets there was only the service door at the end of the corridor. Claudia was briefly confused. Where had the other three gone? Then she realised: it was a no-swipe exit.

As Pierce had said, going into the Underground on the night of Martin's party had been a drunken escapade, a one-off. Claudia wasn't drunk now, not on a few mouthfuls of citizen brew, and she was about to free-move with the clear intention of avoiding surveillance.

She paused, but only for a fraction of a second. The decision was made before her everyday, rule-abiding Level V self could intervene.

Davina and the boys were waiting on the other side, in a minimal-lighting stairwell.

'I thought you might funk it,' said Davina. 'You can still turn back. You could say the citizen brew addled your brain and you went for a pee on the stairs.'

'Here I am,' said Claudia.

In the dimness, Martin winked at her.

'Let's go, then, junior citizens. I will not expect a written report at your next Ideo session.'

They followed Davina down several levels. Another no-swipe exit, and they went deeper. Claudia saw doors marked with service access for the Transit station and an emergency exit for the D-Sector compost unit.

'That's where they process bodies, isn't it, Claudia?' said Martin. 'You're a trainee med tech, don't you get a tour?'

'Not just bodies, all kinds of biowaste,' said Claudia. 'It all gets mixed in together.'

'As we're constantly told, the Dome is a totally efficient system,' said Davina.

'Not quite,' said Claudia. 'There's always something left.'

'Where does it go?' asked Martin.

'I'm not sure,' said Claudia. 'Don't worry, nothing is wasted.'

'Next time Benny gets his fixer pals to glue something up for you, just stop a moment and reflect, with gratitude, on some dead citizen's ongoing contribution,' said Arnie, and Martin snorted.

'Do they ever stop?' Davina said to Claudia. Her tone seemed friendlier.

'They've been like this since Basic,' said Claudia.

Eventually they left the stairwell through a numbered door.

For a few moments, they were in utter darkness and silence. Claudia stood completely still. If she moved even slightly away from the door, which was right behind her, she would be lost, and there was no reason for anyone to come looking.

Arnie was the first to switch on a handylight. It hardly made a dent in the surrounding void.

'Hey, new kit! Did you get that from work?' asked Martin.

'Unofficially,' said Arnie. 'My trainer is good friends with a guy who works in a fixer kiosk and makes all sorts of off-quota stuff. Maybe he recycled some Oldie's pacemaker or knee replacement for the parts. I respect his creativity too much to ask the details.'

Davina turned on her own light. 'I enjoy your banter but keep it down while we're moving. If we can get down here, so can anyone, and they may not be friendly, even if they're not MT.' She suddenly let out a scream. 'Freeding shitfuck Armageddon!'

The beam of her torch had revealed a pair of large yellow eyes. The other three all yelped. The eyes disappeared, and there was a scuttling sound.

'What the freed was that? Davina, is it really safe down here?' said Martin.

'Safe from what? No, this is not a safe environment, you have now been officially informed,' she hissed. 'The Underground is crawling with feral dogs and cats and rats and freed knows what. In the Exodus, people brought animals with them. Their pets, and the other animals they were living off in the Aftermath.'

'Yeah, we had a lesson on this,' said Claudia. 'People used to have strong emotional bonds with animals, as well as eating them and wearing their skins.'

'Sickos. No wonder the world ended,' said Arnie.

'You mean there could be camels and kangaroos and elephants down here? There were some freeding weird animals, before they were all wiped out,' said Martin.

'There's no record of any elephants arriving in the Exodus,' said Claudia. 'Big animals had to be set loose before their people were allowed inside. They weren't part of the planned ecosystem. But people smuggled small animals in, and some of them were highly adaptive. What we saw was probably a large rat.'

This was hypothetical. Claudia had never seen a rat in her life.

'I feel so much better. Let's get a move on,' said Davina.

She seemed to be navigating by the numbers that appeared in luminous paint on pylons and doors. Claudia was intrigued and also unnerved by the parallel city that existed underground, a dark reflection of the one above.

'How well do you know the Underground?' she asked Davina.

'My granddad came down here a lot. He actually worked on some of the early plans before he was thrown off the programme for being a troublemaker who asked too many questions. The idea was that the whole population, or selected people, could take refuge down here if something catastrophic happened. Like, if an asteroid hit the Dome. They had to plan for all sorts of things they couldn't actually imagine.'

'Like the Event. I bet they didn't plan for that,' said Arnie.

'You reckon?' said Davina. 'My granddad had some pretty interesting theories about that.'

She came to a sudden halt and turned her torch off, on and then off. Ahead, another torch flashed on and off. Claudia saw a two-tier bank of modular units.

'Wait a moment,' said Davina. 'I'll see who's here. Citizens' Brigade meetings down here are invitation-only, and I may have used up my guest passes.'

'Citizens' Brigade?' It took Claudia a moment to realise Davina was joking.

'Don't worry, Clau. We won't leave you alone with the rats,' said Martin.

She waited, shivering slightly in the darkness as the other three headed up the metal stairs and into one of the upper units, and wondered at her own recklessness. She was a Level V student without a single demerit on her record; before tonight, she'd never even played an off-system table game or drunk citizen brew. She felt a little afraid of where this would all lead, but the stronger sensation was excitement, the thrill of the new and unknown. It wasn't something she was used to feeling, and it went to her head like hardbrew.

The unit door opened, letting out a long beam of light.

'Come on, then,' said Davina. 'Jim says you're OK.'

The unit where the free spirits were gathered was very similar to a standard three-person res unit but the interior was somehow sharper, cleaner, fresher. Claudia realised that, apart from these meetings, it had never been used. The contrast with Claudia's own unit and most of the Dome's interior spaces, which had been in continual use for thirty years, was sudden and stark. Her whole world was worn and grubby-looking, even though, technically, it was clean and fully functional. Mostly. The kitchen tap in Claudia's unit never stopped dripping, but nobody had been able to fix it.

Now that she was aware of this discrepancy, it would be impossible not to see it from now on.

'Hi, Claudia. We couldn't leave you out in the dark,' said Lisa, smiling.

Claudia saw Jim, Neil and Lily, and several others. They were sitting around the table, some on the divan, others on the stools. They could've been a bunch of Oldies meeting in someone's home, having an Oldie party, if Oldies had parties.

Claudia's first thought was how ordinary they looked. She'd expected free spirits—potential subversives—to look visibly different, the evidence of their deviance stamped on their faces. But there was nothing about these rather tired-looking people, mostly Oldies, to distinguish them from any other citizens of the Dome. A few were wearing deadclothes, like Davina, which made them look scruffy, even dirty. The others wore standard citizen rig, with various functional insignia. The highest Ideo ranking on the younger ones was Level III.

'Hello,' said Claudia. She wasn't used to spending time with Oldies, and she felt suddenly very awkward.

'Hi, Claudia. Couldn't keep away, eh?' said Neil. 'I'm all for encouraging the demon curiosity in junior citizens. We need more of it.'

Claudia's second, slightly self-righteous, thought was that Neil's t-shirt, printed with the barely legible words FOUR HORSEMEN/LAKE OF FIRE TOUR 2046, was more hole than fabric and needed to go to the recycler. The Dome provided everyone with adequate clothing and wearing such an obviously defunct item seemed a kind of criticism. But of course, he was a free spirit.

'Sit down with me.' Lisa patted the divan next to her. 'I heard you ran into a large rat.'

'The place is crawling with them,' said Lily. 'In the old days, we used to eat them.'

'Oh, please, don't remind me,' said Lisa, shuddering. 'Have a biscuit, Claudia.'

She passed Claudia a container of what seemed to be non-standard carb snacks. 'I made them myself.'

'How?' Claudia asked. Private cooking facilities and access to primary ingredients were very limited.

'I'm a food engineer. I can experiment,' said Lisa. 'Nothing does the trick like butter, flour, sugar and eggs used to, but these are pretty good, if I do say so myself. Go on, you won't bust your daily allowance with just one. Kids these days are so skinny.'

'Is that any surprise, with what we eat these days?' said Lily and took three biscuits. Claudia noted that her weight–height ratio was seriously out of balance.

The biscuit was delicious, and she took a second.

Neil picked up Arnie's new handylight, which Arnie had left on the table.

'Interesting design. Haven't seen one of these before.'

'A friend of a friend made it,' said Arnie.

'No. 4 Repair Kiosk, A-Sector, by any chance?' said Neil. 'I think I recognise the handiwork. I see what he's done here. Very artistic use of materials. Are you in materials tech?'

'I'm a trainee,' said Arnie. 'Just clean-and-check so far, in medical.'

After every medical procedure, a technician was responsible for cleaning and checking all the equipment and reporting anything that needed reconditioning or was ready for recycling. Sometimes techs could put together new machines or equipment from the bits of old ones. This required creative thinking and was ideologically a bit dangerous, but such risks were sometimes necessary for the greater good. The machine techs were monitored by DOMUS, which learned from them. Such technology had been strictly regulated in the 2020s, and machine techs were only rediscovering the algorithms. One day, individual creativity would no longer be needed and its dangers could be erased. Until then, people with fixer skills were essential to the efficient functioning of the Dome.

Claudia knew that Arnie was friendly with a few of the older people who supervised his training, which was unusual for people their age, but Arnie was friendly with everyone. Seeing him chat so easily with Neil, Claudia realised that there was a side to Arnie she didn't know, and that his free-spirit tendency went deeper than drinking citizen brew in the D-Sector node.

'Do you want a cup of tea?' said Lisa. 'I've got some hot water.'

'I thought there was no power down here,' said Claudia.

Lisa produced a vacuum flask, the kind normally used in lab work.

'She thinks of everything,' said Lily.

'Can't have biscuits without tea,' said Lisa.

'Or you can have a swig of this,' said Neil. He offered her a cannie, so dented and scratched that surely, like his t-shirt, it belonged in the recycler.

'I wouldn't recommend it, if you value your brain cells,' said Lisa, and she and Lily pulled faces.

Claudia shook her head politely and took a cup of tea from Lisa instead.

'Did you know each other Before?'

'You mean, before all this?' said Lily, with a slight gesture of her head that nevertheless took in the Event and the Dome in all their immensity.

'Lily, Jim and I worked together,' said Lisa. 'At a remote government facility. That's how we survived.'

'I was on the coast,' said Neil. 'Part of a small bush collective, off-grid. I was the only one to make it here.'

'How?' said Claudia. She hardly expected an answer, but she'd never had the opportunity to ask. She felt as if a locked door had suddenly opened a crack.

'They really don't teach you anything, do they?' said Lisa.

'It was a bloody long walk,' said Neil. His eyes crinkled but he wasn't smiling. 'It's something I've tried to forget.'

'My mother was born a few years before the Event,' said Claudia. 'She came here as an orphan. Some Oldies brought her. I think they knew her parents. Then they died, and she was on her own, until she met my father, and then he died. That's all I know.'

She said this as a simple statement of fact, but the three Oldies seemed to flinch. Lily, who was sitting next to her, put her arms around Claudia and squeezed her very tightly.

Claudia was embarrassed. She knew that some Oldies could get emotional, especially around the subject of the Event and the Aftermath, and it was better not to upset them by talking about it.

'I'm sorry I asked. Looking back just creates unproductive despair and socially damaging doubts. That's why they only teach us the minimum that we need to know. I shouldn't be so curious. My mentor is always telling me off. There's no entitlement to excess knowledge. Lisa, can I have another biscuit?'

'Of course, sweetie,' said Lisa and held out the container. 'Take a couple.'

Arnie and Martin had by this time emptied Neil's cannie of

homebrew between them.

'This is good stuff. If brewing was graded, you'd be Level XIV, a full commodore,' said Arnie. 'Have you got any more?'

'No I don't, kiddo. I'm not running a pub down here,' said Neil. 'Should you be knocking it back on a school night? Aren't you in training for the big trial-by-sport event or whatever it's called?'

'Senior Selection Trials,' said Davina. 'I wish it was over already, so I could just get on with my assigned occupation and assigned life course and stop pretending to look like I'm trying. It's not like I'm in any danger of promotion. Not like Claudia here.'

'Why would they promote me?' Claudia protested. 'I'm a social misfit. I don't even hang out in YL nodes.'

'Yeah, tonight was her first time in D-Sector node,' said Arnie. 'She's an innocent. We're corrupting her.'

Arnie's evident satisfaction was annoying.

'Level V and lots of questions, eh?' said Jim. 'That can go several ways. I've seen it happen before.'

'What do you mean?' said Davina.

'People who ask questions, who don't simply accept everything, they're a valuable resource as well as a danger,' said Jim. 'The people at the very top, the Mentargh elite and beyond, they have that same capability, but they turn it to different ends. I don't mean the regular head-banger type, the bully-boys and the enforcers, I mean the ones who make decisions, the ones behind the scenes. Once you get to the higher Ideo grades, it's a different story. Those people need to understand what's really going on, not the mindcrap slogans they push onto everyone else.'

'Are you saying someone can be a Mentargh and a free

spirit? You're freeding with my head,' said Davina.

'I wouldn't use the term free spirit,' said Jim. 'I've known a few of them in my time. Or I thought I did. One old friend was arrested—brilliant guy, very capable—years ago now, and I thought he'd been wiped for D-grade labour, but he reappeared as a Mentargh lieutenant. Had they turned him, or had he fooled them? I've often thought that the most effective subversives would be at the top of the MT hierarchy.'

'And?'

Claudia enjoyed the look Jim flashed Davina. 'It's not as if I could go up and ask him, now, is it?'

'At least you get a massive party out of these Trials,' said Neil. 'Top-quality, designed-for-purpose drugs, AI-generated music to match and a unified feelgood vibe that binds you all together in a loving community, a total emotional journey, amen.'

'Have you been to one?' said Martin, surprised. Beat parties were for younger people.

'Kiddo, I used to design those parties. Back in the day,' said Neil. 'As well as conducting my own extensive personal research on second-generation E.'

Claudia, Martin and Arnie all stared at him, open-mouthed.

'Little faces!' said Neil. He rocked so far back in his chair he almost fell over and had to grab the corner of the divan. 'I caned so much of that shit when it first came out in the 2030s that it almost stopped working for me. Anyway, I wouldn't touch the stuff they make in here. I have a pretty good idea of who engineers it, and it's evil.'

'You're speaking to the original party boy,' said Lily. 'I went to one of his gigs once, out in the bush somewhere. I was flying for days. Didn't want to come back to earth.'

Jim frowned. He didn't look the type to have ever attended a beat party or taken a jenny.

'Jim's a clean-brainer,' said Neil. 'Very old school. Doesn't like to mess with his natural neural processes. That's why he looks so bloody depressed all the time.'

'If people weren't drugged out of their heads to make reality bearable, we might have a different reality by now,' said Jim.

'They can bang on about this all night,' said Lisa fondly. 'Who wants the last biscuit?'

Arnie took it.

'Do you see much of your Mentargh friend?' said Jim.

It took Claudia a moment to realise he was talking about Pierce.

'How do you know—?' said Martin.

'Come on, it's pretty obvious,' said Neil. 'But he didn't seem like a bad kid, from what I could tell. Is he a bit of a free spirit too? That could be interesting.'

'Pierce? No way,' said Arnie. 'But we trust him.'

'He's the brother I never had, the one who isn't Arnie,' said Martin.

'So you're the idiot twins and he's the serious guy,' said Neil and laughed.

'You realise he could be a full MT already, don't you?' said Jim. 'They don't always wear their uniforms right away. It's called unofficial promotion.'

'How do you know that?' said Claudia.

Jim looked at her as if she was stupid. 'I've been in this glass house since day one. I have a pretty good idea of how things work.'

Claudia felt squashed. From across the table, Davina caught her eye, and her expression was almost sympathetic.

'Don't take this personally, junior citizens, but trust is a process and one of your cohort is a baby MT,' said Neil. 'As much as I love to spread the love, we have to be careful.'

'Since when have you been careful?' said Lily.

'I'm still here. Well, bits of me,' said Neil. 'The rest is all salvaged or hacked.'

'We don't see much of Pierce these days,' said Martin. 'The MT keep him busy.'

'Anyway, he came with us the other night, so he'd get in trouble too,' said Arnie.

Claudia remembered her last conversation with Pierce, on the night of Martin's party. He'd said his job was to observe them, not to stop them. She didn't say anything.

The Oldies prepared to leave, clearing away any sign of their presence.

'When we run out of biscuits, it's time to go home,' said Neil to Claudia.

The group left the cabin and dispersed into the darkness. Claudia was glad of Davina's confidence in leading them through the labyrinth.

'What's Ally doing these days?' Martin asked Claudia. 'I haven't seen her for ages.'

'I only see her at training,' said Claudia. In truth, she was relieved not to see so much of Ally, although she felt guilty even thinking this.

'Since she got her implant, she's been chasing after Pierce full time,' said Arnie.

'When did she get her implant? The last I heard, she freaked out and had to bail.' Usually Ally would have confided such a momentous event in Claudia.

Davina cackled. 'Implant madness! Citizen Ally is open for

action!'

Claudia hated the way boys often spoke about girls who'd just got their implants, and it pained her to hear Davina talking the same way.

'Have you had yours?' she asked.

'Maybe I don't need one,' said Davina.

'Everyone has to get one,' said Claudia.

'What about you?'

'Not yet.' Claudia grimaced just thinking about it.

'Rule-breaker! You must be up against the deadline,' said Davina. 'That seems out of character. Or maybe I've underestimated you, and you're a proper subversive after all, plotting to undermine the Dome by free exercise of your fertility. You and Pierce would make cute babies.'

Martin and Arnie laughed, and Claudia was glad of the dark, to hide her embarrassment.

Twelve

When they returned to the D-Sector Youth League node, it was even busier than when they'd left. Four people appearing, at slightly staggered intervals, from the service passage attracted no attention at all. They'd been gone not quite two hours.

'I need a drink. I only got a mouthful of Neil's brew before you two drain-holes sucked it down,' said Davina.

'I'm ready for more,' said Arnie. 'First round on me.'

He produced a plastic chip-card with a crude grinning-face logo. Claudia had heard about illegal credit systems used by people for semi-contraband items, like extra rations or items of clothing, but she had no idea that Arnie was involved. Then again, the chip-cards and the machines that read them—very old technology—were cobbled together by fixer types, like Arnie's other friends, the ones she'd never met.

'I'm going to head home,' she said. Her brain was overflowing and she needed to shut down input.

Martin and Arnie made their usual protests, but Claudia had the impression they weren't trying very hard this time. She was like Jim, a no-fun clean-brainer.

Although, for a Level V study-brain, she'd acquitted herself pretty well turning up to D-Sector at all. Martin and Arnie had underestimated her.

It was a relief to leave the noisy, crowded node and its soupy, synthanol-laced air. Outside, the stretch between the Youth League D-Sector block and the Transit station was very quiet. At the centre of the square was another tower tree, like the one by the Med Block in the Central Zone. Claudia paused and looked up. The leaves were completely still, and in that moment, they seemed strangely fake, although she knew they were very much alive and sustained by a hydroponic column. It was an odd thought to have, and she wondered where it had come from.

Loud voices echoed across the square. At the far side, by the entrance to the D-Sector Transit, she saw a unit of Mentargh and their powerbikes.

Claudia's instinct was to do a hard-turn and take shelter back in the crowded node, but she was halfway across the square and some of the troopers had already seen her.

There was no rule about a resident being in a different sector. She kept walking, going about her legitimate business as a junior citizen, which at this time of the cycle was to get in place, back to her res unit, and bunk down.

Girls like Ally smiled and waved at Mentargh troopers. Claudia wasn't like that. Looking straight ahead, she pretended not to see them. An innocent citizen had no need to interact with troopers or to get in their way.

'Claudia!'

She froze.

Luke broke away from the group and came over. 'I thought it was you. Were you going to walk past without saying hello?'

Banter didn't come naturally to Claudia, certainly not with Luke.

'Uh, hello.' She attempted a smile. Her eyes felt wide and terrified, like those of the giant rat in the Underground.

'You're way out of your sector. What are you doing here by yourself?'

Was it possible that he knew where she'd been?

'I was just catching up with Martin and Arnie and some others in the node,' she said, surprised that this came out so plausibly.

'Would that be Davina? You've made an interesting new friend.' Luke spoke casually, but he was watching her closely. 'Bit of a free spirit, isn't she?'

'She wears her granddad's deadclothes,' said Claudia. 'I guess that makes her a free spirit.'

'What do you think?' he said.

'I think her deadclothes smell.' This just popped out.

Luke's mouth twitched. 'That does tend to be a problem with deadclothes. You can usually smell free spirits before you see them.'

Claudia felt disloyal, but it was true.

'Aren't your team playing first against D-Sector in the Trials?'

She hadn't checked the gameboard yet. 'Are we? I've been concentrating on my junior squad, to be honest. I'll think about the Senior Trials when I've got my kids through.'

'Admirable community spirit,' he said. 'I'm sure you'll do very well, when the time comes.'

Claudia didn't know what she should read into this.

'Thank you.' She smiled, like a good junior citizen.

A low whine signalled the arrival of a Transit shuttle. Claudia looked up at the platform. From D-Sector to B-Sector, she could take the inner or outer line.

'I need to get that,' she said, relieved.

'I'll give you a ride,' said Luke.

Claudia looked over to the other troopers, who were talking and laughing among themselves. 'But you're on duty. I'm fine, honestly. I'll get the Transit—'

'Elliot can manage on his own. We're just doing the usual rounds,' said Luke. 'In fact, we're about to visit the D-Sector Youth League node with the Party Machine. I don't think you've been for a trip since Martin's party, have you?'

'No.' Claudia struggled to keep her voice neutral. Was Luke going to insist that she go back into the node and take a trip?

Overhead, the doors of the Transit shuttle hissed shut. At this phase in the cycle, not many shuttles were in circulation, and it would be a wait for the next one.

'It'll be much quicker by bike,' said Luke. 'Come on.'

She had no choice but to follow him to where his unit was waiting.

'I'm going to take a run across to B-Sector. Elliot, you know what to do.'

'Sure, boss.' Elliot leered at Claudia. 'Enjoy the ride, citizen.'

The powerbikes were parked in a neat row around the back of the pylon. Luke took a second helmet from beneath the seat of his bike and handed it to Claudia. She put it on carefully and then fumbled to adjust the chin strap.

'Haven't you ever been on a bike? I thought Pierce might have taken you for a ride.' Luke leaned over and tightened the strap for her. In that brief, alarming moment of proximity, she remembered the night of Martin's party and how his face had been right up close by hers.

'I didn't know he could ride.'

'Of course he can.'

Pierce had never mentioned being able to ride. Claudia remembered what Jim had said about unofficial promotion. Then again, Pierce might have learned just from living in the Barracks.

She got on behind Luke, put her feet up on the rests and, very carefully, put her hands on his waist.

'You'll have to hang on a bit tighter than that, or I'll leave you behind.' He pulled her hands closer around. He was wearing black gloves, made of the same lab-leather as the rest of his outers.

As the bike moved off, she was very conscious of being pressed up against him. His back was broad and solid.

Out on the Ring, Luke accelerated. The press of air was startlingly cold against the thin fabric of her blues and the earth blurred beneath them.

She had never travelled so fast in her life. She should've been terrified, but she was exhilarated. She forgot she was hanging on to Luke and gave herself up to the sensation of being hurled through space by a powerful machine.

All too quickly the lights of B-Sector rushed up and the bike slowed. She expected Luke to stop by the main entrance, which was by the stairs to the Transit station, but he took her, going very slowly, right into the residential complex and up to the door of her building. Nobody was about and the pathways were empty.

Claudia dismounted, a little shakily, and took off the helmet.

Luke lifted his visor. 'How was that?'

'It was like flying,' she said, and this time she didn't have to force her smile.

'It's the nearest we can ever come,' he said and took the helmet from her. 'How are things with your mother?'

'You know about her?'

'It's my job to know things about people. Your mother's situation isn't unusual, sadly.'

'She's home again, but I don't know how long that'll last,' said Claudia. She glanced up at the hundreds of windows, although it was impossible to pick out her own.

'Hearing about other people's parents, I think Pierce and I are lucky we grew up in the Barracks,' said Luke. 'I don't know any Survivors who aren't deeply damaged, even the ones who were too young to remember much. The ones born in the Aftermath are just as warped as their parents. That kind of trauma can take generations to breed out.'

Was he expressing something close to sympathy or just stating facts?

'Thank you for the ride, Commander,' said Claudia. She had the strangest sensation of wanting to prolong the moment, but she had no idea how.

'Here to serve, citizen,' he replied, and put down his visor and rode off.

Thirteen

The Junior Selection Trials were coming up soon and Claudia's squad of eleven-year-olds was uncontrollable. Two had almost concussed themselves in completely unnecessary tackles, and while she was seeing to them, several others disobeyed her order to run laps and started playing some game of their own devising, which involved a lot of shrieking and one bloody nose. Claudia rebuked the malcontents for individualistic behaviour and made them run extra laps, to much complaining. Unlike Juanita, whose squad both feared and worshipped her, she struggled to find a balance between being friendly and being strict.

Claudia's squad captain, Daria, was particularly precocious and liked to push limits. Claudia had promoted her to harness her energy and talent, and also to exploit her authority over her peers. Delegation was key to leadership, she had learned, in the tedious mandatory seminars for Senior Youth League officers.

'Daria, it's your job to make sure your team members follow my orders when I'm doing something else. When people are injured, that has to be my priority, and I depend on you to look after the others. What happened today?'

The various scripts suggested by the Youth League mentors

never seemed to work on Daria.

'They didn't want to run laps, and neither did I,' she said, pouting. She was a pretty girl, and she knew it. 'We've already run more than we needed to today. I'm bored running laps. Playing a round of Short Game seemed a more effective team solution.'

'Is that what you call it? Giving each other nosebleeds? I decide how many laps you need to run, and you make sure everyone runs them, you as well. If you want to get promoted, you need to obey orders.'

Claudia did not have a way with children, and children knew it.

'I watched the seniors training yesterday,' said Daria, giving Claudia a sideways look. 'Me and some friends. Pierce took his shirt off. We all think he's hot. You're doing it with him, aren't you?'

'That's none of your business,' said Claudia sharply.

'I'd do it with him.'

'Sounds like you need to get your implant done early. I'll put a note on your records.'

Claudia was pleased to see Daria flinch. Some girls did start early; often, older boys were involved. As Daria's squad leader, Claudia had the authority to make such suggestions.

Over Daria's head, she summoned the rest of the squad, gave them a stiff talking-to about pulling it all together and finished by telling them she was confident they would all do well, the standard spiel. She'd already put in her recommendations and did not expect to be surprised by any of the results. On Daria's report, she had noted a need for discipline, along with individualistic tendencies and lack of team spirit. On the last two, she wasn't so different from Daria, but she knew to conform, and Daria needed to learn.

Perhaps it was a failure of her own leadership, and under someone like Juanita, Daria would have flourished. Since going into the Underground, Claudia was constantly noticing new individualistic and potentially subversive traits in herself.

Coming out of the change rooms, she saw Martin and Arnie standing together in the spacious entry hall of the Youth League training facility. They headed to the senior canteen together, moving against a press of squealing juniors going in the opposite direction. Claudia glimpsed Daria amid a group of her cronies, the natural leader.

The canteen had large windows that looked out over the sports ground on one side and the SYL parade ground on the other. By the windows were arrangements of low chairs and table games; the centre was taken up by bench and table seating, which at this time of the cycle was mostly full.

The three friends joined the food queue. Claudia told them about Daria.

'There's one in every group,' said Arnie. 'If you don't take control, they take over and it's hell.'

'Juanita manages,' said Claudia. She didn't really care about the Game, but it rankled to be outdone by Juanita, even if Juanita had only reached Level IV Ideo.

'But she's scary,' said Martin. 'If I were eleven, I wouldn't mess her about. I mean, she's had pre-Trials promotion to the MT. She has that special intimidating quality that they look for.'

'Do you think Pierce has it?' said Claudia. 'I haven't seen it.'

'Nah, he's a softie,' said Arnie. 'Can't believe he's the same gene pool as Luke.'

'I don't know about that,' said Martin. 'I saw him with his

squad once; one kid was playing up, really out of line, and Pierce suddenly turned on him, not shouting or anything, quiet but really intense, not like himself at all, and I could see the kid almost shitting himself inside out. I don't know what Pierce was saying to him, but then he saw me and switched it right off and just winked. There was a moment, though, when I copped the dead-eyed stare, and it was freaky. Gave me a jolt.'

Arnie started doing impressions of Pierce in blank-eyed Mentargh mode, with Martin acting the frightened junior, and they were all laughing when Claudia spotted Pierce and Ally at a nearby table and hushed them.

'Oh freed,' said Martin. 'Do you think they heard?'

Pierce and Ally were sitting across from each other. Between them existed either an intimate silence or an intimate vacuum. Ally kept pushing back her hair and smiling, while Pierce poked at his food and seemed moodily absorbed in his own thoughts.

'Yikes. I think Ally could use some conversational help,' said Arnie.

They fetched their food trays and joined the other two.

'Hey! I haven't seen much of you lot lately,' exclaimed Pierce, suddenly animated.

Ally seemed relieved to see them, too, but in her eyes, Claudia detected a glimmer of reproach. Claudia avoided her gaze.

'Any room for me?' That was Juanita, suddenly appearing behind Martin. 'Hey, this is great! We haven't been all together since Martin's party.'

She squeezed herself into the space next to Arnie and the girl on the other side was forced to move up to make room.

She was only a second-year SYL officer and Grade II, and Juanita simply took for granted that she would cede the space to Juanita, a final-year officer.

'Are your kids allowed to sleep or have you got them on stims?' Arnie asked her.

Juanita took this literally. 'Of course they're allowed to sleep! Sleep deprivation is counterproductive. If I thought anyone was using performance-enhancing drugs on children, I'd report them right away. I hope you're not cutting corners.'

Arnie did have a reputation among his friends for finding work-arounds.

'Absolutely not! I use the pure force of my personality to spur them on to ever-higher achievement for the greater good,' he protested.

Martin was sitting next to Claudia, and she felt him kick Arnie under the table.

'I guess your squad are all in top shape and fully prepared,' said Pierce to Juanita.

'Pretty much, but I don't want them to peak early, so I've had to build in some light days,' said Juanita, with her usual lack of modesty. 'I have a couple of kids I think are leadership material.'

'I have one, and the little freeder's giving me orders,' said Martin.

'So on the big day, you'll be out on the parade ground marching and the kid will be sitting up with us,' said Pierce.

Juanita looked scandalised. The others laughed, and eventually Juanita got the joke.

'Seriously, though, Martin, if you need some help straightening out this problem kid, just let me know,' she said.

They chatted for a while, and something of their old

camaraderie returned.

Juanita was the first to leave, saying she had extra training. She wished them all well for the upcoming Trials, senior as well as junior, and Claudia felt that she actually meant it.

'Every time I think she's too much, she does something that reminds me she's my friend, and I feel really mean for teasing her,' said Martin.

'I know,' said Arnie. 'Davina thinks we're completely soft.'

At the mention of Davina, the camaraderie dissipated like vapour.

'Are you still hanging out with her?' said Pierce.

'We're in the same Science Ed stream,' said Arnie. 'If you call that hanging out.'

This was an evasion rather than a full lie, but Arnie did it very well. At the same time, Claudia could tell Pierce wasn't fooled.

'I don't like her,' said Ally and looked at Pierce.

He seemed to be on the verge of saying something, but Arnie got in first.

'Cadet-Trooper, if you're trying to read our minds, you need to give us the appropriate drugs. Whatever went into today's protein slurry is working on my bowels but not my brain.'

Usually Arnie's jokes could lighten any mood, but this one did not.

'Talking of bowels, I need to get over to the Med Block. We're doing Basic Gastro,' said Claudia and stood up. 'Next time anyone does a massive synthanol puke, I'll know exactly what to do.'

'Get the freed out of the way,' said Arnie, but his comeback was a little flat.

Claudia was relieved to escape the sudden chilly vibe. In

fact, she had some time before her afternoon Ideo session, and she was planning to sit under the tower tree and read ahead on her tablet. The Ideo chapters were only released on the day of the lesson, otherwise Claudia would've read all of Grade V already.

Coming out of the toilets in the entrance hall, she saw Pierce, his gear bag slung over his shoulder, standing alone. The lunchtime crowds had thinned out and she couldn't avoid him.

'What's going on with you three?' he asked, straight out.

'What do you mean?' Unlike Arnie, Claudia was not very good at evasion.

'You know what I mean. I'm not going to say it.'

She returned his stare.

'OK, don't tell me. Actually, it's better that you don't. But listen, hanging around with people like Davina—as fascinating as you all obviously find her—gets you noticed. Why do you think she's suddenly popped up in Arnie's Science Ed stream? She was held back six months for remedial training. Attitude problems. Her granddad was big in the old Biodome Project, and someone's protecting her, otherwise she wouldn't still be getting around in that stupid hat.'

'How do you know this? Did you check her file?' said Claudia. 'How do you even have access? You keep telling me you're just a cadet-trooper and you don't know anything.'

'I know enough, and she's trouble,' said Pierce.

Claudia recognised another evasion. None of her friends were being fully honest.

Pierce pressed on. 'And since when do you go all the way to the D-Sector Youth League node to hang out, Claudia? Dodgy D-Sector, a total sleaze pit, the problem quadrant. Arnie has form—he's into all sorts of shit—and Martin goes along with Arnie, but you're a straight student, why freed it up now? With Level V Ideo, you could be promoted to the MT, you know that.'

'No, I don't know that,' said Claudia. 'You're not serious. I can't even control my freeding junior squad. And what about you?'

'What about me?'

'Have you been promoted? Unofficially, I mean.'

'What the freed are you talking about?' Pierce's surprise seemed genuine, but Claudia was no longer sure what she believed. 'Has Davina told you some crap?'

'No.' This was true: it was Jim who had mentioned unofficial promotion. 'And how do you even know I was in D-Sector?'

'I heard from Luke that he gave you a ride.' Pierce said this reluctantly.

'He told me that you can ride. You never said anything about that.'

'Everyone who grows up in the Barracks learns to ride, but I don't get priority access to a bike. I'm too junior. I'm just a freeding cadet, Claudia. I can't roar around and give people rides and use a bike as a chick-magnet.'

'What the freed?' Claudia almost shouted. 'Chick-magnet? You are out of your freeding mind.'

'Are you two arguing?' Ally had come up without either of them noticing.

'I have to go,' said Pierce shortly. 'See you both around.'

'Everyone's behaving weirdly these days except for Juanita,' said Ally, watching him walk out the main doors. 'I hate it. I wish we could go back to the way things were before Davina turned up.'

Claudia ignored this. 'I'm running late too. See you later.'

'You don't tell me anything these days,' Ally complained.

Fourteen

Across the astroturf of the Senior Youth League oval, senior squads were being shouted through a tough circuit routine by the head coach, a Mentargh lieutenant called Ash and known as the Beast. The end of the active cycle was drawing to a close, signalled by the deepening grey and the descending chill as the Meteorological Bureau lowered the temperature to the nocturnal optimum of 16°C.

Claudia's t-shirt clung damply to her back and her muscles were beginning to shake. Ash was pushing them all to their limit. The rumour was that he did this every year, that people who couldn't handle the max-out sessions would fail the Senior Trials before the actual day. Everyone hated him, except Juanita.

Claudia was not going to fail. She had spent her entire childhood working towards an A-grade graduation from Youth League, following all the rules and rituals with the required diligence of a model junior citizen. Her ambitions had been dictated to her and she had followed them unquestioningly, until now.

What did she actually want, beyond her assigned role as a medical technician? Pierce's comment about being promoted to the MT had unsettled her. That had never been an ambition or even a possibility.

In the Mentargh, there would be no limit to her ideological training. She might even gain access to the Survivor Archives.

Claudia forced herself through the final laps, trying to pace herself against the other dim figures moving, ghost-like, around the oval. She was aware of Juanita passing her, the white soles of her trainers flashing in the gloom. Somewhere behind her was Arnie. Ally and Martin were in the centre, going through a high-intensity routine of planks, squats and lunges.

One of her feet snagged, and she fell hard on the astroturf. By the time Ash had run over to scream at her for being clumsy, she was holding the culprit, the sole of her own shoe, which had half come away.

'I'm sorry, sir. I was trying to keep these going until the Trials,' she said, wincing in pain and resisting, very hard, the urge to cry. As part of the Inheritors generation and a Senior Youth League officer, she was supposed to be tough and resilient.

The lieutenant swore under his breath. Amid the throbbing of her ankle, Claudia reflected that the production delays had been caused by subversive sabotage and that she was possibly more to blame, very indirectly, than Ash could imagine.

'Freed, Claudia, you OK?' Arnie kneeled beside her.

'You get back on the track!' barked Ash. 'You are borderline already! You have no excuse!'

'Yes, sir.' Arnie stood up, very slowly, returning Ash's stare. 'Take it easy, Clau, I'll check in with you later.'

Claudia worried for Arnie. He'd always had a playful attitude, but since meeting Davina, he'd developed an edge that could get him into trouble, quite apart from his new

Underground associates. Claudia recalled Pierce's comment the other day. What else was Arnie up to? How well did she know any of her friends anymore?

Ash examined her ankle, none too gently.

'Looks like a simple twist. If it swells up, go to medbay for an injection. You can take tomorrow off. I want you on top form for the final practice Game. And get another pair of trainers from the MT distro. You can't freeding go to the Selection Trials in bare feet. Tell them I sent you.'

Being given time off was a major concession from Ash, who believed in working through pain.

'Thank you, sir,' said Claudia.

She hobbled over to the sideline benches. It was almost dark now, save for the pale ambience of the circuit lights, and she could hardly recognise any of the sweating, straining bodies still out on the oval. In Claudia's exhausted state, the spectacle was like something from one of her nightmares.

'You look like yesterday's lunch,' said Martin, handing over her jacket. He used a word to describe Ash that Claudia had only heard Davina use, part of her large repertoire of crude and colourful Oldie phrases.

'Does it hurt?' said Ally, sitting down next to her.

'It's OK,' said Claudia. 'Really, don't fuss, Ally.'

Her foot didn't feel OK, but she didn't want any help from Ally.

She was one of the last to leave the SYL stadium. Martin and Arnie said they had remedial Ideo class; Juanita had a meeting of her local Citizens' Brigade, as a youth rep; and Ally, possibly miffed, went off with another girl who lived in the same residential block. Claudia could've asked any of them for help getting home, but she didn't want to be a burden.

Limping down the front steps, she felt sorry for herself.

'Come on, junior citizen! Pull it together! You're Mentargh material,' she muttered, and the idea seemed even more preposterous.

If Pierce wanted to show off his chick-magnet bike mastery, she thought, now was the time to offer her a lift.

At that moment, she heard the quiet drone of a powerbike. It circled around from the side parking bay and pulled up in front of her. The rider, all in black, pulled up their visor. It was Tia, Ash's second-in-command. She was also a med tech trainee, several years ahead of Claudia.

'Heard you twisted your ankle. You're B-Sector, aren't you? Want a ride?'

'Yes please, ma'am.'

Amid her relief, Claudia was also aware of disappointment; she'd wanted the rider to be Luke. This realisation shocked her, and she pushed it out of her mind.

When she swiped herself into the unit, the lights were on. Claudia's heart sank. She was physically drained, and she wanted to be alone.

'Is that you, Claudia?' Her mother sounded almost sober.

'No, it's the freeding Rehab team come to take you away,' Claudia muttered. 'Yes, of course it's me.'

The living area was clear of the usual mess of used food containers, dirty clothes and empty cannies, and two places were set at the small table.

'I thought we could have dinner together, for once,' said Faye. 'I picked up two pilaffs from the distro. You used to like these when you were little. I'll put them in the mike.'

Claudia put down her bag. Faye's voice trembled, as did her

hands, and there was still a whiff of roughbrew about her, but when someone had been drinking it for a long time, the smell took a while to wear off, seeping out of their pores instead of sweat.

'Come on, sit down with me. Tell me what's been happening.'

'The usual. I go to school, I go to training, I come home.'

'Don't you have some sort of test coming up?'

'The Selection Trials, Mum.' Claudia sat down. She was starving. If Faye was actually going to prepare her dinner, she'd take full advantage.

'Is that what they call it? Selection for what, exactly?'

'I've told you already.' Roughbrew destroyed short-term memory, and Claudia had no patience for repeat explanations.

'Don't shout at me.'

'I'm not shouting.'

'God, you can be unpleasant to live with.'

'Me? You're the one who's drunk most of the time.'

'What's the point of being sober? I don't know why other people bother.' The microwave pinged and Faye went to open it.

'Self-pity is a destructive outgrowth of individualism and interferes with social functioning and productivity,' said Claudia. Even as she spoke, she was aware of her own very recent lapse. 'A correct attitude of resilience and gratitude at all times prevents the development of this negative tendency.'

'Don't quote that shit at me!'

Faye reached into the microwave with her bare hands, then screamed and dropped one of the trays. The pilaff spattered all over the floor.

'Look what you made me do!' she screeched, shaking her

burned fingers.

'Freed, here we go again,' said Claudia under her breath, and got up slowly from her chair. She pulled her mother's hands to the sink, not at all gently, and ran cold water over them.

'Stay there. I'll take care of it,' she said.

It was always easier that way.

She squatted to scrape up the food and wipe the floor, ignoring the pain in her ankle. There were tiny grains and specks of vegetable matter everywhere. By the time she'd finished cleaning up, the other tray of pilaff, still sitting in the microwave, was cool enough to eat.

Faye had retired to the divan. When Claudia put her head around the corner to ask if she wanted the remaining pilaff or something else, her mother was asleep, her mouth hanging slightly open. Her breath came in wheezes, sometimes laboured.

Claudia's mother had been signed off minimum citizen activity protocols for a very long time. Physically as well as mentally, she was a wreck, a total waste of resources. There was no difference, really, between Faye eating the pilaff and Claudia throwing it in the organic recycler. Looking at her, Claudia felt a wringing combination of pity and disgust.

She ate the pilaff in the kitchen standing up, her weight on her good foot. Tia had given her some painkillers, stronger ones than she'd normally get from the dispensary. MT medics had special access. Claudia took one, to get her through the night, and saved the rest for her next training session. She knew people who only managed training at all with the help of painkillers, especially with Ash as their coach. Did he give anyone stims? She remembered the lunchtime conversation between the friends. She was supposed to be the intelligent one, but there was so much she didn't know or notice compared to her more worldly, less naive friends.

She'd already showered in the SYL change rooms, which had more generous timings than domestic showers. Once she'd cleaned her teeth, Claudia retreated to her cabin and snibbed the door. The painkillers were taking effect and she was ready to sink into her bunk.

Two missed messages showed up on her screen, both from Kate. As Claudia was considering whether to call back—she really didn't want to talk to Kate just then—another call came through. It was Kate, again.

'Well, hello, citizen! You're hard to catch these days.'

Claudia took a deep breath and managed a smile.

'Hi! Things have been really busy. You know, with the Selection Trials.'

'I know, I just wanted to check in. I heard you sprained your ankle at training today.'

'Yeah, my trainer gave out. Ash said I should get a new pair at the MT distro.' Claudia should have left it at this. 'Which is a bit weird, because I thought there were no new clothes or shoes for six months, after that sabotage incident.'

'Well, of course there are still some supplies from before the incident,' said Kate. 'These are available on a needs-basis, and obviously you have a need. We can't have you bombing out of the big day because you don't have a pair of shoes, can we?'

'And I'm very grateful,' said Claudia. 'I was just wondering. But of course.'

'I know, you're always wondering. So many questions!' Kate smiled, as if Claudia's curiosity was a naughty little secret between them. 'But seriously, Claudia, how are you feeling? Even a minor injury at this stage can throw you off course, and I know you've been working very intensively. Actually, I've noticed quite a few stress spikes on your health monitor, and I can see you're having nightmares again.'

As a trainee med tech, Claudia was only just learning the extent of what was monitored via each citizen's bodychip. Most people had no idea.

'Yeah, I've been feeling pretty stressed. And Faye's back home again. That never helps. She's a nightmare in person.'

Kate was not distracted by any sort of levity. 'Claudia, is there anything you're not telling me?'

'What do you mean?'

'That bad trip, and now the nightmares. When you withhold things or repress them, they come out in other ways. We've talked about this before. You need to be completely honest with me, so I can help you.'

'I know, but I'm so tired. I'm worried about the Selection Trials.'

'Why are you worried? You're totally on track. Your Ideo grade is higher than it needs to be, your med training is going well, and apart from today's little accident, your phys ed and Game are excellent.'

Claudia almost asked *Am I really on track to be promoted to the Mentargh?* but this would sound presumptuous and even cheeky.

'I'm just stressed, that's all.'

All she wanted was for Kate to leave her alone.

Perhaps Kate picked up the irritation in Claudia's tone. Instead of signing off, as Claudia too obviously wanted, she continued to scrutinise her.

'Claudia, something's up with you, I can tell.'

Claudia returned her gaze, trying to look innocent, but she could feel her mouth settling into a sulky line. Her ankle was throbbing. Annoyance seeped out of her like putrid water from a backed-up drain.

Kate took a few moments to speak, as if deciding exactly what to say. Her manner was still calm and caring, but the undertone was quite different.

'Claudia, if you won't tell me what's going on, so I can help you, I'll have to refer you further up the line.'

Claudia's irritation turned instantly to shock, and there was no hiding it.

'I thought that'd get a reaction,' said Kate. 'It's not a step I'd take lightly. The interrogation process is tough. You dread it at first, the relentless probing—probing—probing, and you fight against it because you think you're stronger than they are. Then you begin to realise they're helping you, and you even start to look forward to your sessions, because you want to be a productive citizen, not a social burden and a liability.'

'You were a ... subversive?' Claudia whispered.

'Not quite, but close enough. At your age, I was a free spirit. I even wore some awful deadclothes. You wouldn't have recognised me.' Kate grinned. 'They were so gross! I ponged like you wouldn't believe, but of course I wouldn't listen to anyone. I thought I was so clever, that I could make my own rules and get away with it. I was arrogant and selfish. But they saw through me, of course. They always do.'

Claudia's lungs constricted, and for a moment, she could hardly breathe.

'You have so much promise,' Kate was saying. 'It would be a shame if you took a wrong turn now. A loss to the community.

It's my job to make sure that doesn't happen. If I refer you, it'll be for your own good, as well as the good of everyone else.'

Tears began to trickle down Claudia's cheeks.

'I'm so tired,' she said. 'I'm just so tired.'

Kate seemed to make some private calculation and relented.

'OK, we'll talk later, when you're fresh. Have a good night's sleep! And don't take all those pills at once! I know they feel nice, but don't!'

The screen went blank.

As Claudia fell asleep, it crossed her mind, very fleetingly, that Kate had said nothing about Luke finding her in D-Sector and giving her a ride home.

Fifteen

Limping slightly, Claudia was joined by Martin as she headed out of the Med Block to the Transit station.

'Hey, how's the ankle?'

'I've got another few days off training,' said Claudia. 'I had to get some more painkillers because Faye found my last quota. She actually broke the lock on my cabin door. Apparently they go really well with roughbrew, a one-person head-party that lasts for days. Too bad if someone else actually needs them. I have to take them everywhere with me.'

'Sorry about that, Clau. You can always stash your stash at mine,' said Martin. 'Any plans for this evening?'

'Uh, sleep?'

'Oh, boring,' said Martin. 'What I'm actually saying, without wanting to be too obvious, is that you're invited to friendly D-Sector node tonight.'

Claudia stopped. 'Does that mean what I think it means?'

'Freed, Claudia! So many questions! Just go with the flow. Unless you'd rather go straight home to bed.'

'Going with the flow' was a Neil expression. Claudia wondered how often Martin and Arnie had been to the Underground without her.

'No remedial Ideo tonight, then?'

Martin grinned guiltily. 'Sorry, Clau. For a smart person, you can be a bit dim. I love hearing your long Ideo quotes, truly, but the downstairs cohort aren't entirely convinced. The Oldies seem fine with you, but the younger ones are still suspicious.'

'I don't care about Luma. I like talking to the Oldies,' said Claudia. 'And that's all they seem to do, and eat off-quota biscuits. They don't seem dangerous.'

'I know, they just seem old,' said Martin. 'But come on, Claudia, do you really think they could chat like that in a community centre? Can you imagine Neil in a Survivors' Group, harshing on their happy drugs?'

There were special meetings for Survivors who couldn't get over their trauma and adapt to reality, with a version of the Party Machine and drugs. Faye used to attend when Claudia was little but had been ejected for being disruptive. She'd started early on roughbrew, like many Survivors. The resultant cognitive and personality decay was known as roughbrew brain-rot; even medics used this term rather than the official one.

'So who's decided that I'm OK? Has Davina convinced them?'

'Actually, Jim seems to have taken a shine to you,' said Martin. 'Anyway, are you coming or not? The sleep of the righteous in B-Sector or the free-spirit thrill of D-Sector? Anticlockwise or clockwise?'

Since Kate's threat, Claudia had had two more sessions with her mentor. The pain meds had relaxed her and she'd been more herself—the self she routinely presented to Kate. They'd had their usual talk, and Kate had seemed taken in by Claudia's curated anecdotes and manufactured enthusiasm.

The night Claudia had hurt her ankle, she'd lost her usual control. She would never let that happen again.

'Let's go, then, citizen,' she said. 'I can sleep when I'm old and on low rations.'

***

Claudia had just accepted her first biscuit from Lisa when Luma and another young woman came in.

'What the freed, Level V?' said Luma's companion, looking Claudia up and down.

'What's she doing here?' said Luma. 'I didn't agree to this.'

'She likes my biscuits,' said Lisa.

Her manner was calm but Claudia could sense the antagonism between Lisa and the younger women.

'Hi, Debs. She got kicked off a Party Machine. It spat her out for having subversive thoughts,' said Martin.

'Not being able to hack jennies doesn't make you a subversive,' said Luma. 'It makes you weak.'

'I don't handle drugs well myself,' said Lisa. 'I suppose that makes me weak, does it?'

Luma seemed briefly ashamed. 'Well, I still don't like it. This'll have to be a social meeting.'

'That's what we scheduled,' said Lisa. 'If you want to discuss changing the world, or what's left of it, that's Thursday night.'

Claudia wasn't sure if she was being sarcastic. Only Oldies used obsolete time-units like 'Thursday'.

'Whatever,' said Debs, and she and Luma pointedly went to the far end of the unit and started talking with Davina, Arnie and some other people, including Jim.

Lisa shook her head. 'They were told, but they come and go on their own schedule. If Jim thinks you're OK, that's enough for me.'

'That was awkward,' said Claudia. 'Thanks, Martin.'

'No worries. She's like a negative version of Juanita,' he said. 'Anyway, I've been waiting to see the new shoes. To be honest, I'm jealous. You still haven't been to pick them up?'

'How does anyone get new shoes here?' asked Lisa. 'I've had the same pair for years now. They've been fixed to death and into the next life.'

Claudia explained. She hadn't been to the Barracks yet. Until she was ready to start training again, it was easier to put it off.

'I could've got you a new pair of trainers,' said Neil, who had come over for a biscuit and taken several. 'Easy-peasy-lemon-squeezy.'

'But how? What actually happened in Recycling? Do you know any of the people involved?' This was a very daring question, and Claudia was almost shy to ask it.

'Kiddo, I work at the depot, and there wasn't any sabotage,' said Neil. 'Every so often, something breaks down, but that's because the whole system's getting a bit old and creaky. Like me.'

'They just blame it on subversives, shut down supplies of certain things, and get everyone riled up or scared,' said Lisa.

'So there was no sabotage at all? You mean, they completely lied to us?' said Claudia, and Martin also looked troubled.

Neil and Lisa burst out laughing, Neil spraying crumbs.

'Did you really think it was Neil in the Recycling Depot? With his spanner, jamming up the works?' Lisa made an exaggerated ramming gesture with her fist.

'It's not as simple as that.' Claudia felt a little defensive. 'Before the Event, society had huge material wastage rates. Our society is 99% efficient. It's like a perfect machine, which doesn't lose any energy through friction or noise or heat. Subversive elements are like dirt clogging up the mechanism. A subversive isn't necessarily a person who wants to break things and literally sticks a spanner in the works. Someone who becomes slack and individualistic, who loses their sense of duty to their fellow citizens and community, is a subversive. This sort of attitude can spread, and you end up with petty system-cheating, corruption, laziness and low efficiency. Basically, a subversive is a person who resists and rejects the Ideo, who thinks independently of it and acts according to individual motives and feelings. Just by being down here makes us kind of responsible for what happened at the Recycling Depot.'

She took a deep breath. Lisa and Neil both blinked.

'If it wasn't for yours truly, that bloody Recycling Depot would've broken down a long time ago and you'd all be playing special rugby in your bare feet,' said Neil. 'And 99% efficiency is complete bullshit. We're hardly at 84% regeneration, and it's going down. Natural material attrition. We are going to be in big effing trouble within a generation.'

'Do you have to memorise all that for Level V, Claudia?' said Lisa. 'Crikey. No wonder they give you kids so many drugs.'

'And not even good ones,' said Neil.

'Before the Event, I had fifty pairs of shoes,' said Lisa. 'I left most of them in storage because I didn't need them out at the facility. Then I wore the same pair of trainers for three years, tying them up with bits of bandage or wire or tape or whatever I could find. When I was accepted into the Dome, everything I had on me was taken away for decontamination and I never got anything back. I've worn one pair of shoes, more or less, ever since.'

She stuck out her feet, showing off a pair of very worn standard-issue utility shoes. Her ankles were quite thick, indicating to Claudia that Lisa suffered fluid retention, common to women her age.

'I often think of all those gorgeous shoes I left behind, vaporised in an instant,' she said.

'You were *allowed* to own fifty pairs of shoes? What were they all for?' Claudia asked.

Lisa sighed deeply, as if this was beyond explanation.

'She was a human centipede,' said Neil and guffawed. 'I could tell you about capitalism, kiddo, but that would take all night and then some, and we don't have enough biscuits.'

A younger man came over from the other side of the cabin and took some biscuits.

'Neil, we need to chat about chips,' he said, glancing at Claudia and Martin.

The slogan on Neil's t-shirt was NO SWIPE, in a circle with a line through it. Following Claudia's eyes, Neil grinned. 'That's me, the original no-swipe. Invisible man. Nobody knows where I go unless I want them to.'

'Don't you have a chip?' asked Martin. 'Everyone has one.'

'I used to have a lot more than one. I practically had a motherboard inside me,' said Neil. 'I was into bodyhacking, big time, but all my chips were fried by radiation, back in the day. The piece of crap they stuck in me when I got here! I hacked that in five minutes flat.'

'Neil,' said the younger man, looking again at Claudia and Martin.

'Oops, me and my big flapping mouth. Information wants to be free. Goes against the grain not to share,' said Neil, winking, and followed the younger man over to the corner.

'Are they planning something?' said Claudia.

'You ask a lot of questions, for someone your generation,' said Lisa. 'I thought they trained that out of you. I'm not involved. I don't want to know. I've been through enough in my life, and I'm not going to live long enough to see what happens next. That's up to younger people. But Neil's right, something will have to change. This place is not sustainable in the long term.'

It took a moment for Claudia to realise that 'this place', which Lisa said in a dismissive, almost disrespectful way, was the Dome.

'So why take the risk of coming down here at all, if you're not involved?' said Martin.

Claudia had the sudden and clear impression that he knew more than he had told her.

'Because I can talk normally with other people who talk normally, and we don't have to pretend,' said Lisa. 'And because sitting around an empathy projector being drug-happified with a bunch of brainwashed old farts in senior citizen community node brigade, or whatever they call it, is not my bag. And because nobody down here is going to ask difficult questions about where my biscuits come from.'

The door of the cabin was flung open. A man burst in, panting. He wasn't wearing a jacket and his t-shirt was sweat-stained under the arms.

The energy in the room changed immediately.

'Jay, what's up?' That was from Debs.

'Something's going down. I came through the second D-Sector portal. The MT are all over the place.'

'Not just the routine D-Sector clean-up?' said Luma.

'No, there was no warning this time,' said Jay. 'Something real is happening. The upper levels have been powered on.'

Claudia felt a jolt pass through the entire cabin.

'We need to engage evacuation protocols,' said Luma.

'We need to get the hell out,' said Neil. 'Leave it up to me, citizens.'

From an ancient blue backpack he produced an equally ancient-looking monitor, which he unrolled on one of the tables. Everyone gathered around. Peering between Martin and Lisa, Claudia glimpsed detailed plans of the Dome flashing up.

'Yeah, I can see what they're doing,' said Neil. 'D-Sector is the hot zone tonight. Central and the other sectors should be safe, but we don't all want to pop out the same hole like a family of bloody wombats.'

He quickly assigned exit routes and rolled up the monitor. As he shoved it back into his pack, he winked at Claudia.

'You didn't see a thing, right? The MT net is totally secure, absolutely bomb-proof.'

The pack bore the word BILLABONG. Claudia wondered if that was his original family name. In the Dome, everyone was simply a citizen; all other identifiers were suppressed. In the Old World, conflicting identities had caused social unrest and fragmentation.

Claudia didn't know her family name. People her age didn't.

The group quickly dispersed in different directions into the darkness. Neil told Claudia, Martin and Arnie to follow him.

He put on a pair of smart glasses. Claudia had seen them used in medical settings, in the course of her training, but they were restricted-access tech, like personal comms devices.

'This is so I can keep track of the situation,' he said.

He also wore a head torch, which he powered up without using any manual controls.

'Super-efficient! I want one,' said Arnie.

'OK, I was lying when I said all my chips were fried,' said Neil. 'My mates used to call me the cyborg.'

He didn't seem particularly perturbed by the situation and led them through the labyrinth as if they were simply going on a long walk. They went down, and then down again, and along an endless corridor, coming out into a vast hall. Three columns loomed in the centre, as tall as buildings, with pipes running up their sides and a platform at the top.

'Backup reactors,' said Neil. 'Haven't been touched since before the Event. Mint condition. Nobody ever comes down here. It's like a time capsule. Now, are we all good with heights?'

Narrow metal stairs zig-zagged up the far wall. When Neil gestured up with his head, the light from his head torch vanished into the distance.

'Don't know why I bothered asking because we don't have a choice. Come on, up we go.'

Claudia concentrated on the steps, her hand never leaving the narrow rail. Behind her, Arnie was breathing heavily.

At the top, Neil stopped on the gantry that ran the whole circumference of the reactor chamber and touched one arm of his glasses.

'Just checking,' he said. 'We're below C-Sector now. D-Sector is still busy, but not much is happening here. Ideally you would've popped out in D-Sector, kept the circle tight and closed, but the MT have gone through the YL node and it'd look pretty dodgy if you suddenly appeared there out of the blue.'

They followed him through a door and emerged out of the darkness into a minimal-lighting corridor.

'If I had more kit with me, I could re-swipe you right to your door,' said Neil. 'The best I can do is swipe you into C-Sector, so if they do a quick check, it looks OK. If they don't have a reason to back-check, then nobody will notice. It's not like the system is watertight, anyway. If your chip faults, you're effectively in ghost mode and you only find out if you can't get your rations anymore because DOMUS thinks you've croaked. Hold out your arms, citizens.'

He produced a small scanning device from another pocket in his pack, pressed in a setting and swiped their wrists in turn.

'That's you. Safe to go. Now, keep going along here, go up the ladder, and you'll come out the emergency exit for C-Sector utilities control, which is not currently locked. More nefarious subversive activity, no doubt, but what would I know?'

'Aren't you coming with us?' said Martin.

'Nah, I have other places to be,' said Neil. 'Mr Invisible has choices that you don't.'

He winked and went back into the reactor chamber.

The three friends looked at each other and started to laugh from relief.

'Freeding freed,' said Martin. 'I thought I was going to pass out and fall off those stairs.'

'I had my eyes shut,' said Arnie.

'I was watching your feet the entire way,' said Claudia to Martin.

They came out on the edge of the Ring, the same exit they'd used the night of Martin's party. Ahead, several hundred metres or so across the bare earth, they could see the lights of the C-Sector residential blocks and the towers of the Moisture Regeneration Plant behind them. Unlike the first time they'd gone underground with Davina, everything was faintly illuminated. A full moon Outside occasionally added a white, eerie light; perhaps it was one of those phases. But for the Event, the Dome would've been on the moon. It was a strange thought.

'I don't think I've walked so far in my life,' said Martin and yawned hugely. 'The Transit will be on slow for a few hours yet. Come to my place and bunk down. I'm going to be wrecked for training tomorrow.'

Trudging along behind the two boys, Claudia became aware of a faint hum. Lying in her bunk at night, when it was very quiet, she sometimes heard a hum, the sound of the Dome's massive, tireless life-support systems vibrating up from the depths. This hum was higher and thinner and coming rapidly closer.

Turning, she saw a rim of single lights heading from the far side of the Ring, from Central Zone. It took her a few seconds to realise what they were.

'Bikes! Run!'

They ran. The air burned in Claudia's throat and her injured ankle screamed. The humming came nearer and nearer, and it seemed that any minute they would be overtaken and surrounded by a swarm of Mentargh on powerbikes. She had never run so fast, not even when shouted at by Ash. Every atom of her being was focused on the familiar lights of C-Sector ahead. She plunged through the pale light as if she were flying.

The sound of bikes began to recede, but the three didn't stop running until they had entered the residential precinct and gone several buildings deep. Martin was bent over, gasping, and Arnie simply dropped to the ground and lay splayed out. Across the Ring, the lights had turned and were heading towards B-Sector.

'You two are breathing too much. Stop it, you'll wake everyone up,' said Arnie, and Claudia knew they were safe.

'Freed me, Ash never trained us for that,' she said, her breath coming in gasps.

'Citizens! Evading the Mentargh involves many special skills,' intoned Arnie, between deep breaths. 'Entering reactor chambers and climbing a thousand stairs and trying not to look down. Sprinting until you want to vomit, to outrun a fleet of powerbikes. Your guide in the following challenge course is an Oldie jacked up with pre-Event chips who can ghost his way around the entire Dome. At a crucial moment, the old freeder will disappear on you.'

Martin and Claudia laughed helplessly.

'Arnie, you need to write the table game for that,' said Claudia. 'A special pirate table game for the D-Sector node.'

At this moment, she almost felt she belonged in D-Sector node.

'We don't need the Selection Trials,' said Martin. 'We're Inheritors, as tough as freed and fully sustainable. Let's tell Ash tomorrow and go for a drink instead of doing any more laps around that freeding oval.'

They didn't notice the two black-suited figures approaching, and then it was too late to do anything but try not to look horrified or guilty. Arnie got quickly to his feet.

Martin suddenly grinned. 'It's Pierce! Thank freed, it's Pierce!'

He was about to run over, but Arnie grabbed his arm. 'Who's the other guy? And why is Pierce in black? He never said he'd been promoted to his blacks.'

They stood and waited for Pierce and his colleague to reach them.

'Hello, citizens,' said Pierce. 'Strange time of the cycle to be out. You look like you've been running.'

'Extra training. Laps around the res block,' said Arnie. 'One of Juanita's hot tips. Don't sleep, just train more.'

'This is Byrne.' Pierce inclined his head towards his partner, a thin-faced boy, who nodded in acknowledgement.

'Strange time of the cycle to be on patrol in a res block,' said Arnie. 'Is something up?'

'Nothing you need worry about. It's all under control,' said Byrne. 'We're just doing a final sweep. We'll need to scan you.'

'I'll take care of that,' said Pierce to Byrne. 'I know them, I'll deal with this. I'll catch up with you in a minute.'

Byrne nodded and moved on, but not before he'd given them a final scrutiny, as if imprinting every detail of their faces on his mind.

Pierce waited until he was out of earshot before he spoke again.

'What the freed are you doing out at this time? Don't tell me you've been partying, I know you haven't.'

'We were just hanging out,' said Arnie. 'Burning off some stress. There's no rule against that, is there?'

There was a new coolness in his tone.

'No,' said Pierce. 'But there are some nights when being out of place could attract a whole lot of unhappy attention your way.'

'Like when the Mentargh are hunting someone down?' said Claudia.

'When were you promoted to full blacks, Pierce?' said Martin. 'You never said anything. We could've had another party to celebrate.'

Pierce did not look at Claudia. 'It's not really a promotion. I sometimes do extra duties.'

'Like chasing people on a powerbike? Sounds like fun,' said Arnie. 'Since when did you learn to ride? We could've had excellent times.'

'They learn young in the Barracks,' said Claudia.

'Yeah, you had that discussion with Luke,' Pierce retorted. 'After he gave you a ride home from D-Sector the other night.'

The other two turned to Claudia.

'Freed, Clau. You never said anything,' said Arnie.

She managed a shrug. 'I ran into him when I was going for the Transit. It's not like I had a choice. It was … weird.'

Before Martin's party, she would've shared this extraordinary event with her friends, and they would've laughed about it. Well, maybe not Pierce.

'Let's get this over with.' Pierce detached a scanner from his belt and they held out their wrists. He looked at the display, scrolled down and frowned. 'Did you re-enact the Exodus tonight? You've been all over the place.'

'Those Transit scanners must be playing up again,' said Arnie.

His defiant manner seemed to trigger something in Pierce. 'Whatever,' he said, and put the scanner away. 'You're just lucky I found you and not someone else. Now do yourselves a favour and get in place. You're not supposed to be out and about for another couple of hours.'

He was speaking to all of them, but his gaze was directed, disconcertingly, at Claudia.

'Thanks for the advice, Trooper,' said Arnie.

There was a flash of hurt in Pierce's eyes, but he only nodded and took curt leave of them.

The three watched him walk away and join Byrne.

'Freed, he looks just like Luke in that uniform,' said Martin.

'You're telling me,' said Arnie. He was uncharacteristically grim. 'He knows freeding well we were in D-Sector and that we didn't get here on the Transit.'

'Do you think he'll report us?' said Martin.

The other two didn't reply.

Martin sighed. 'We went to the same Zone Nursery. I've known him all my life. It feels weird not to trust him.'

'Nothing personal, but I don't think we can anymore,' said Arnie. 'I don't think Pierce wants to betray us, but if he knows too much, he'll have to. We can't always expect him to protect us if he's put on the spot.'

'I didn't like the look of that other guy,' said Martin.

'Yeah, spending a long night on patrol with Trooper Byrne wouldn't be much of a party,' said Arnie and reverted to his usual grin. 'We definitely had more fun.'

* * *

On the early morning Transit back to B-Sector, Claudia tried to organise her own feelings towards Pierce.

He'd lied to her. If unofficial promotion was supposed to be secret, then he couldn't have told her, but his denial had been so natural. She'd believed him without a single twinge of doubt.

In full MT blacks, he looked like a different person, and the resemblance to Luke, as Martin had noted, was unnerving.

Until that night, she hadn't believed that he'd betray them, but now she was no longer sure.

It saddened her that Martin and Arnie were beginning to doubt their long-time friend too. They'd always been so close, a complete and indivisible unit. Their friendship had survived the petty arguments of Basic Ed, the separation of professional training, the often disruptive transition from Junior to Senior League. True, Juanita was also Mentargh, but she was still the same person, and they'd always understood the built-in limit. Ally was just Ally. Pierce was different.

As she got off the Transit, her ankle throbbed. She'd need two painkillers to get to sleep. Instinctively, Claudia reached into the pocket of her daypack for the reassuring shape of the pill packet. Faye could be quite cunning in searching things out.

Sixteen

Claudia had never been in the Mentargh Barracks before. The entry to the secure compound was double-swipe, and she had to explain to a lieutenant at the first barrier why she was there. The lieutenant did a cursory check on the system and waved her through.

'Can't let subversives undermine Ash's straight run of Senior Trial Game victories, can we?' he said and winked at her.

'No, sir,' said Claudia.

'You're in Pierce's cohort, aren't you?' He took another look at the system, then back at her, less casually.

'Yes.' She waited for something more, but he simply pointed across the far side of the Barracks quadrangle. 'Commissary's that way.'

It was shift-change in the morning cycle and the quadrangle was milling with Mentargh, in both black and grey uniforms. Claudia felt conspicuous in her standard rig, and she was aware of people noticing her, although nobody said anything.

The quadrangle was very large. To the right were the administrative and operational buildings; to the left, the residential blocks, mess halls and common rooms. At the far end was the stadium used for Mentargh-only matches and training, along with the large gym. The Barracks even had its own medical block. This was where Pierce had grown up, the self-contained miniature world that mirrored the Dome and also controlled it. It was not uncommon for orphaned children to be taken into the Mentargh, if they were perceived to have potential. This had happened to Luke and Pierce. If Faye had succumbed to roughbrew earlier, Claudia might have grown up in the Barracks herself. She'd thought of this more than once, and the Barracks had not always seemed the worse option.

A small group around Claudia's age, in standard rig and wearing black armbands, were at the commissary ahead of her, accompanied by a training lieutenant. Among them was Juanita. Seeing Claudia, she grinned broadly.

'I wasn't expecting to see you here!'

'Ash sent me, for new shoes.'

'Yeah, I remember. Is the foot all good? We want you in fighting form for the big day.'

'If I survive the rest of Ash's training schedule,' said Claudia.

'Positive thinking, citizen!' chided one of Juanita's companions.

'She's just modest, Dillon,' said Juanita. 'Guess what! We all heard this morning we passed our basic training and we're getting our greys.'

Her excitement was infectious, and Claudia had to feel pleased for her. There had never been any doubt about Juanita's trajectory.

'Congratulations, citizens.' Claudia included Dillon in this, smiling to disrupt his scrutiny. If he was practising basic face-scanning, she wasn't having it. 'Juanita, did you know that Pierce is on probationary full black duty?'

'No, but it's not usually announced or anything,' said Juanita. 'How do you know?'

Dillon resumed his scrutiny.

Claudia relaxed all her facial muscles and shrugged. 'I was around at Martin's the other night and we met him on patrol around the res blocks, with another guy.'

'You guys need to slow down the partying,' said Juanita. 'At least until the Trials are over.'

Unlike Arnie and Martin, Claudia didn't have a reputation for partying, and it was strange to be included.

'I heard something went down the other night. Lots of bikes were out,' said Dillon.

'Really?' said Claudia. 'We didn't hear a thing.'

The lieutenant bawled out to the remaining probationers. 'Hurry up! Unless you want to wear blues the rest of your life!'

Claudia was used to waiting in distro queues. She mentally revised her last Ideo lesson ('Money and the consumer society'), waving to Juanita and ignoring Dillon's last passing stare as they came out with their new clothing issue.

The supply clerk scanned her and disappeared into a long aisle of shelves. As far as Claudia could see, the Mentargh commissary was well-stocked, with no empty shelves in view. In the most recent Ideo session, the trainer had explained how rampant pre-Event consumerism had contributed to planetary degeneration on a vast scale. Consumer activity had originally taken place in 'shops', which to Claudia's mind must have looked something like the commissary. In-person shopping had been partly replaced by virtual consumer activity over the internet by the 2020s and 2030s, but many people had still enjoyed viewing and selecting goods in the physical sphere and as a social activity in an otherwise atomised and alienated society riven by loneliness.

Claudia could see how it could be fun to explore the commissary shelves, even though she knew pretty much what she would find.

The clerk returned with a pair of trainers in her size.

'Try them on, but unless you've grown extra toes, they'll fit.'

This was an oddly imaginative comment from an MT supply clerk, and Claudia was reminded briefly of Neil.

The shoes fit perfectly.

'Wow, these are so comfortable!' Claudia walked up and down in front of the counter and bounced a little.

'Yeah, only the best for the guardians of society,' said the clerk. 'Watch out someone doesn't flog them when you're in the change rooms.'

Claudia didn't quite understand what he meant. Everyone had shoes, so why would anyone take something that wasn't theirs?

Coming out of the commissary, she felt pleased to be in possession of a new pair of trainers, clean white lab-leather with a black stripe between the sole and the upper. It was a frivolous feeling, almost individualistic, and Claudia reminded herself that the purpose of the shoes was to enable her participation in training and then the Selection Trials, an important shared activity that contributed to social cohesion. Any pleasure she had from a new pair of shoes was irrelevant.

She thought of Lisa's fifty pairs of shoes, vaporised in the Event, and understood, just a little, how Lisa must have felt each time she acquired—'bought'—a new pair. Each pair must've been different in some way, otherwise there would be no point having fifty of them. Also, Lisa must have chosen them herself, rather than simply having them assigned to her.

Pondering the matter of new and excess shoes, Claudia didn't see Pierce until he was walking alongside her.

'What are you doing here?' he demanded.

She hadn't seen him since the other night in C-Sector. He was wearing greys today and looked more like himself.

'Don't worry, I haven't been arrested,' she said.

'That's not something you should joke about.'

She explained about the shoes, and Pierce relaxed. 'Ash is famous for wearing out people's gear. And people.'

'Am I really in danger of being arrested?' Claudia said this with a lightness she didn't feel.

'Come and have a coffee with me in the MT canteen,' he said. 'We've got some time before the next shift-change.'

'Sure. I've never had coffee at your place before,' she said. Her instinct was to get out of the Barracks as soon as she could, with her beautiful new trainers, but she was also curious.

He took her up some wide stairs and into a spacious lobby. A massive version of the 30th Anniversary poster hung on the rear wall, flanked by two banners wishing young citizens all the best in the upcoming Junior and Senior Selection Trials. The same posters were displayed all over the Dome, part of the visual landscape that Claudia hardly noticed. Here, they could not be ignored. The images and slogans impressed themselves on her vision, somehow surreal and sinister, although there was no reason for her to feel this.

Announcements flashed up on several electronic boards, including codes and abbreviations she did not understand. Everyone else was in black or grey. Claudia had the very strong sense of trespassing.

'Am I even allowed to be in here? I don't even have a black

armband. I'm just a civilian.'

'You're with me,' said Pierce, as if this answered everything.

The panoramic windows of the MT canteen overlooked the stadium. Pierce fetched two coffees from the machine and led her to some seats right by the windows, not near anyone else. At this time of the cycle, a few people were sitting alone or in groups, with coffee cups and snacks, working on screens or talking. The next shift break was lunch and the fug of cooking was beginning to seep out from the kitchens. Claudia wondered if the Mentargh had different food.

She sipped her coffee—it was better than what she got at the Med Block or Youth League canteens—and waited for Pierce to speak.

'That night you saw me on patrol with Byrne, someone had escaped from the Re-Education Centre,' he said. 'You know what that is, don't you?'

Claudia's stomach clenched, but she wasn't going to be cowed. 'Where subversive elements go for recycling. This is a waste-free society, after all. No human being knowingly wasted.'

'Freed, Claudia! Every time you speak now, it's like I'm hearing Davina instead of you. How do I get through to you? Why do you keep going back?'

Claudia involuntarily looked around. 'Is this really the place to have that conversation?'

'It's the safest place in the Dome for this conversation. The worst place is hundreds of metres below.' Even so, Pierce lowered his voice. 'Claudia, you've always played by the rules. What's different now?'

'Nothing's different. You know I've always been curious.' Claudia lowered her voice as well, although nobody was near enough to hear. 'They're just free spirits. I learn things from them I don't hear in Ideo.'

'If you just like chatting to Oldies, you could do community service in a Senior Citizens' Circle, for freed's sake. Claudia, if you want access to real information, off-script stuff, then you should be in the Mentargh, not no-swiping around the Dome with Davina and her crew. Whoever jacked your chips the other night could've wiped you off the system and then you'd be as good as composted. Believe me, your friends downstairs already are.'

A chill passed through Claudia. 'What do you know? Pierce, if Martin and Arnie are in danger, you should tell them.'

'What the freed do you think I've been doing?' He fell back in his seat and ran both hands through his hair. He and Luke had the same deep black hair.

He leaned forwards before speaking again. 'Since Davina came on the scene, they don't trust me. If they keep hanging out with her, in a year, or even six months, they could be doing D-grade labour in the sewage plant with a vocabulary of a hundred words. That's how it goes.'

Claudia stared. 'You never mentioned any of this before.'

'Of course I didn't! I don't want to know half the shit that I know! Martin might get off more lightly, but Arnie, no way, he's coded high risk. You're a valuable resource, so they'd want to rehabilitate you, and you really don't want to go through that, trust me on that at least.'

'Kate said she'd been rehabilitated,' said Claudia. 'She said she used to be a free spirit.'

'What exactly did she say?' said Pierce. He seemed less surprised than he should've been.

'She said it was tough, but that she was better now. She

even said that she used to wear deadclothes, can you believe that?'

'You're not going to hear the full story from Kate,' said Pierce.

'You're saying I shouldn't trust her? But she's my mentor.' Claudia was aware of testing him.

'I know you don't trust her, because if you'd been telling her the truth for the last couple of months, we wouldn't be sitting here now,' said Pierce. 'Claudia, the other night, you and the others are so freeding lucky it was me who found you. One day it could be someone like Byrne, or even Luke.'

As he said the name, his gaze moved past Claudia's shoulder and his face suddenly stiffened. 'I don't freeding believe it.'

'Hello, junior citizens,' said Luke, ignoring Pierce's scowl. 'Claudia, I haven't seen you in the Barracks before. Is my brother showing you around?'

'Ash sent me to get some new trainers.' Claudia's voice went a little high. It was disconcerting to see Luke, although of all the places to come across him in the Dome, the Barracks was the most obvious.

'Kate mentioned you'd had a fall. All good now?'

'Almost. I'll be back training any day. Pierce, thanks for the coffee, but I should go.' Claudia stood up. So did Pierce.

'I'll walk you to the gates,' said Luke. 'Cadet-Trooper, don't you have an Ideo session starting in five?'

'Yes, sir,' said Pierce. He saluted, his face sullen. 'Claudia, I'll see you around soon.'

Watching him walk off, Luke said, 'My brother is such a moody little shit. Sometimes I just want to sit him down on a Party Machine with me and find out what the freed is going on inside that stubborn head.'

Did Luke expect Claudia to tell him?

'I don't have any brothers or sisters,' she said carefully.

'I know,' said Luke. 'Come on. And don't forget your new shoes.'

Flustered, Claudia had almost left the shoes behind.

She picked up the empty coffee cups in her free hand and dropped them in the recycling bank on the way out.

Crossing the quadrangle with Luke, she attracted more attention than she had on the way in.

'Do they think I'm under arrest?' she said, because she was compelled to say something, however stupid.

'Believe me, if you were under arrest, it would be obvious,' he said. 'Anyway, why would you be under arrest?'

'Why else would a civilian be inside the Barracks?' she said, panicking slightly.

'New shoes? A cup of coffee with a friend?'

Claudia felt even stupider. She glanced sideways at Luke, and he returned the glance with a quizzical expression.

'Your attitude to the Mentargh is worryingly negative, especially for a Level V student.' He said this as a simple observation, but Claudia felt another clutch of fear. 'One who could potentially be recruited after the Senior Trials.'

'That's what Pierce keeps saying, but I don't understand.'

They reached the first security gates.

'You should listen to him,' said Luke. 'Pierce's duty is to protect both his friends and the Dome. If it comes down to protecting the Dome or his friends, there's only one choice he can make. That would be very difficult for him, but I know he'd make the right one. Claudia, I don't want my brother put in that situation. Do you understand?'

Her mouth went dry. 'Yes, sir.'

'Good. Now, I'd give you a lift to your next session, but I have somewhere else to be.'

He nodded to the trooper on duty at the gates and left Claudia to swipe out.

Seventeen

The Youth League parade ground was milling with juniors being bawled into formation by their captains. Claudia stood at the sidelines watching Daria go through her paces. The girl was naturally bossy, even though she resisted being bossed around herself. Claudia was confident that she'd do her best now the final day of Junior Selection Trials, the biggest day, had finally arrived, out of individualistic pride if not genuine community spirit.

'All present and accounted for, ma'am.'

Claudia returned Daria's salute and joined her squad. The assembled children were all conspicuously smart and in perfect formation. As she looked them over, they seemed to hold their breath as they stood at attention.

'Don't forget to breathe,' she said. A few kids always passed out during the Junior Trials parade. 'That's an order!'

A hush fell over the vast stadium. The four speakers at each corner crackled into life, and the familiar opening chords of 'The Inheritors' echoed overhead.

Looking across the congregated children, Claudia wondered how many of them had questions or doubts. At that age, nobody wanted to stand out. The parents of her own squad had been born in the Dome themselves, with no memories of Before, and it was rare for people to have grandparents, as Davina had. Living knowledge of the past was dying out, and the Archives, the only records that still existed, were controlled by the Mentargh. If Claudia ever had children, what could she tell them?

The final refrain of the anthem suddenly struck her as ironic, almost cruelly so: what golden future were any of them going to inherit? The greatest achievement of the community living in the Dome was survival; they had already arrived at their only possible future and nothing could ever change.

The whistle blew for stand-at-ease, jolting her out of this pointless and troubling reverie.

Four black-clad figures mounted the dais at the far end of the stadium. One, a tall, athletic woman, stepped up to the microphone and saluted. The massed children returned the salute with equal precision. This was Commodore Nira, the ultimate leader of the Junior Youth League.

'Junior citizens, welcome!' she began, her voice echoing stridently overhead. 'You've worked very hard to get to this day, and we're proud of you. Your gradings and social placements will be announced in the next week. Those of you who have been selected for entry into the Senior League will be ranked as cadet-corporals. Those who are leaving us to start work as manual or production techs will be assigned to the appropriate Citizens' Brigade or workplace community unit.

'We will also bid farewell to our present senior officers. Soon they, too, will undergo Trials for gradings and activity placements and, above all, selection for the Mentargh. Only an elite few will be chosen for this honour. Some among you have already been singled out for service. However, the majority of seniors, who will not be selected, must not forget their responsibility to society. They all have a position to fill in our community and a duty to the other citizens of the Dome. I must stress that individual achievement is unimportant in itself, but the better grades you gain personally, the better it reflects on us all. Remember, survival is a team effort! We must all strive together for the common good. On the sports field, we are not fighting for survival, but your performance and attitude there carries over to your future work, which contributes to the continuing survival of us all. Individual achievement belongs to the collective and has no meaning without it. The selfish wants and whims of individuals have no place in the Dome.'

Claudia winced. Thinking the golden future a bad joke was just a random thought, with no immediate destructive effect, but it indicated a frame of mind that could infect, first, her own actions and, then, potentially those of people around her, especially impressionable children. Amid the rows and columns of juniors, she felt herself culpable. Had she unwittingly passed on negative attitudes to her young charges? What damage had Davina done to hers? Somewhere in the stadium, Davina was standing in formation with her squad, the *hordes of screaming little freeders* she couldn't wait to offload.

Claudia accepted the fact of her own free-spirit, even subversive, tendencies, but she didn't want to mess up anyone else's life.

'Do your best today, junior citizens, and every day after. That's the most we ask of you and each other. I wish you all luck in your future lives. It has been a privilege serving you.'

The Commodore saluted and stepped down from the

microphone. The massed children cheered and pumped their fists, as they had been instructed.

The Sub-Commodore took her place. 'We will now observe a brief silence in memory of all those who died during the Event and in the horror of the Aftermath.'

A whistle blew and everyone bowed their heads. Claudia had observed hours, possibly days, of silence in her life remembering what she only knew second-hand, in fragments and distortions. She thought of Neil's long journey from the coast to the Dome, a secret location. From knowing Neil just a little, Claudia wasn't surprised that he had discovered it. Lisa, Jim and Lily had all known each other Before and had made the journey together, but across what kind of landscape? Claudia could not even visualise it. The only images she had of Outside were Jemima's tatty photographs.

The whistle blew again, and the Sub-Commodore recited the Memorial.

'The series of catastrophes that we remember as the Event began on 26 September 2052. An ordinary day, by all accounts. Except on this particular day, the anarchy that had been building for decades reached its apocalyptic climax, leading to the end of global human civilisation in all its rich variety. Billions died in the first weeks and months; then millions more, from injuries, from radiation, from famine, from disease, in the chaos that followed. Our poisoned planet offered no relief for those who survived.'

Claudia knew the words so well she hadn't listened to them properly for a long time, and she was struck anew by the horror they described, an unimaginable horror that had become banal by repetition.

She found herself looking up, over and past the buildings

that surrounded the stadium, at the Dome itself, and wondering what the sky behind looked like. Even if the planet was dead, the sky still existed, indifferent to the fate of the selfish, stupid humans beneath it who had destroyed themselves.

It must have been a reflection or a trick of the light as constantly adjusted by DOMUS, but Claudia had the briefest impression of a gradation of colour on the other side of the Dome, as if clouds had been pierced by a sudden shaft of sunlight.

'As the only survivors, it is our duty to nourish the small flame of human existence for as long as it burns, until the very end,' finished the Sub-Commodore.

'Until the very end,' murmured the children.

Claudia realised that her eyes were wet and blinked quickly before Daria or any of the other children could see.

The parade began.

With practised efficiency, the squads began to move.

The routine for this year's Junior Trials was unusually complex; it would be performed again for the 30th Anniversary celebrations. Unlike the mixed-age drill, when the younger ones fumbled and had to be prompted, not infrequently causing traffic jams, the final-year juniors executed the manoeuvres smoothly and precisely, without hesitation. Synchronised marching was a discipline every junior citizen was expected to submit to and master; to move in perfect time through intricate formations as a single, coordinated, anonymous mass.

The parade concluded with the recital of the Allegiance, led by Commodore Nira.

'We, the survivors and citizens of the Dome, recognise that we owe our survival and continued existence to the July

Covenant, its institutions and representatives.'

'What do we pledge as our civic duty?'

'We pledge our loyalty and obedience; to fulfil to the best of our abilities whatever responsibilities are assigned us; to diligently study and uphold the principles of Ideology; to strive for the common good and resist individualism; to fight the subversion in all its pernicious and subtle manifestations, and to work ceaselessly for the continued survival of humanity.'

'Lest we forget.'

Heads bowed as the melancholy refrain of 'The Survivors' echoed over the parade ground. The music was engineered to evoke certain feelings; Claudia knew that, but this knowledge didn't block the effect. In those few minutes, the Event and the Aftermath became a personal tragedy rather than a dim historical catastrophe. Billions of people had actually died; human civilisation had been annihilated, a civilisation that she, with her limited experience of the Dome, could hardly begin to comprehend. The natural wonders of the planet Earth had been destroyed, transformed to a poisonous wasteland. The course of history had been drastically altered and once omnipotent humanity reduced to evading extinction.

The usual, concluding feeling was one of gratitude and belonging, centred on a tiny, brave community existing under a thermoplastic dome, a low steady light in the darkness.

As the final notes faded out across the parade ground, Claudia's thoughts lurched shockingly off-plan.

We are pathetic.

Then the triumphant opening chords of 'The Inheritors' thundered overhead, and the assembled children snapped to attention.

Eighteen

Claudia had no genuine interest in the Game, but the final matches of the Junior Trials exhilarated her. Standing on the sidelines with the other senior officers while her squad played, she found herself shouting and screaming along with everyone else with every goal, foul, misstep, defence and tackle. Had she finally submitted to the common mood rather than standing back in her individual shell, as Kate had often described it?

Her conversations with Kate had almost relaxed back into their old pattern. Claudia hadn't been back to the Underground since Neil had led them out via C-Sector, the night someone had escaped from the Re-Education Facility, and she felt she had nothing to hide, although she had bad dreams almost every night. Oddly, Kate hadn't mentioned this, although the sleep disturbance would show up on bodychip monitoring.

When her squad lost their final match to Juanita's team by one goal, Claudia and Juanita hugged each other, and Juanita picked her up and spun her around.

'Good play! Excellent match!' said Juanita.

Claudia was so hyped that losing by one goal still felt like a victory. She went onto the pitch and hugged all her squad individually and then as a group. Daria was crying because she felt she'd failed and Claudia walked her off with an arm around her shoulder, actually feeling fond of the little brat. Had DOMUS put something in the water that day? Mood regulation was technically part of the total environmental control system, so this was not impossible.

After the closing ceremony, Claudia gave a final scripted talk to her squad in their change rooms. They were exhausted but still buzzing. In a few hours, there would be celebrations in the Youth League stadium, with music, games and other activities designed to bring the whole experience and life phase to an emotionally satisfying close. This was the last occasion at which seniors would supervise their squads. About halfway through the event, at a 'release from service' ceremony, junior squad leaders would make a speech and play a (pre-approved) practical joke on their senior officer and then the seniors would all exit the stadium and leave the juniors to party on their own.

Some senior officers remained close to their charges, es-pecially if the children had no other functional adult figures in their lives. Kate had been Claudia's Junior League leader. Strangely, Claudia had no memory of her wearing deadclothes or being any kind of free spirit, much less disappearing for a period of re-education.

Perhaps Claudia would be instructed to mentor Daria, who had a strong and potentially wayward personality.

In the few hours before the celebrations began, juniors were sent home for down-time. Some parents had come to watch from the stands and were waiting by the exit to meet their children. Seeing families gave Claudia an odd feeling. She saw Daria run up to a man in standard citizen blues, wearing the insignia of an Infrastructure (Buildings) worker. He gave her a big hug, lifting her off the ground.

'Stop it, Dad, I'm too old for that now!' she protested, wriggling.

The only person who gave Claudia big, powerful hugs was Juanita, who had no family at all and had lived in a Senior League res block until her recent move into the Barracks.

'See you in the C-Sector node for a quiet one before the big party?' said Martin, coming up beside her.

Junior League parties were strictly synthanol-free, so supervising seniors often had a pre-drink to make their duty bearable. This was all part of the recognised tradition, and as long as seniors weren't obviously intoxicated, no sanctions were applied, although certain zealous juniors had been known to report such infractions. Such 'mini-Mentargh' were not generally popular with their peers. Knowing what, when and if to report at all was part of a citizen's unofficial socialisation.

'Yeah, sure,' said Claudia. 'You're not going to D-Sector?'

'I figured I should stay closer to home on this occasion. People are beginning to miss me, and D-Sector has been a bit hot lately.'

'Are Davina and Arnie coming?'

'I don't know. Maybe later.'

'Martin, is something going on? You know what I mean.'

Martin glanced around them at the steady stream of people leaving the stadium.

'They won't tell me. You know, it's not just a history chat club down there, Claudia. There are other meetings, other people. Arnie already knew some of them. He's in deep. He says it's for my own good that I don't know too much. I'm worried, but I don't know what to do. I even thought of asking Pierce—'

'No, don't!' said Claudia. 'Pierce knows too much already, and if he knows anything more, he has to report it. When I was in the Barracks to get my new trainers, I ran into Pierce, and then Luke turned up and gave me a little talking-to, which was no fun at all.'

'Hyper-freed, Luke! What does he know? But if the Mentargh know something, why haven't they done anything?'

'That's not exactly a question I could ask Luke,' said Claudia.

Martin swore again.

'Guys! Why so serious?' From behind, Ally put an arm around each of them. 'Claudia, you should be freeding ecstatic! Your team almost beat Juanita's! You're coming to the C-Sector node, right?'

'Yeah, totally,' said Claudia. 'I'm just going home for a bit first. I'll see you there later.'

She left Martin to deal with Ally's high spirits.

* * *

The unit was dark when Claudia got in. For a blissful moment she thought Faye was out, but when she turned on the light, she saw her mother slumped over the table. Around her were several cannies, the dented kind that usually signalled roughbrew. The smell was dense and sour.

'Freed's sake.' Claudia adjusted the ventilation setting to high. 'Are you trying to gas me?'

Moving carefully and quietly around Faye, she showered

and changed into fresh clothes. Occasionally Faye muttered and wheezed in her stupor, and even seemed to stop breathing for moments at a time. Each time, Claudia waited, half-hoping that she would quietly die, but also wanting Faye to start breathing again so that she wouldn't have to make a choice. Claudia knew all the medical and civic protocols; there was a first responder kit at the end of the communal hall, and she was more than capable of sustaining CPR until a med team arrived. She also knew that, given Faye's level of addiction and advanced physical degeneration, limited resources would be spent reviving her. If Claudia did not intervene at all and allowed her mother a 'compassionate release', this would be considered a sound and even admirable judgement call. The people who had set these standards had come through the Aftermath; survival had required brute pragmatism, not sentiment.

Claudia was not quite ready to make that choice.

She heated up Citizen Meal No. 14, a mildly spiced slurry on a bed of protein-boosted grain, and ate standing at the kitchen counter, scrolling through public announcements and messages on her screen, trying to ignore the snoring and occasional hacking from the living area.

'I don't know why they keep sending you home, you freeding wreck,' she muttered, thinking Faye couldn't hear, and then the noise abruptly ceased.

'Claudia? You say something to me?'

'Oh freed, not now.' Claudia crushed the food tray into the recycling bin, which was almost overflowing, as always. 'Go back to sleep! I'm on my way out.'

Cannies crashed to the floor, and there was the sound of shuffling. Leaning heavily against the wall, Faye looked around into the kitchen. Her eyes were yellow and bloodshot.

'Where the fuck are you going? You're always out.'

'I have a life. I'm not your personal care attendant.'

'A life! You have a life!' Faye's laugh curdled into more hacking and choking. Respiratory distress was a common comorbidity of advanced roughbrew addiction, Claudia had learned, and Faye was a textbook example.

'Well I'm really happy for you. I never had a fucking life.'

'You've had the same life as everyone else!' flared Claudia. 'People survived the Aftermath and came out of it as functioning human beings.' She thought of Lisa and her biscuits, Neil and his t-shirts. 'You grew up in the Dome. You had food, shelter, medical care, order and security. What is your freeding problem?'

'Oh, I'm the problem, obviously,' said Faye. 'I'm the square peg in the round hole, the nail that sticks out and needs to be hammered down. I disrupt the smooth and efficient functioning of our ideal society.'

At a certain phase of inebriation, Faye became morosely eloquent. Claudia watched as her mother went through the recycling bin, scattering rubbish over the floor, and pulled out another canister.

'You don't have to bother hiding it.' When she was younger, Claudia had gone through a phase of emptying her mother's stash of roughbrew down the drain. The comeback had been ferocious, and it was easier to just let her mother drink herself into a coma.

Faye popped the top of the canister and took a swig.

'Roz came by today,' she said. As well as being Faye's friend, Roz was the leader of her work unit. In Claudia's view, Roz was far too soft on Faye. 'Told me they were organising something at the Plant for the 30th Anniversary. Citizens' Brigade Committees and all that nonsense. I told her to piss off.'

She laughed raspingly.

'And what did Roz say to that?'

'Told me I needed to get my act together. Gave me the tough talk. Rehab won't have me back. I'm a drain and a burden, and I don't contribute my fair share to the efficient functioning of society.'

Roz had always managed to get Faye into Rehab before. Claudia was aware of protocols for non-contributing citizens, such as the very old and the chronically ill. When disability could be seen as self-inflicted, the rules were different, harsher.

'So naturally you went on a massive brew bender,' she said, although she knew it was better not to engage with Faye when she was in this frame of mind.

'I'm celebrating the glorious 30th in advance,' said Faye. 'In my own way. I should've died like an abandoned baby rat in the Aftermath, but two kind people brought me in from the chaos. It would've been kinder to leave me out there.'

'Here we go, the pity party,' said Claudia. She had heard it all before.

'Don't patronise me! Claudia, you're very intelligent. I know you think outside the box. All those questions when you were a little kid! I did my best to answer, the way Arturo and Celia had answered my questions, until your Basic Ed leader came for a special chat and said it would be better for your development and happiness and overall efficient functioning if I shut the fuck up and stopped interfering with your social programming. Who was I, anyway? Just your mother. It's better not to know about what you can't have. Ignorance is bliss.'

Faye was blocking the way out of the kitchen, and Claudia was forced to listen.

'I'm glad Arturo and Celia didn't live long enough to see how things turned out,' Faye went on. 'They'd already gone through hell, moving countries for a better life. We're constantly told we're living in a glorious new epoch, a golden future, but look at us! A tiny pack of refugees under a plastic dome, a totally artificial environment, living in a superbly efficient, correctly functioning, highly unnatural and paranoid society. Oh, yes, we've survived—but at what a price! We're trapped in here, hooked on our security and rations of fungus and algae slop and predetermined, totally predictable lives. Glorious future? It's the dim fucking twilight of human existence!'

Remembering her own thoughts that same morning, during the opening ceremony, Claudia recoiled. Had she inherited her taint of subversion from Faye? Would her doubts fester inside her until she took to roughbrew as well and became a bitter wreck of a human being?

'I have to go,' she said abruptly, and pushed past Faye. Even this brief physical proximity disgusted her.

'Claudia, don't go.' Faye reached out and caught one of her arms. Her bony hand felt like the grabber claw of a machine. 'Stay in with me just this once. Let's talk. I know there's something going on with you. Talk to me. There's so much I want to tell you, and I don't have much time left.'

Claudia shook off her mother's hand. 'Don't touch me!'
'Claudia, please!'

Faye reached out again. Claudia pushed back, and her

mother stumbled and fell against the kitchen bench. She swore and dropped the cannie, and it crashed on the floor and rolled until it hit the wall, leaking roughbrew everywhere.

'Go, then, you little bitch! Fuck off and leave me alone!'

She squatted, with difficulty, and picked up the canister, shaking it to check how much was left inside. It was as if Claudia had already gone.

Nineteen

Claudia and Martin arrived together outside the Youth League hall. Crowds of seniors were gathering in knots and groups, ready for the beat party that was always held for them after the Junior Trials.

There was a buzz in the air and lots of squealing and ecstatic hugging as friends met up.

'Freed, are people on drugs already?' said Martin. 'The jennies for this are meant to be pretty special, no need to come pre-amped.'

'Look, there's Arnie and Ally.' Claudia waved at them over all the heads, and Ally waved back with both hands, bouncing up and down.

Pierce and Juanita joined them soon after. Both were wearing their grey uniforms.

'Is Davina coming as well?' Claudia asked Arnie.

'She's kicking off with her own cohort,' he said, glancing at Juanita. 'But we'll see her around.'

'I think it's great we're all together, just us,' said Ally. She threw her arms around each of them in turn, giving Pierce an especially lingering hug.

'Hey, party girl! Don't wear out your vibe before the show starts,' said Arnie, reeling slightly from the force of Ally's affection.

Several Mentargh appeared at the doors and the crowd surged forwards. Claudia recognised Elliot, Luke's second.

'Luke doesn't come to these, does he?' she asked Pierce. They hadn't spoken since her visit to the Barracks, although they'd been at the C-Sector node pre-drinks before the junior party the other week.

'Not unless there's a problem,' he replied. 'This kind of party control is more Elliot's thing. And he might find himself a fresh girlfriend.'

Claudia recoiled at the thought. The behaviour of certain Mentargh officers was no secret. At big beat parties, there were good reasons to stick with your cohort.

Inside the hall, they could hear the opening music slowly stirring up. As the six moved towards the doors to be swiped in and receive their party pill, Claudia remembered Neil's comment about designing parties and his contempt for jennies. *Evil shit.* Just inside the doors, Tia was one of the officers handing out the pills with cannies of water. She winked at Claudia. It did not seem possible to Claudia that Tia would give her something bad. Drugs in the Dome were made to very high laboratory standards, with pure ingredients, not like Before, when social drugs were illegal and contained all sorts of toxic substances.

Claudia took a pill from Tia and swallowed. She and Ally and Juanita held hands and skipped into the hall together.

As the hall filled up, the lights went down and the tempo of the music picked up. Instead of standing and talking with their friends, people began to dance. The jennies given out at parties were designed, along with the music, to provide a certain kind of experience, like the Party Machine but bigger, more expansive. Claudia felt the swell and then the rush as the drug took effect, lifting her out of the everyday. Time stopped. She was utterly at peace, almost floating and bodiless, a flame of pure feeling. Next to her, Ally and Juanita smiled back at her, feeling it with her. The boys joined them, and they danced as one, their bodies woven by the music and the drugs into a blissful, throbbing whole. All around them, people were feeling the rush. The shared energy filled the hall. Nothing mattered but this.

As the music intensified, Claudia had the sensation of flying. For a moment, she felt herself back on the bike with Luke, hurtling across the Ring, but the thought pulled her away from the moment and she repressed it.

'What's up?' Pierce said in her ear. 'I could feel you were thinking something.'

'Nothing,' said Claudia. 'It was nothing.'

She put her arms around his neck and continued to dance. Nearby, Davina and Martin, not breaking their rhythm, were grinning at them. Martin gave her a quick thumbs-up behind Pierce's back.

Juanita went off with a friend from her team. Ally disappeared.

Claudia didn't know who moved first. Their faces seemed to come together naturally; with the special clarity of the pills, there was no doubt or hesitation. When Pierce's mouth met hers, she felt another powerful rush. Nothing could ever feel as good as this: being held by Pierce and kissed in this particular, infinitely expanding moment.

After what could've been hours, the music seem to lighten and relent, and they realised they were both desperately thirsty. They headed for one of the tables at the edge of the hall, where cannies of water and snacks were set out.

'All good, kids?' said Elliot, who was standing nearby. 'Need a top-up?'

Claudia shook her head, a little too violently. In her super-sensitised state, Elliot's presence was revolting.

'We're fine,' said Pierce, holding Claudia close.

'Yeah, I can see you're doing extremely well,' said Elliot, with his usual leer. 'I'll leave you to it, Cadet-Trooper. About time.'

Claudia pressed her face into Pierce's shoulder, because now she could. 'He's so gross.'

'Shh, Clau! I know, but you're so obvious!'

'I can't help it.' Shivers ran up and down her entire body.

They moved back onto the floor and joined Arnie, Martin and Davina. Other people from their teams and training cohorts merged with them for a while, then broke away again and dissolved into the heaving crowd, like a series of oil bubbles. Juanita was briefly visible with her friend, a short but very athletic girl. In her peripheral vision, Claudia glimpsed Ally with Elliot at the side of the hall. She assumed Ally was accepting a top-up and blocked any further thoughts.

As the atmosphere thickened and deepened, the music changed as well. More people were accepting top-ups. The energy took on a different, harder quality, as the dancers pushed through their physical exhaustion. Other people were beginning to wind down. Some were sitting on the floor, wiped out. Around them, other couples were variously pressed together, standing in the middle of the dance floor or even half-lying on the stairs, beneath the huge banner celebrating the Junior and Senior Trials. The lights were very low.

Claudia and Pierce found a secluded spot behind the stairs and continued kissing. Claudia had her back to the wall. They were both very sweaty. She slipped her hands beneath his t-shirt and ran them over the hot, damp skin of his back and then his chest and shoulders. Pierce had a beautiful torso; she didn't need a freeding presumptuous eleven-year-old to tell her that.

As she pressed herself against him, she could feel his erection. He moaned and pulled her closer.

'Is Faye at home?' he asked, his hands under her t-shirt, arriving at her waist and then pushing up to her breasts.

'She's at Roz's.'

'Let's go to your place.'

Claudia wanted more than anything at that moment to be somewhere private and alone with Pierce.

'I haven't had my implant yet.'

He pulled back sharply. 'Freed, Claudia. You need to get one! It'll go on your record if you don't.'

'I know, I know, I just haven't got around to it.' She kissed him, drawing him closer again.

'Mentargh babies are pre-approved.' He was joking, of course. Pregnancy was curable, but the stigma of getting pregnant without permission or even having sex without contraception was not.

'Do they wear little black baby suits?'

He kissed her with renewed force. Undoing the top of his trousers, he took one of her hands and closed it around his penis. She could feel his warm, silky flesh and the surrounding wiry hair. He guided her hand up and down, faster and harder, and eventually he let go and gave himself up to the sensation. Then he groaned, and her hand was suddenly wet and sticky.

He leaned back against the wall, his eyes closed. Awkwardly, Claudia pulled her hand free and wiped it on her trousers, which needed refreshing anyway.

She felt strangely clear-headed, sad and flat, as if all the jenny and the party vibe had suddenly drained out of her system.

'I'm going to head off now.'

Pierce seemed to come to himself again. 'Claudia! Wait!'

She pushed her way across the dance floor to the doors, past Tia's questioning face, and ran towards the Transit station. A shuttle was just coming in. She turned around, briefly, before swiping herself through the gate, but he hadn't followed her.

* * *

The next day, Claudia made an appointment to have her implant. She felt she'd been punished enough for the delay, and she didn't know if she could trust herself next time. If she hadn't ruined everything and there even was a next time.

Twenty

A few days later, the hall of the Senior Youth League stadium had reverted to its usual utilitarian appearance, drained of its twilight party magic.

'What the freed happened with you and Pierce?'

Martin and Claudia had crossed paths heading in for a late afternoon training session.

'What do you mean?' She wasn't ready to talk about what had happened with anyone. The pain and disappointment were simply unsayable.

'Oh come on, Clau, don't pretend. We all thought you'd finally got it on, at last, and then he suddenly turned up alone and said you'd gone home. Huh? What the freed?' Martin spread his hands. 'Pierce was not a happy trooper. When we rescued Ally from Elliot—we peeled her away—we almost had to rescue Elliot from Pierce. I've never seen him like that. He was about to go for Elliot. Not that Ally seemed to want rescuing, but suddenly she was all over Pierce like he was saving her from a fate worse than D-grade sewage duty. Freeding hell, Elliot would've mashed him into Citizen Meal No. 1. He's built like a nuclear reactor. And then Luke turned up out of nowhere, in that weird way he has, told Elliot to pull his head in, and dragged Pierce off by the scruff of his neck, more or less. That's when we bailed. Until then, it was a proper ten-megaton blast.'

'Yeah, it was,' said Claudia. 'And Juanita got lucky.'

Martin broke into a broad grin. 'Yeah, J's a happy trooper. You know, I reckon she often feels a bit lonely around us because we're not on the same wavelength anymore and she's always the odd one out. Now she's got someone of her own. I'm really glad for her.'

He didn't ask any more about Pierce, and they went into their respective change rooms.

* * *

With the Junior Trials out of the way, the seniors could concentrate on preparing for their own Trials, with extra training on top of their final Ideo exams and their annual Occupational Ed assessment. Claudia was glad to be away from her res unit most of the time. She ate in the Youth League mess or the Med Block canteen with the others or alone, and came home late, going straight to her bunk and falling into a deep but troubled sleep. She hardly saw Faye at all. Roz left messages, either to say that Faye was with her or to ask if she knew where Faye was. Claudia didn't always bother replying.

She didn't have time to even think about going into the Underground. Martin didn't mention it, and Claudia didn't ask.

It was a shock, then, to come face to face with Luma. A practice game had been scheduled with a team who trained in a different slot, and unfamiliar faces appeared in the change rooms. When Claudia saw Luma getting changed next to her, she had to quickly shut down her face. It wasn't as if Luma and the other free spirits existed only in the Underground; they all had regular lives and citizen identities above ground.

Luma flashed her a quick, cool look of recognition. 'What position do you play, Level V?'

Claudia told her.

'So do I. So we'll be chasing each other for the ball.' Luma did not say this in a friendly way.

She bent to fasten her shoes and let out an expletive that only Oldies used.

'Fancy trainers, citizen! Advanced promotion?' She looked up at Claudia with undisguised loathing. 'Or have you been one of them all along?'

She said this under her breath, although nobody else was nearby.

'My coach got them for me.' Claudia's MT-issue trainers had attracted a few admiring comments from teammates in their first few outings, and even one icky suggestion about what she'd done for Ash in return, but nobody hated her for them. 'Otherwise I'd be competing in bare feet, thanks to that sabotage incident at the depot.'

She'd believed Neil and Lisa when they said subversives had nothing to do with that, but Luma was right in her face and the words just came out.

'You're spying on us, aren't you? I tore strips off Davina for bringing you all down. You and your MT boyfriend. Yeah, I've seen him around, in his grey uniform.' Luma lunged at her, pushing Claudia up against the lockers. 'You bitch! I'm going to shut you up for good.'

'Get off me, you stupid cow!' Claudia knew cows had been

used in dairy production and that 'cow' was an insult for women, used by Oldies, but her mental image of a cow was very vague.

She pushed back, but Luma put her hands around Claudia's throat and pressed with her whole body weight. She was too close for Claudia to kick or knee her.

Was this the end? Strangled by Luma in the change rooms? Claudia thought fleetingly that she'd never get another chance to kiss Pierce.

Luma was suddenly jerked away by a much greater force.

'What the freed, citizen?' Juanita's face appeared behind Luma's red angry one. She slammed Luma against the lockers and held her there with one arm. 'What's going on, Claudia? Who is this crazy bitch?'

'Rescued by your MT mate,' Luma said, gasping. 'That figures.'

Juanita had just arrived and was still in her greys.

'Citizen Luma took exception to my trainers,' said Claudia, rubbing her throat.

'I'll have to report this,' said Juanita. 'I know feelings can get high before a match, and we've all been under a lot of pressure, but this is straight-out assault. Clau, are you OK?'

Claudia nodded. 'I think Junior Citizen Luma has been taking too many stims.'

It was true: Luma's eyes had the red, staring quality of someone who had been over-using performance-enhancing drugs.

'Has your coach got you all cranked up?' Juanita demanded. 'If you're all on stims, this match is totally skewed.'

'This is a purely independent initiative,' said Luma. Her expression was defiant, even pinned against the lockers and grabbing helplessly at Juanita's arm. 'My coach is a total rulesbody citizen. If it wasn't for me, we'd never win a freeding thing.'

'Where did you get them from?' said Juanita.

'Listen, don't bother reporting it,' Claudia said to Juanita. 'Citizen Luma's not going to give me any more trouble. Who knows, all those stims might give her a heart attack on the pitch.'

Juanita withdrew her arm and Luma slid down onto the bench with a thump.

'On this occasion, I'll let it go, but you're on notice,' she said. 'One more freeding thing, any little thing, and you're mine.'

While grateful for the intervention, Claudia was a little chilled by Juanita's new authority and her use of this Mentargh phrase. *You're mine.* A record of reports and arrests all added to a trooper's rank and reputation. Ambitious junior officers were always on the lookout for signs of individualism, minor non-conformity or petty rule-breaking. Dedicated monitoring could often reveal an actionable pattern. While overenthusiastic surveillance was discouraged as a waste of resources, the rumour was that the arrest and processing of innocent people was occasionally allowed for practice and to boost troop morale.

If Luma's brain wasn't completely warped by stims, she'd know to keep well out of Juanita's way from now on.

Twenty-one

The Director of Medical Education summoned Claudia out of class to break the news. It was an Ideo session, one of the last before the final exam. She followed the Director down the hall, wondering what could be so important.

Waiting in her office for Claudia were Roz and several people Claudia recognised as Faye's colleagues. There was also the director of the Hydroponics Plant, a medical officer, the district administrator and the Citizens' Brigade captain for B-Sector, Res Block E. Claudia stared at them blankly, confused by their concerned, apologetic faces.

'Still no answer from Kate?' the Director asked her assistant, who shook his head.

'Claudia, I'm so sorry,' said Roz.

From the faint grimaces that flashed across the other adults, Claudia understood that Roz had spoken out of turn and disrupted the script.

'Your mother,' began the Hydro director, and then looked at the district administrator and the medical officer.

'She's dead, Claudia,' said Roz. 'She died this afternoon.' Her voice cracked. 'I tried so hard to help her.'

'You went way above and beyond, citizen,' said the Hydro director.

Roz went over to Claudia and grabbed her in an almost stifling embrace.

Claudia's arms hung limply at her sides. 'What happened?'

'There was quite a bit of damage,' said the Hydro director. 'When she fell.'

'She was a very sick woman,' said the district administrator quickly. 'We can't blame her for that.'

'Of course not,' said the medical officer. 'Although we did everything we could to help. Every resource at our disposal.'

Claudia thought of all the times she had called her mother *a waste of resources*. By the standards of the Dome, she was. Had been.

'A terrible loss to the community,' said the Hydro director. 'We do all we can as a society, but addiction is an individual tragedy.'

'She was a special woman. We had some wonderful conversations, before the roughbrew got her.' This was another of Faye's colleagues. 'She had a unique way of looking at things.'

'She was so proud of you,' said a third colleague, sniffing and wiping her eyes. 'You were all she had after your father died. You're very much like her, you know. It's a pity things didn't go so well between you both in the last few years.'

They were talking about another person, one Claudia had never met.

'How did she fall?' Having no access to her emotions, Claudia resorted to seeking information.

'She jumped,' said Roz. 'Right from the top. She went through the glass. We were sitting on the terrace and I went to get us some coffee. I heard the crash.'

Her embrace tightened and Claudia felt several sobs jolting

through her.

'It was lunch break,' said the Hydro director. 'Lots of people saw. Very distressing. We've had to send people home.'

What did they want her to say? *I'm sorry my mother disrupted the workday and damaged colleague morale by killing herself.*

'You can go home, of course. I'm still trying to get hold of Kate,' said the Ed Director.

'You can come home with me,' said Roz.

'Can I go back to class?' said Claudia.

Nobody said anything. Roz let her go, and Claudia immediately stepped back.

'Are you sure?' said the Ed Director.

'I've got exams next week,' said Claudia.

They all looked at each other as if they couldn't decide who was responsible for her, and nobody wanted to be.

'I'd advise against seeing the body,' said the medical officer, to the others more than to Claudia, and they all quickly nodded.

'All the arrangements will be made,' said the district administrator. 'You don't need to do anything.'

'Thank you,' said Claudia.

'Is there anyone else we can call for you?' said the Ed Director. 'Anyone from your cohort? One of your friends?'

'No, they're all really busy preparing for the Trials,' said Claudia.

'Claudia, you really shouldn't be alone,' said Roz.

'I'll be fine,' she said. 'Can I go now?'

'Of course,' said the Ed Director.

Claudia had the impression she had made them all very uncomfortable and that they were relieved to see her go.

Behind, she heard one of the Hydro workers whispering,

a little too loudly, to Roz, 'They're all like that. Cold as ice. They don't have feelings. I can't understand them.'

'Everything alright?' her instructor asked when she returned to class.

Claudia nodded and went back to her seat.

Going home on the Transit that evening after training, she passed the Hydroponics Plant. Workers suspended on ropes from higher levels and wearing headlamps were already repairing the glass panes. Productivity would not be impeded by the selfish actions of one individual.

The area below was taped off. Looking down, Claudia glimpsed shattered glass all over the ground.

Had Faye deliberately chosen to kill herself in such a public and destructive way, rather than quietly poisoning herself with roughbrew, as an act of sabotage? Did this make her mother a subversive?

There's so much I want to tell you.

Sunk in her addiction, she never had, and Claudia would never know.

A day later, the repairs were finished, with no trace of what had happened. There was a short announcement over the news channel that a Citizen-Survivor had given in to individual despair and roughbrew poisoning. The loss of an individual, even a non-productive one, was regrettable, as was the destruction to community property. The Mentargh would be pursuing roughbrew production and distribution with renewed vigour.

Twenty-two

Her life continued: training, studying, Youth League meetings, all the usual activities, intensifying as the Selection Trials approached, and with a new absence where once there had been a constant background stress. When Claudia returned to the unit, usually late, it was exactly as she'd left it, with ready meals in the foodstore, no mess of cannies or overflow from the recycling bin. The moment she swiped herself in, she still braced a little, from habit, and then remembered: it was alright now, she was on her own at last.

The pervasive roughbrew stench had finally been purged from the unit. She'd rammed Faye's stained, reeking bedding into E-Block's textile recycling bin and collected a fresh set from the depot. She'd also requested a new mattress.

Faye's death freed her of the awful, dragging misery that had been the backdrop of her entire life: a sudden, liberating absence. And there was plenty to fill the hole: more training, more study. She was fine. Life was so much better now. She'd always wanted to be free of Faye, and now she was.

'Are you OK, Claudia?' said Martin, as they left the stadium one evening. Her friends had been strangely careful around her, as if she were both fragile and combustible.

'I'm fine.' She meant it. She felt numb and invincible.

It wasn't a bad feeling. 'I guess I won't need to apply for independent housing now.'

She grinned and shrugged, and Martin grinned back, although his grin seemed tight and forced.

'You seem weird,' said Davina, when they had lunch together in the YL canteen. 'Have they put you on something, just to get you through Selection Trials? That would be freeding typical.'

'My mentor wants to send me to drug-assisted grief counselling, but I won't go. I don't need it,' said Claudia.

'Oh, freed, that,' said Davina. 'I don't blame you. The Citizens' Brigade captain tried to get my granddad to go when my gran died, and he told them to get stuffed. He said he was entitled to feel what he was feeling, in his own time, and if it interfered with productivity for a bit, then too freeding bad.'

'I'm not grieving,' said Claudia. 'I'm getting on with my life. I'm working really hard. They should be pleased with me. I know they're pleased that she's finally gone, although they'd never say it. The only one who cares is Roz. She's the one who needs the guided grief party. She keeps sending me messages and wanting to talk. I wish she'd just leave me alone.'

Claudia had despised Faye for being completely prey to her own eviscerating misery, and she wasn't about to go that way herself, although people suddenly seemed to expect it.

Pierce came up to her after a YL meeting.

They hadn't spoken since the night of the Junior Trials party. Alone in her bunk, she'd often imagined Pierce lying there with her. She remembered the imprint of his body on hers and the smell of his sweat. If they'd gone back to her unit, she wouldn't have been able to stop herself, whatever the consequences.

Seeing Pierce now, fully dressed and in everyday surroundings, what had happened between them no longer seemed real.

'I'm really sorry about your mother,' he said.

There wasn't much to say. 'Thanks. She'd been on a downward slide for ages, so I was expecting something bad to happen. And now it's happened, and it's all over, at last, and I can get on with my life.'

Pierce winced. 'I know things were pretty tough, living with her, but still.'

'The Hydro director was annoyed about the damage,' Claudia went on, the words just clattering out. 'He was trying not to show it, but I could tell. Maybe she did it on purpose, to sabotage his production figures. He was always giving her a hard time. He would've relegated her ages ago if it wasn't for Roz.'

As a Citizen-Survivor Rep, Roz had a certain amount of influence, and punishing Survivors was not straightforward.

'Yeah, she certainly chose a spectacular way to go,' said Pierce.

They were standing outside the Youth League hall, and people were heading in from the Transit station for the next training session. Claudia had to be at the Med Block for a review lesson.

'Listen. I'm really sorry about the other night. At the party.' Pierce couldn't quite look at her. 'I was a dick. That's not how I wanted it to be.'

'It's OK,' she said quickly. 'Really. It was my fault. I've got my implant now, like a good citizen. I should've had it ages ago.'

She said this casually, so he wouldn't think she was begging for another chance. The process itself had been uncomfortable but swift. The technician had noted that she'd just made the deadline. 'Another month and you would've been up for a warning.'

Maybe she had scared Pierce off with her blank face and empty voice; whatever she might have hoped for in making this announcement did not happen. The memory of that night became a torment, and she needed to forget.

In the change rooms, Ally, having exhausted all expressions of sympathy, asked, 'So, what's happening with you and Pierce?'

'Nothing. What does it look like?' Claudia snapped. 'What about you and Elliot? I heard the others had to pull him off you. He's awful. What were you thinking?'

'Everyone else was having fun, even Juanita. I didn't need rescuing,' she said. And then, with a mean little emphasis: 'I got my implant ages ago.'

What the freed did Ally know? Had she seen Claudia and Pierce up against the wall? The thought that Ally had watched them made Claudia feel violated.

'Well, aren't you a good little citizen. You can do the entire Mentargh.'

She slammed her locker shut and walked off.

* * *

Every night she dreamed about the man on the overpass, the one she'd seen on her way back from Martin's party. She'd forgotten about him, and now he invaded her dreams. She now knew why he had been standing there by himself, looking down. If the Transit had passed a few moments later, she would've seen him jump. Suicides weren't always announced. At that time of the cycle, few people would've seen and the aftermath could've been cleaned up quickly. A dutiful citizen with no known physical or mental debilities had simply decided to take the short road home; no need for a public service announcement. It may have been premeditated; it may have been a sudden, overwhelming moment of recognition, of exhaustion, of not wanting to live out whatever time was left. The official suicide rate in the Dome did not match the actual figures, which were classified. Claudia only knew this because she'd overheard the Human Recycling Services manager at the Composting Facility comment to her medical trainer, on that study visit, that they had a backlog in the storage units from all the elective deaths and that the non-supervised numbers were much higher than she was allowed to say.

'What a surprise,' the trainer had replied, in a sardonic tone that indicated the opposite, and then they'd both seen Claudia listening and gone quiet.

* * *

There were a few low-key parties leading up to the Senior Selection Trials, but Claudia didn't feel like partying. She soaked up what little excess time she had training in the gym with Juanita and her new friend Mickey. Although Juanita now had access to the MT facilities, she still used the Youth League gym so she could train with Mickey. Mickey was short but very strong, and she and Juanita spotted for each other. Apart from quiet words of encouragement, the two didn't speak much, either to each other or to Claudia, but on the periphery of their togetherness, she felt included.

* * *

Alone in the unit, she took the fresh pillow from the empty bunk that used to be Faye's and held it when she went to sleep. She allowed herself, briefly, to imagine lying next to Pierce, but the lost opportunity was too painful.

When Claudia was very small, after her father died, Faye used to get into bed with her, holding her tightly from behind. Claudia would try to wriggle free but Faye held her firmly, her face pressed into Claudia's hair. The smell of synthanol and, later, roughbrew was stifling. Her mother's loneliness and despair were like radiation; Claudia had felt herself saturated and defenceless.

She could no longer remember at what age she'd begun to snib the door shut, but she would always remember the rattle of the door and her mother pleading, or swearing, if she was drunk. A few times, Claudia was afraid her mother would break in, but eventually the rattling and muttering would stop and she'd be left in peace to sleep alone.

There was no longer any need to lock the door, but Claudia found it hard to break the habit.

Twenty-three

In the first week of the Senior Selection Trials, Claudia's team played against Luma's. Everyone was in peak condition and the game was hard and fast. Claudia was constantly aware of Luma's presence on the pitch, glaring and hostile. In the final few minutes, Luma moved towards the ball; rather than going for the ball herself, Claudia ran straight at Luma and smashed her to the ground.

There were shouts from the stands and the sidelines, but they seemed very distant. Stunned, Claudia lay on the ground, a wetness running down one cheek, around her ear and into her hair. Somewhere nearby, Luma was moaning and swearing. Claudia stared up at the non-sky, not caring if she never got up again. She felt strangely calm and oblivious to any pain. Above her, she could see the pale, cold shape of the sun at zenith. Outside, it was noon.

The sun was blocked by the duty medic leaning over her, checking her pupils and quickly scanning her body. He nodded and got up, and then Ash appeared overhead, his face vast and furious.

'What the freed is wrong with you? Tackling is not your play!'

He hauled her up and half-carried her off the pitch, and the game continued.

In the medbay, an assistant swabbed at her head.

'What the freed was that about?' he asked.

'Ask her,' said Claudia, nodding in Luma's direction.

Luma was on the next bed, having her arm bandaged. She shot Claudia a vicious look and said nothing.

Outside, the crowd roared as the next game began.

She was shaken awake by Ash. Luma had gone.

'Did we win?' she asked groggily. One side of her body throbbed, along with her head.

'Yes, but no thanks to you,' he said gruffly. Claudia could tell he was pleased; if they'd lost, he would've screamed at her. 'You're one lucky citizen. I've spoken to Commodore Nira and we won't be taking this incident further. We've been told that Luma assaulted you in the change rooms, which you should've reported at the time. Luma's a strong player but she has an attitude problem.'

'Did Juanita say something?'

'How we know is not your business.' Ash sighed deeply, crossed his arms and looked down at his feet. 'You know I don't believe in going easy on people, but it's been a tough time for you, with your mother. If you'd been to grief counselling, you'd be handling this a lot better. This is what happens when you go into lockdown. You can't take it out on people like Luma, even if she deserves it. If I was her coach, none of this nonsense would've got off the ground.'

When she was allowed out of medbay, the day's matches had finished and the stadium was empty. The med tech had given her some painkillers for the next few days, but she wouldn't be back on the pitch for a while.

All those months of intensive training, and then getting

over the sprain, and now she was out of the Trials, and it was all her own fault.

When the Transit slid into the B-Sector res station, she did not get off. She was not aware of any desire to go elsewhere, only that she didn't want to return to the empty unit.

None of the adults in the carriage paid any attention to Claudia. She was just a junior citizen in dirty athswear with a dressing on her forehead, a casualty of the Selection Trials. For Survivors, people her age were like another species, one they didn't understand or trust.

She stayed on the Transit until it almost did a full loop. Eventually she got off at the C-Sector res station, thinking she'd see if Martin was home. Of all her friends, he was the one she felt she could speak to just then. But there was no answer. Maybe he'd gone to the D-Sector node with Arnie and Davina. She knew they often went without inviting her. Since Faye's death, she hadn't been much fun, and she wasn't much of a drinker.

Would they ask her back to the Underground with them? She'd just trashed her good citizen credentials in spectacular fashion. Would Arnie applaud her for behaving like a noxious antisocial element? Luma wouldn't want her down there, that was for sure.

Claudia didn't know where to go next, and so she kept walking along the corridor until she came to G4-5-41.

'You're the girl from the party, aren't you?' said Jemima when she opened the door. She was wearing the same scruffy pink slip-on footwear. 'One of Martin's friends. Come in, come in. It's not often I get visitors. Actually, I was wondering when I might see you again. We had such an interesting chat last time.'

The party had been ages ago. For an Oldie, Jemima's memory was pretty good, Claudia thought.

She followed Jemima into the main room. There were a few empty cups and a tray of half-eaten food on the table.

'What happened to you? You look like you've been mugged,' said the old lady, taking in her dishevelled appearance and the dressing. Claudia was aware of dried blood in her hair and along the neck of her t-shirt.

'I was playing a match. For the Senior Trials,' she said.

'Oh, the Game.' Jemima rolled her eyes. 'I thought it was meant to be non-violent. Designed for maximum inclusivity and all that. Did someone tackle you? You're not really built for it.'

'I kind of tackled someone else. I wasn't supposed to.'

'Oh dear,' said Jemima. 'Did they have you on performance enhancers? That used to be a problem with the last generation of military-grade drugs. I'm not up on the current state of social medication. God knows what they put in the water these days.'

'I wasn't on anything,' said Claudia. 'It was just me. A stupid moment. I've never done anything like that before. What's mugged?'

'Mugging is violent theft, a negative social phenomenon that was widespread in the Old World but unknown in the Dome, because all needs are perfectly met and aggressive psychopathology is chemically managed for the greater good,' said Jemima.

Claudia hadn't expected to hear an Oldie quote Ideo.

'What level is that?' she asked, impressed.

'I don't know. Probably the higher levels. I see you're Level V. That's quite high for someone who's not in the Mentargh, isn't it?'

'I'm not Mentargh, and I never will be. Especially not after today.' She'd never aspired to be a Mentargh, but the sudden demotion from star junior citizen to liability and troublemaker was psychologically as well as physically bruising. The implications were still seeping through: as a civilian med tech, the highest Ideo rank she could achieve was Level VI, and only if it was deemed necessary.

'Really? I'd be very surprised if they didn't recruit you,' said Jemima. 'They pick up all the bright ones early. Better to have them in than out. Also, human intelligence being an even more severely limited resource than before, they need as much of it as is left. Tea or coffee?'

'Coffee, please.' As she replied, Claudia realised she was ravenous. The remains in the food tray, a lab-meat stew with a green leafy vegetable and fungi, which she recognised as Citizen Meal No. 5 (soft rations, reduced portion), were congealed and unappetising.

'It'll be a bit weak, I'm afraid,' said Jemima. 'I go through my ration rather quickly. I used to get top-ups from a friend who couldn't bear the taste of it, but he popped his clogs a while back. What do they call it now? A final release? A compassionate release? That's the glorious future we live in.'

She shuffled into the kitchen. Claudia heard a brief splash of water and then humming, a tune that did not resemble any of the music played on the official channels. There were rumours that some Oldies had retained recordings of music from before the Event, although the devices that played such music no longer existed.

While she was waiting, Claudia wandered over to the shelf and pulled out one of the books. It fell open in her hands, and the paper gave off an odd, dusty smell. Two photographs were lying between the pages.

In the first, a younger Jemima was surrounded by dense green foliage, similar to the photograph with her husband. In this one, she was wearing a bright pink jacket, its hood pulled up over her head and close around her face, like something a lab tech would wear. Although she was obviously very wet, she was grinning hugely.

The next photograph showed a group of people, including the younger Jemima, apparently celebrating something. They were all dressed in different, colourful clothes, and they were holding up drinks and smiling in the direction of whoever had taken the photograph. Behind them was a banner with writing in another language, spiky and square.

Jemima came in with two cups of coffee, which she put on the table. 'Ah, you've found some more photos. I haven't seen those in ages. I'd been wondering where I put them. I lost thousands of pictures in the Event when the cloud servers were fried. Fifty years or so of digital storage, a massive archive of human experience, wiped out. All I had left were the printouts I had on my office notice board.'

'Sorry! I shouldn't have touched anything.'

'Not at all. Thank you for finding them. Have you seen many photos? I don't remember if visual material is included in the education design. It was quite controversial at the time. Bring them over.'

As Claudia sat down at the table, there was a soft impact noise next to her. Staring at her was a small furry creature just like the one she'd seen in the Underground, except that its eyes were green.

She screamed and jumped up.

'Oh, here's Lucky, come to say hello. She's usually very shy,' said Jemima. She stroked the creature and it emitted a low throbbing noise. 'She's harmless, mostly. She likes being petted on her back and chin.'

Claudia reached out and touched the cat. Its fur was the softest thing she'd ever felt. Beneath the fur was a small, densely muscled body.

The cat turned to look at her, blinked slowly, and looked away. It moved, with liquid elegance, to the other end of the table and began to lick itself.

'How—?'

'We share rations, although Lucky is very fussy,' said Jemima. She picked up the first photograph. 'Ah, that was up the north coast, in the rainforest. Jorge and I did a walking holiday back in 2039. It rained almost every day, but it was glorious.'

'Weren't there massive droughts then?' Claudia sipped the coffee. It was indeed very weak. As fascinated as she was by the photographs, she couldn't keep her eyes off Lucky, who was now completely ignoring them.

'In some places, yes,' said Jemima. 'Other places got more rain than they'd ever had. The weather had been changing for decades. Some places became more liveable. Other places became uninhabitable.'

She picked up the second photograph.

'I had a fellowship at Tsinghua University's Climate Change and Governance Centre during détente. Met some wonderful people. And not so wonderful. I don't suppose you've heard of Antek Lisowski?'

Claudia shook her head.

'He had some rather … harsh ideas about how a society with very limited resources should be governed. In the years running up to the Event, the outlook was increasingly grim, and some extreme political theories were gaining ground. Lisowski's book, *The Limited Society*, was the big one. The Chinese were very interested in his ideas, and he spent a lot of time in Beijing. A very clever man, but not in a good way.'

'Was he on the Survival Committee?' Claudia was struggling to keep up.

'Oh, no,' said Jemima. 'Although various key people on the Committee were great admirers. Hah! Antek and I had a few good ding-dongs when we crossed paths in Beijing, and I was persona non grata. I didn't draw any attention to myself when I arrived here. Kept my head down, didn't interfere. I could see what was happening, and I didn't like it, but I didn't have a choice.'

There was almost too much information for Claudia to process.

'What was it like in the Aftermath? Was it really that bad?' she asked.

'Oh yes.' Jemima's eyes clouded over. 'They haven't lied to you about that part. The destruction, the death, everything dying and rotting and stinking and falling apart. Starving people murdering each other for food, the sickness, the Earth itself dying all around us, like a huge corpse. We were maggots scrabbling to survive on the surface. The world was a vast cemetery. We were the human debris, the flotsam who survived in the wreckage. People fought to stay alive without knowing why. Everything was brutal and savage: mindless violence and mindless survival. There was nothing to give us any hope. As far as we knew, the whole world had been destroyed. Lots of people ended it themselves rather than endure any more.

'Unlike most people, I had inside knowledge about the Biodome Project. It had been kept very secret. Its location was protected by image blockers, the best and latest stealth and concealment tech, and very few people knew where it was. A former colleague, who was passing through the survivor collective where I lived for a while, said he knew how to find it. I knew other people had died trying, but the situation in the collective was getting, what can I say, a bit primordial for my liking, and I needed to get away. Hetty and Jorge were dead, and I had nobody left and nothing to lose. So I abandoned the collective and went with him.

'I could write a book about that journey, if there was still such a thing as books. God, sometimes I still can't believe I got here, and the last thirty years haven't been some sort of ghastly prolonged brain-death hallucination. We met all sorts of people on the way. Some of them helped us and we helped them; some we had to kill before they killed us. The will to survive is monstrous, and survival can leave you less human than before.

'When we finally saw the Dome in the distance, on the horizon, it was like arriving at the gates of heaven. But to get in, we had to go down, not up, through the Underground.'

As she listened to Jemima, Claudia could almost see and feel what she was describing, as if they were on a Party Machine together and Jemima was guiding her through what she had experienced all those years ago. A long concrete corridor, the walls dense with pipes and vents, like some Claudia had passed through in the Underground herself, dim and filled with the din of voices, sobbing, moaning, children's cries setting off shrill echoes. The stink of fear and desperation and sick, unwashed bodies. Some people pushed ahead with new hope; others were broken by pain and fatigue, their eyes set in pale, emaciated faces. The laborious ascent up narrow gantries that creaked beneath their collective weight. The expectancy, like an electric current, as they jostled through the final doorway. Then the heart-stopping wonder as they emerged into the Dome itself, a vista poignantly reminiscent of the cities of Before.

'People cried just to see the tall, gleaming buildings. Everything was whole and clean and untouched. To us it was everything we had thought lost forever,' said Jemima. 'The Committee had created a whole new society, one where everyone had food and shelter and medical care, even jobs and recreation, if you can call that mongrel sport a form of fun. After the horror of the Aftermath, we were ravenous for order, security and routine. Anarchy had exhausted us. To regain the faintest semblance of our old lives, however limited, was a miracle. After surviving like animals, we were only too grateful to accept what was offered. Nobody can blame us for that.'

'Nobody does,' said Claudia.

'No,' said Jemima. 'They managed that very well.'

She glanced around her unit and Claudia saw it through the Oldie's eyes: the dingy walls and the sparse functional furniture, the low, claustrophobic ceiling and single porthole window that looked out over the Ring. On the far side, the Central Zone was just visible, an orderly array of concrete shapes, grey in the Dome's fading light.

Claudia put down her cup of coffee, suddenly revolted by its metallic taste.

'Not very nice, is it?' said Jemima. 'Thirty years and they still can't get it right.'

'I should go,' said Claudia. One side of her body had begun to throb and stiffen. She needed a hot shower, however brief, and some more painkillers. And some food.

'Yes, you should be in bed. You look like hell. You must have quite a headache after your unfortunate collision,' said Jemima. 'I enjoyed chatting. Come again. I don't have anyone else to talk to these days, and Lucky seems to like you.'

The cat looked up, as if recognising its name, then resumed licking its deep furry belly.

Twenty-four

'Where have you been?'

The screen in the main room came on the minute Claudia came home, as if Kate had been waiting for her.

'I was in the sick bay. I had an accident on the pitch.' Ravenous, Claudia went straight to the foodstore, letting Kate yammer on behind her.

'Yeah, I heard about the accident.' Kate's tone made it clear that she knew the collision had been no accident. 'Out of the finals with minor concussion and bruising, and all your own fault. Ash told me Commodore Nira let you off.'

'Well why are you asking me, if you've heard it from him?' Claudia was so hungry that she opened the topmost food tray, a grain and protein mix, and started to eat it cold.

'You were released from sick bay over two hours ago. I need to know where you've been all this time. I've been trying to get through to you. I can see on the system that you've been to C-Sector, but Martin's not there. He's out in D-Sector with Arnie and that Davina. What were you doing in C-Sector, Claudia?'

'I waited. I thought Martin might come home. Maybe I fell asleep. I was pretty tired.' Claudia didn't even care that these excuses were weak. She wanted Kate to shut the freed up and leave her alone. She swallowed two of the painkillers.

'Why are you lying to me, Claudia?' said Kate quietly.

'Why does it matter where I've been? I've had a really crappy day and I'm fed up with everything.' The grain mix tasted particularly horrible and Claudia checked the expiry date, but it was fresh.

'Claudia, sit down and look at me when I'm talking to you!'

She took the food tray and sat at the table, looking sulkily in Kate's general direction.

'I know you've been lying to me for a while,' Kate went on. 'I didn't mention it. I wanted to give you a chance to be honest. There have obviously been some new influences in your life that haven't been entirely healthy.'

'Davina's just a free spirit,' said Claudia, poking at the food. It really was disgusting, but she was desperately hungry. 'If she's such a bad influence, why don't you arrest her so she can't infect people with her individualistic attitudes?'

'We'd hope that someone with your level of Ideo would be able to resist and push back,' said Kate. 'Claudia, we didn't allow you to study Level V because you like history. Your individual interests and curiosity are irrelevant. I can see you've been quite curious in the last couple of months. Tell me, why did you look up "anarchist"? "Bodyhacking"? "Anzacs"? "Capitalism"? And what the freed is a "sheeple"? Either that's graded above my head or it doesn't even exist.'

Claudia knew some people used their training tablets in off-script ways and that there was a way to erase your search record, 'deep-cleaning', but this was not general knowledge and as a diligent student with no ill intent, she'd never thought to find out, or that her occasional searches would be checked.

'I just overheard people speaking. That's all,' she said,

pushing the food tray aside. A hole seemed to be opening up in front of her and she wasn't feeling strong enough or sufficiently in control to pull back.

'What people?'

'I don't remember. Maybe on the Transit or the distro queue.'

'Maybe in D-Sector? I saw on your movement record that you've been going to the Youth League node there.'

'With Martin and Arnie,' said Claudia.

'It's good to keep up with your Basic cohort, but sometimes you need to move on. Martin and Arnie are going in different directions. You'd be better off keeping up with Pierce and Juanita.'

Claudia sat mulishly silent. The painkillers were beginning to take effect and her mind began to fog pleasantly. Paying attention to Kate was an effort she resented having to make.

'We've given you some leeway, because of your mother, but after what happened today, you need to pull yourself together,' said Kate. 'At this point, Claudia, things could go well or really badly for you. You need to get to grief counselling and sort yourself out, for the general good as well as your own. Your mother chose the worst time to kill herself. Not that she was thinking of anyone else, least of all you, when she smashed up the Hydro Plant on the way out.'

'Maybe she did it on purpose!' Claudia shot back. 'Instead of quietly OD'ing, like a good citizen, she put on a proper show, an individual one-way celebration of the 30th Anniversary, to make people think about how we live. Maybe she's been a subversive all along, and maybe I inherited it from her, my very own golden future.'

Where did all this come from? It was like another person

speaking in Claudia's voice.

Kate's face curdled. There was suddenly a stranger looking out of the screen at Claudia, a cold, hard-faced stranger who bore no resemblance to the cheery Kate she'd trusted since Junior League.

'Claudia, that's a bad attitude you have there.'

She stared at Kate, horrified by her own rashness.

'I'm worried about you, Claudia,' Kate said, but there was no concern in the stony eyes. 'I see I misjudged you very badly. I trusted you, and this is how you repay that trust. This is what happens when you lie: it rots you from the inside. It's a lot worse than I thought. I'm going to have to take this up the chain, and the next person who deals with you won't be so nice.'

Kate's voice seemed disembodied, weaving in and out of Claudia's consciousness.

'I'm sorry. I didn't mean that. I'm just so tired,' said Claudia, but her voice came out as a whisper and Kate showed no signs of hearing.

Twenty-five

The painkillers sank her into a mercifully deep sleep, but she woke up early, aching from yesterday's collision. The routine that had held her together no longer applied; she was out of the Selection Trials Game and on notice for attitude.

Her heart began to flutter and she broke into a sweat. What was wrong with her? She was losing all control of her emotions. A lifetime of dutiful study and training, trashed in one stupid outburst to Kate.

Had talking to Jemima infected her? She wasn't just any Oldie. Her casual and dismissive mention of Lisowski, Ideology and other aspects of Dome life were all the more shocking the morning after. How did she know so much? Surely the Mentargh were aware of her? And yet she was living freely, without any chemical restraint, with a collection of artefacts that should've been classified and locked away.

And the cat. Its green, inhuman stare and impossibly soft fur.

Jemima was very old, but she wasn't crazy, not at all.

Did Kate know she'd been to visit Jemima? How presumptuous, to think that she could keep secrets from Kate and make her own judgements about what was acceptable.

Claudia thought, *I'm like my mother: mentally and emotionally weak.*

One day she might also throw herself off something, make a big mess and bring production to a halt for an hour or two.

Amid her sweating fear, Claudia felt the tiniest spark of satisfaction. Kate had underestimated her, and so had Davina and Luma. Her own mother had done more damage to the Dome in a few seconds than any Underground meeting, and Claudia had the same sick, antisocial, mutant seed of individualistic discontent inside her, which had obviously taken root and was sprouting, like one of the rogue non-food plants that sometimes took over a level in Hydroponics and had to be destroyed.

Everyone else was at the Game. Claudia was adrift, with nowhere to go and nothing to do except wait. If she hadn't been injured, she would've gone to the gym. She briefly considered some gentle cardio, but she felt too stiff and sore, and any sort of exercise after mild concussion wasn't a good idea. She was a half-trained med tech, after all.

She opened up her Ed tablet, wondering if her access had been restricted, but all her coursework was there, and the usual newsfeed, with upbeat messages about the progress of the Senior Trials. Nothing about an unfortunate incident on the pitch, an out-of-control subversive element sabotaging all her coach's hard work.

It was unbearable sitting alone in the unit, so she got dressed and went out, taking the Transit in the usual direction, towards the Med Block training facility in the Central Zone. Would she at least be allowed to continue her medical training? She could still be a useful citizen.

She sat down by the tower tree and waited. When they were ready for her, they could come and find her. There was nowhere for her to hide unless she went into the Underground. How long could she survive down there, sustained by Lisa's biscuits? It wasn't a serious thought.

Eventually, a trooper appeared at the far side of the square and headed right for her. She watched him approach.

'Junior Citizen Claudia X69-398?'

She held out her wrist to be swiped.

'It would've been easier if you'd stayed in place at home. Any particular reason you came here?' he asked, sounding almost grumpy. He was only a few years older than her.

'I'm not used to being at home this time of the cycle. I'm usually here.'

'You're required to attend the Barracks now, reporting to Commander Luke.'

Claudia was shocked out of her strange detachment. She hadn't expected Kate to report her directly to Luke. Her heart began to thump so hard it was like being punched from the inside. If Kate was monitoring her physical stats, she'd have the satisfaction of knowing Claudia was now completely terrified.

As he led her to where his bike was parked, Claudia was aware of glances from other citizens, some curious, some almost sympathetic, others indifferent. Despite his youth, in his blacks, the trooper carried about him a certain atmosphere, a low-level menace, and nobody was going to interfere.

At the Barracks security gates, Elliot was waiting on the other side of the second barrier.

'I'll take over from here, Trooper,' he said. 'Come with me, citizen.'

His usual knowing grin was replaced by an altogether more threatening demeanour. Next to him, Claudia was aware of his height and bulk. She thought of Martin and Arnie trying to pull Ally away from Elliot on the night of the party, and then Pierce having a go at him. Pierce was well-built for his age, but next to Elliot, he was still a boy.

Elliot took her to the main administrative block and up to a floor that was swipe-entry. In either direction stretched a corridor of numbered doors. Claudia did not recognise any of the function codes on the door plates.

She was right at the centre of Mentargh operations. If Luke had intended to intimidate her, he had already succeeded.

At the end of the corridor, Elliot pressed the intercom on the last door.

'Junior Citizen X69-398 for the Commander.'

The door buzzed and Elliot pushed it open. 'In you go,' said Elliot, and he seemed to smirk as Claudia passed him.

The door closed behind her with a click.

The room was large and dim. A detailed dynamic map of the Dome showed various metrics and functions. Luke was standing in front of a bank of screens.

'Junior Citizen.'

She wondered if she should salute, although she wasn't MT. Even at their last meeting, in the Barracks canteen, he'd still been Pierce's brother. Now, as a senior officer, he was distant and formal.

'Do you know why you're here?'

'Kate said she was going to refer me.' Her mouth dried up. 'I didn't think it would be you.'

'I have responsibility for your sector.' He turned around from the screens and looked her up and down in a regretful, searching way. 'It seems that you've developed some … attitude problems and have been withholding information.'

She directed her gaze over his shoulder, concentrating on one of the screens behind him, a data feed of incomprehensible code and red or white squares that suddenly zeroed in on particular areas of the map. On another screen, surveillance camera footage flashed up in short sequences, some faces highlighted. There was more going on in the Dome at any one moment than Claudia could comprehend, and all that information was fed back here.

She had never been in such a room. She knew that all citizens were constantly monitored, a banal fact of life that was almost abstract; she'd never seen the other end of it. How could anyone presume to hide anything?

'I'm sorry about your mother,' he said, unexpectedly.

'It was going to happen eventually, and it happened.' Claudia kept looking over Luke's shoulder as she spoke, avoiding his face. 'If it hadn't been for Roz, she would've died ages ago or been recycled or whatever you do to people like her. I suppose it's for the greater good that she's finally dead.'

'What do you think we do to people like your mother?' said Luke.

'They're a social problem. A drain on common resources. I know that. There wasn't anything I could do.'

For a moment, Claudia's throat constricted, but she kept herself steady.

'Nobody blamed you,' said Luke. 'If the trained people at the Rehab Centre couldn't help her, nobody could. It's important—it's our duty to the community—to accept help when necessary, and she rejected it. Now you're rejecting grief counselling.'

'I'm not grieving,' said Claudia, almost interrupting him.

'Then what the freed happened yesterday on the pitch?

Claudia, that was completely out of character. I know you better than you think. And why Luma? What's going on with you two?'

'She doesn't like me,' said Claudia. 'I don't know why.'

'You're withholding,' said Luke. 'I can tell. Something is going very wrong with you, Claudia. You know, Pierce is so worried about you that he actually came to me.'

'Pierce reported me?'

'No, he didn't report you. He said he was worried about you, that you were all locked down since your mother's death and he was afraid you were going to do something stupid. He didn't get more specific than that.'

'I'm not feeling anything. Isn't that a good thing?' she said. 'Feelings are an individualistic luxury and have no part in the efficient functioning of society.'

'That's not a quote,' he said quietly.

'Not yet,' she said, and when she finally dared to look at him, his gaze was both penetrating and opaque.

'Has my brother ever mentioned special interrogations?' said Luke.

'No.'

Glancing over his shoulder, he made a gesture and the screens blanked. 'I wouldn't expect him to. A special interrogation is … an intensive conversation for the extraction of information a person won't give up willingly.'

Claudia's ability to breathe almost deserted her.

'Don't look at me like that!' said Luke. 'We're almost in the twenty-second century, I'm not going to torture you. A special interrogation is a special trip on the Party Machine. I'm not going to hurt you. For freed's sake. Is that how you think of the Mentargh?'

It's how we all think of the Mentargh, Claudia thought, and she had the impression that Luke knew what she was thinking, all the more so because he was standing right in front of her.

'If you do, that's either a reflection on you or on us,' he said.

She did not reply.

'Sit down.'

A Machine was already unfolded on the table. She sat down. Luke fetched a blue water cannie and something else from a small storage unit. He held out his palm. On it was a jenny, but not the kind the Mentargh passed out at parties. This one was blue.

She took it and he waited for her to swallow before he took another one, which was yellow. He took off his uniform jacket and hung it on the back of the chair. Underneath he was wearing a plain white t-shirt, no different to Claudia's. The jennies could make you sweat, at higher doses.

His shoulders were broader than Pierce's, she noticed, and his torso was more filled out. There were five or six years between them. Their middle sister had died young.

'You're going to show me what happened when you last went on the Party Machine. It seems you've managed to avoid them ever since that bad trip at Martin's party.'

The effort of trying not to remember had the reverse effect. As she put her hands on the Machine, it came to life, the familiar colours swirling across the surface as the usual program started up.

'The Dome is a perfectly balanced and efficiently function-ing society,' Claudia said, trying to open her mind to the neuro-animation and all its positive emotions, but it was like trying to eat plastic waste.

'Anyone can quote Ideo,' said Luke, his own hands on the

screen opposite hers, almost touching. 'When you see the Dome, what does it make you feel? I want to feel it too. Show me.'

She saw the Dome as it had been the night of Martin's party, when they had set out along the edge of the Ring. Beautiful, but also ugly. *A machine for survival.* Trying to escape this thought, her mind jumped to the parade on the last day of the Junior Selection Trials. Her fresh sadness on hearing the Memorial recited was overlaid by the cold cynicism of her reaction to the anthem. *What golden future?* It was like biting on something hard and bitter in a sloppy protein stew. *We are pathetic.*

She forced herself to think about training, focusing on the sense of camaraderie, the practice matches that had gone well, all the positive community feeling, and then suddenly she saw Ash's face overhead, screaming at her, for falling over, for bashing into Luma. And then Luma's face, right up against hers. *You bitch! I'm going to shut you up for good.*

The surface of the Machine became hot and the colours leapt and flared. Claudia could feel the sweat trickling down the side of her face.

'Tell me about Luma,' said Luke. 'Where have you met her before?'

Resisting, Claudia thought instead of Lisa. *Have a biscuit.* Her head felt heavy and under pressure, like a certain kind of headache. *Have a biscuit.* Briefly, she saw Neil's face and his head torch, and heard Arnie's admiring voice: *Super-efficient!* Efficient was a good word, a safe word; there was no harm in thinking it.

'Who's Lisa?' Luke's voice, breaking through the images.

Neil's voice: *She was a human centipede.*

'She had fifty pairs of shoes, but they were all vaporised,' said Claudia, trying to get rid of Neil.

'You had a new pair of trainers from the Barracks commissary. How did that make you feel?'

Claudia saw herself walking between the shelves, an infinity of shoes on both sides.

She heard her own voice: *I don't understand. Where did they all come from?*

And then Lisa's voice: *Nobody down here is going to ask difficult questions about where my biscuits come from.*

'Who are these people?'

If Claudia could have willed herself unconscious, she would've obliterated herself. Last time, the Machine had thrown her off, but now it seemed to hold her. She could feel Luke's will pitted against hers as surely as if he were physically overpowering her.

'Oldies. Nobody.'

'What happened on the night of the party, Claudia? That's when it all started, isn't it?'

The memory was as vivid as if she was reliving it: being hurled off the Machine and waking to see Luke looking down at her with his dark, inscrutable eyes. She tried to pull away but her hands were held fast to the screen. He might even have been holding them there.

She wrenched her mind away from Martin's unit and the press of faces and bodies, leaping over the hours to the next morning. Alone on the Transit, she watched the pale dawn creep across the outer surface of the Dome shield as the carriage swung close to the barrier. Below, she saw, again, the man on the overpass, standing alone and looking down.

A few moments after her shuttle had passed, he had hauled

himself over the barrier and plunged the equivalent of twelve floors onto the hard-packed earth below, the same way Faye had, somehow, despite her physical weakness, crawled over the rail of the Hydro Plant terrace and smashed through several panes of glass, leaving a trail of blood and torn fabric.

The Machine suddenly went dead and Claudia was released, thrown back on the chair.

Luke was staring at her, his face slick with sweat. His eyes were no longer hiding anything.

'You saw him? The man at the overpass?'

Claudia nodded. Her mouth was too dry to speak, and she drank from the cannie of water that Luke had left on the table, her hand shaking. As soon as she put it down, he took a long swig himself.

'I didn't see him jump,' she said.

Luke grimaced. 'We were called to the scene. It was almost the end of the shift. We'd done a few more parties after Martin's and we were heading back to the Barracks when the call came through. Abrupt extinction of life, no medical precursors. There was no point calling a med team. We had to get a sanitation team out to clean it up before the dawn shift. It was horrible. Elliot puked his guts up. Don't tell anyone I said that. I know he's not your favourite Mentargh.'

'Is he anyone's?' Looking across the table at Luke, Claudia had a sudden sense of him as a person beyond the uniform. It was probably just the effect of the jenny, but there was a new familiarity between them, almost an intimacy.

'Ally seems to like him. Although your friends didn't approve.'

'I wasn't around to see that,' she said, and bit her lip.

'Yeah, I heard. What happened with you and Pierce that

night?'

She shut her eyes, as if she could block him from reading her mind. 'Is the interrogation over now?'

Across the table, she could feel Luke shutting down as well, retreating into his official persona.

'Yes, citizen, that's enough for today. I'll call someone to escort you out.'

Twenty-six

A female trooper led her to a small windowless room, gave her an electrolyte drink and scanned her to check her physical stats.

She spoke into a comms device: 'X69-398 cleared for release.' Turning to Claudia, she said, 'You're good to go. I'll take you down and you can swipe yourself out.'

Emerging from the dimness of the Admin Block, Claudia almost blinked in the neutral light of the quadrangle. The comedown of the jenny made everything both distant and hyperreal, and seeing all the black figures moving about the compound triggered a feeling of dread.

Pierce was waiting for her outside. He grabbed her arm.

'What happened? I heard you'd been called in to see Luke. I checked on the system, and I saw the code for special interrogation.'

'Luke said you'd been to see him about me because you were worried. What did you think would happen?' Claudia's emotions were too dulled for any sort of indignation.

'Of course I'm worried! Claudia, you're losing the plot, and we know it's not just your mother. You won't get a free pass for much longer. Smacking into Luma is small stuff. You know how I feel about Luke, but I didn't know who else to ask. I thought he'd just … talk to you, make it clear how close you are to serious trouble. I didn't know he'd go straight for a special.'

'I had a run-in with Kate,' said Claudia. 'She reported me. So it's not your fault, if that makes you feel better.'

He was still holding her arm. 'Actually, it is. I'm supposed to keep track of my friends, report any anomalies.'

'And you have system access?'

'In the Barracks, yes. Everyone's always checking up on their friends. It's part of our training. It's our … job. If I'd done mine properly, you wouldn't have ended up on the Party Machine with Luke.'

'I don't think he saw that much,' she said. 'If it makes you feel any better.'

'You don't understand,' said Pierce urgently. 'It's more subtle than that, and this is only the first time. You know how the jenny makes you feel connected to everyone else who takes it, and the Party Machine amplifies the connection? In a special interrogation, you feel close to the interrogator. It makes you trust them. But it's not real, it's your brain chemicals being messed about. And the pill he took isn't the same as yours.'

'But it still works both ways. I could feel and see him as well.'

She told Pierce about the man on the overpass.

'They know what they're doing,' Pierce insisted. 'Luke knows what he's doing. If he lets you in and shows you something, you're being manipulated. They're trained to do this.'

'And one day you'll be doing it as well,' said Claudia.

'No. I don't have the aptitude for it. Not many people do.' He let go of her arm. 'I didn't want that to happen to you, and certainly not with him.'

'Are you feeling sorry for yourself or for me?'

'I'm sorry he did that to you. I'm also sorry because you're my closest friend, and it feels like he's taking you away from me.'

Claudia felt Pierce's pain as a sudden stabbing sensation inside her. If they hadn't been standing in the Barracks quadrangle, she would've put her arms around him and closed the awful distance between them.

'No, he's not,' she said, but it seemed to her that he was already giving up.

* * *

She met Davina and Martin under the tower tree in the square outside the four Ed blocks in the Central Zone. The final results of the Selection Trials had yet to be announced, but occupational training and work placements had resumed. The graduating cohort of Senior Youth League were now full citizens and had to fulfil their duty to the community.

'What the freed is happening with you? I heard you'd been called in by Luke,' said Martin. His face showed both concern and a new wariness.

'Did Pierce tell you?'

'No. He's totally airlocked,' said Martin. 'Anyway, special interrogations are classified.'

'So how do you know?' said Claudia.

'Word gets around. The Barracks leaks like a drain,' said Davina. 'Technology fails, but humans are the weakest link, my granddad used to say.'

'Freed, Clau. How much do they know?' said Martin.

'Nothing from me. You have nothing to worry about. I managed to block him.' Claudia said this with more confidence than she felt. Just to remember sitting across the Party Machine with Luke in that small, dim room made her break out in a sweat all over again.

Davina looked sceptical. 'From what I hear, the jennies they use in specials are a lot stronger than the party pills. You think you're having a nice shared experience with Luke, I dunno, like another sexy powerbike ride across the Ring, while all the time he's going through your memories like DOMUS tracking down a system malfunction.'

'You told her about the ride?' Claudia looked at Martin.

'Why wouldn't I?' said Martin. 'I still think it was weird you didn't say anything to us.'

'I told you, I was freaked out of my mind! I didn't want to think about it.' Her powerbike ride with Luke still set off a disturbing mix of emotions in Claudia. 'And it's not like the MT came down the hole after you.'

Davina looked narrowly at Claudia. 'The D-Sector node was flushed out by the MT just after you left that night. They handed out some heavier than usual drugs. Really intense trip. Of course, being whacked on homebrew didn't help. At first it was just Elliot, and then Luke appeared. I felt like my head was being turned inside out. A few people even puked.'

'To be fair, that could've been the homebrew,' said Martin. 'The stuff going around that night wasn't a good batch.'

'I want to come down again,' said Claudia. 'I want to be a part of what's happening down there, whatever it is. I'm not on the MT track. I don't have a golden future, and I don't believe we're living in one. Don't you trust me?'

Even as she said the words, shocking herself by this sudden confession, spilling out from some part of her mind hidden even from herself, she could feel their resistance, an invisible wall as palpable as the Dome barrier itself.

'No.' Davina said this without hesitation, her voice implacable. 'You're under observation. You're going to have more special interrogations, because there's always more than one. I know you're curious about the past, and you have doubts and lots of questions that are never going to be answered officially, but it's much bigger than your individual curiosity and your *divergency issue*'—Davina put a sarcastic emphasis on this—'and expecting us to take a massive risk just so you can eat Lisa's biscuits and chat about her fifty pairs of shoes is a bit freeding selfish and *inefficient*, to be honest.'

'Martin?'

'Sorry, Clau.' He seemed pained by Davina's harshness but accepted it. 'Not that I think you'd deliberately say anything, but sometimes they have a way of just knowing things.'

She stared at them both, feeling lonelier than she'd thought possible.

'By the way, where's Arnie?' she asked, affecting a new coolness. 'I haven't seen him for ages. Is he living down there?'

'Arnie is just fine. Do him a favour: don't think about him. In fact, forget him,' said Davina. 'Especially when you're having private parties with Commander Luke.'

'I've known him all my life. I know him better than you!'

'That's what you think,' said Davina, not hiding her scorn. 'You've never even played a table game with him in D-Sector. Oops, almost out of time for the next shift, gotta go.'

Martin lingered a moment.

'To be honest, the powerbike ride sounded pretty hot to me,' he said. 'You used to tell me stuff like that. Ally would've had a hysterical meltdown.'

'Yeah, I know,' said Claudia. 'Maybe she'll get a ride from Elliot before long.'

Martin grinned ruefully. 'I think we might have wasted our resources trying to rescue her.'

The second shift-change klaxon sounded and they went their separate ways.

Twenty-seven

Nobody came to escort her to the next interrogation. She received a simple instruction over her screen to present herself at the Barracks security gate at the beginning of the third shift. There was no need to inform her trainer; her locator code would indicate a necessary absence.

A trooper was waiting at the swipe gates to escort her up to Luke's office. This time, there were no questions, although he looked her over in a close, unfriendly way, as if trying to work out what she'd done that required such serious measures.

'It's clear that you have some ambivalence about the Dome,' said Luke. 'We need to explore that some more and see how deep it goes.'

As before, he waited for her to take the pill before swallowing one himself. Beneath their hands, the Machine lit up, and Claudia felt the usual rush as the boundaries of her mind seemed to expand and dissolve. She was no longer an individual entity; she was floating, bodiless, in a vast sea of colour and sensation. In that sea, Luke's presence became stronger as the drug took effect on them both.

That powerbike ride sounded pretty hot, to be honest.

As she stifled the memory of Martin's words, she could feel Luke's attention gather and focus like a surgical laser.

Already hiding? Why don't you trust me?

Of course I don't freeding trust you. Her resistance arced like a solar flare before she could temper it.

Luke seemed to retreat and she was left alone.

She saw the Dome, not the usual enhanced version offered up by the Machine but as it was, completely unedited, its colourless, functional, utterly familiar everyday appearance. There were no emotional prompts. She could feel Luke waiting.

She was waiting under the tower tree by the Med Block, wondering if the tree was alive, and thinking what a poor imitation it was of the rainforest in Jemima's photographs. What did that rainforest look like now? A wasteland by a poisoned sea? A sudden wave of grief and anger passed over Claudia, emotions that belonged to the Oldie and had somehow transferred themselves to her.

She shut down the thought of Jemima, hauling her attention back to the tower tree and letting it rest there, neutral.

Do you blame the Dome for your mother's death?

Had Luke misread the grief and anger?

My mother was to blame. She made the choice. Nobody forced her to drink roughbrew.

That's harsh.

She remembered Faye crawling around the floor, scrabbling for the painkillers. *You little bitch.* She could feel him recoil.

Want to see more?

If that's what you want to show me. Follow your feelings, Claudia. It works better that way.

* * *

'I've been called in for special interrogation,' she told Jemima.

This time, she'd brought the Oldie some of her snack allowance, some fruit pods and vitamin jellies, because Jemima looked so thin and had so few teeth left. Claudia also brought a few protein chews for Lucky, who sniffed them suspiciously, licked one, and turned her back.

'Special interrogation? Is that what they call it now? What have you done?' Jemima spooned the first of the jellies into her mouth like a greedy child.

'I've been withholding from my counsellor. The last time I came around to see you, after the … incident on the pitch, she was trying to find me. She wanted to know where I'd been, and I didn't tell her. I was pretty tired, actually, and I kind of mouthed off at her.'

'Oh dear. You had a teenage moment.' Jemima's mouth twitched. 'How socially inefficient.'

'I was in pain, actually.' Claudia felt that the Oldie wasn't taking her seriously.

'Yes, you did look rough that day.' Jemima's tone became kinder.

Lucky came up beside her on the table and butted her hand, her tail upright and hooked at the end. Claudia watched as Jemima stroked the animal. Her hands were almost fleshless, the bones netted together by thick purple veins. Lucky arched her back, her eyes closing in pleasure.

'And you've come back, even though it got you into trouble the last time.' Jemima looked up suddenly, her gaze sharp. 'What's so compelling about a crazy old woman and her imaginary cat?'

'I don't have anyone else to talk to.' The words came out before Claudia was conscious of formulating a reply.

'What about your mother?'

Claudia took a sip of her coffee. She'd also brought Jemima some of her coffee ration, but the Oldie had still made it very weak.

'She died last quarter.'

'Bloody hell. I'm sorry.'

'It's OK. She was in a bad way for a long time. Roughbrew brain-rot,' said Claudia.

'Vile stuff,' said Jemima. 'Although I can understand the human impulse to seek oblivion, and on your own terms, rather than being drugged off your nut for the greater good. But all that had already started Before. Endemic depression, loneliness, alienation. The pharmacological solution for social breakdown. The line between therapeutic use and social management was getting very thin. There was loads of funding for neuropharma research, and from some very dubious quarters. I knew some of the people doing it. Fascinating stuff, don't get me wrong. I was involved in some off-books experiments, pure curiosity, not my field at all, but towards the end it was a bit of a free-for-all. The new generations of empathetic and psychedelic drugs had astounding possibilities; an evolutionary step in human connection, the ability to share feelings and even thoughts. In the Aftermath, it saved my life a few times. But the downsides were just as radical: the ability to mould and control minds, the total end of privacy. If the Event had one benefit, it was to stop certain lines of research, although I sometimes wonder if they haven't been continued in the Dome.'

She glanced at Claudia, a brief but penetrating look that reminded the girl strangely of Luke. 'Do you want another cup of coffee? I'll make it a bit stronger this time.'

* * *

Thinking of Jemima's unit, the grubby walls, the mean little window with its partial, grey view of the Ring and the distant Central Zone, the worn, functional furniture, Claudia felt sadness, even disgust. But these were not her feelings. The single-person unit was no different from any other in the Dome, and she had known nothing else.

Pulling her attention away from Jemima, who was just out of sight, somehow hiding in a corner, she focused on the photographs. Looking at the two sisters in the sea, she was standing in the water herself, feeling it rush around her ankles, as she had on the night of Martin's party.

Where's this?

It's the sea.

Luke was there, watching. Had he ever seen a picture of the sea? Claudia showed him the rainforest photograph. Inhaling, she could feel the dense, moist air in her nose and throat. She put her hand out and touched the rough, wet trunk of a tree. The Dome's tower trees had no trunks, only massive vertical hydro-frames.

Is this where you'd rather be?

It doesn't exist any more. If I was there now, I'd be dead. I'm lucky to be alive in the Dome.

You can't hide by giving the right answers. It's not that easy.

* * *

'It's a shame you can't access the Archives,' said Jemima. 'You'd find a lot of very interesting answers to all your questions.'

'I've read extracts, in Ideo class, but not much.' Claudia's second cup of coffee was marginally stronger.

'After I arrived in the Dome, I recorded for weeks,' said Jemima. 'Of course, it's all highly classified now. If you were in the Mentargh, at the right level, you might be allowed a look. Unless certain people have decided, for the greater good, to destroy it. That wouldn't surprise me at all.'

'How much do you know about the Mentargh?' Claudia asked.

The Oldie spoke in a familiar, almost casual way. 'The MNT Group—Merrivale Norris Tanner, if I'm remembering correctly—was the security contractor for the Biodome Project, back in the day. The people behind it had some connection to a neofascist group, lots of that about in the years before the Event. There was a scandal when it came out, but nothing seemed to come of it. Politics was getting very strange, towards the end, and the media was completely bogus. You had to go on the alt-net to know what was going on.'

She paused. 'You have no idea what I'm talking about, do you?'

'Was Antek Lisowski a ... neofascist?' Claudia was doing her best to keep up.

'His ideas on extreme and survival governance were popular with far-right types, and the people who wrote the Ideology. Anyway, an MNT Group team lived permanently on site. They were here when the first refugees arrived. They'd been here since the Event, and a lot of their own people had already joined them, the ones who'd survived and could manage the journey. When the rest of us arrived, we had to make some compromises, to fit into their system. There was a protracted settling-in period, you could say. I kept my head well down. Nobody takes any notice of a silly old woman who wears pink fluffy slippers.'

Jemima finished her third jelly and started on the fruit pods.

* * *

She was riding across the Ring, on the back of Luke's bike. *That powerbike ride sounded pretty hot.* Again, she stifled Martin's comment, but Davina's words popped up instead. *Sexy powerbike ride across the Ring with Luke.*

Quickly, she overwrote them with her own thought: *Just like flying.*

The nearest we'll ever get.

Overhead, the pale shape of the moon, a smudge against the Dome barrier.

Claudia was standing in the centre of the Ring, the same red earth beneath her, but instead of the usual greyness, she was looking up at a limitless spread of stars, a vault of speckled light that stretched overhead into the infinite distance. The desert night was crisp and dry, teeming with invisible life. The sense of space was so overwhelming that she almost lost her balance.

This is what it looked like before they built the Dome.

Next to her, Luke was feeling the same wonder.

Who showed you this?

There had been no such picture on Jemima's shelf.

* * *

'I've been talking to some other Survivors,' said Claudia. 'Not as old as you, though.'

'No offence taken,' said Jemima. 'I really should have croaked by now.'

'One of them works for the Recycling Depot,' Claudia went on. 'He said 99% efficiency was a lie, that the Dome wasn't fully self-regenerating and sustainable, and that we were going to have problems down the line.'

'That old ratbag!' Jemima laughed. 'I thought they would've recycled him for spare parts by now. He used to call himself the Anarchist Motherboard. I won't even ask what he's up to these days. Best not to know.'

Claudia's head was spinning. She wanted to ask more about Neil, but she needed an answer to her previous question.

'Yes, everything in the Dome is getting old and decrepit, not just me,' Jemima went on. 'Incremental degradation and wastage. Neil's right. We only have a few generations left.'

'How do you know for sure?'

Jemima took a few moments before replying. 'I haven't talked about this for a long time, but I used to work with Amelia.'

'Professor Amelia Liu-Martinez? The scientist who invented the Dome?'

In her shock, Claudia regressed to Level I Ideo.

'The one and only. Total bloody diva. Brilliant mind, but very difficult to work with. We worked on SRAE together, until we didn't. I disagreed with her over the 99%. There was no such thing as totally self-regenerating, infinitely renewable, not back in 2052. We still needed some level of external input to keep the system going. Amelia was obsessed with totality, but it wasn't possible, not with the tech we had then. The magic number wasn't 99%. No way. But corporations and governments had massive amounts invested. Amelia wasn't going to disappoint them. She was sure we'd get up to 100%. That was her dream, and she wouldn't listen to people who said it wasn't possible, not yet. Including me. That's why I was thousands of kilometres away from the Dome when the balloon went up. So was Amelia. She was at some elite feelgood jamboree, maybe the Singapore Human Futures forum, giving her usual spiel. Maybe some trillionaire spirited her away in his personal rocket, and they're now colonising Mars, who knows. They certainly never bothered to come back and check up on the rest of us.'

'So eventually the Dome will reach its limit, and we'll all die?'

'Possibly, but not necessarily,' said Jemima, and waited.

Claudia could barely think the words, let alone say them. Once she had voiced them, there would be no turning back.

'But it's dead Outside.'

Their whole existence in the Dome was based on this unquestionable truth, the very foundation of Ideology.

'That,' said Jemima, 'is open to question. Nuclear winter and nuclear summer were only ever theories. It's not like we could test it. There were all sorts of debates about the planet's powers of regeneration, very politicised, which didn't help the science. After the Event, of course, our capacity to measure and monitor was extremely limited, but there were some small signs of recovery, or at least that the damage wasn't total. The bombing never reached saturation levels, we knew that much. Did some of those old warheads fail to launch? Had they been taken offline? Was there a human decision not to launch? Was it just an accident that triggered a limited series of counter-strikes? What actually happened? It's possible the social damage was far worse than the long-term damage to the planet. Maybe the planet was trying to offload us so it could heal.'

'But didn't they know all this back then? The Survival Committee?' Claudia's whole world was falling away beneath her.

'The Committee had their self-contained little totalitarian survivor colony, the perfect set-up for Lisowski's grim ideas about post-democratic governance,' said Jemima. 'Why undermine that? And in the Aftermath, it didn't seem like the worst option, I can tell you. But that was thirty years ago.'

All this time, Lucky had been lying on Claudia's lap, purring as she was stroked. She suddenly twisted around, raked Claudia's arm and jumped onto the floor, where she sat calmly washing herself, with her back turned.

Her claws left three deep marks on the inside of Claudia's wrist.

'Lucky changes her mind very quickly,' said Jemima. 'You should go and wash that scratch.'

* * *

A little girl, in a yellow overall, squatting on the ground and building a stack of plastic bricks, with great concentration. She had the same black eyes and hair as Pierce and Luke. The same girl, older, in regular blues, marching in a squad of other girls, her expression serious. Then, smiling, her knees grazed and bloody after a Game. And then, in a medical bed, the centre of a nest of tubes and machines, her dark eyes large and frightened.

Julia. The middle sister.

Claudia could feel Luke's pain, a surge of raw, real emotion that rushed beneath her defences and enveloped her. She had no defence against it.

He'll share with you, to make you trust him, but you can't.

I lost my sister. I won't lose my brother.

** * **

He pulled his hands away from the Machine and the screen went dead.

Claudia could feel the sweat trickling down her temples. Each session left her more drained. She lifted a hand to wipe her face, and Luke grabbed her wrist. The marks from Lucky's claws were still red and angry, slightly raised.

'What happened?'

'I must have scratched myself. Maybe in a prac session.' Claudia tried to pull away, but Luke held fast. He was very strong.

'What did you scratch yourself on?'

'I can't remember. I don't even remember doing it.'

'It doesn't look like something you wouldn't notice. It looks like it would've hurt. It looks like you might need it seen to. It could be infected.'

'It's fine. I'll put something on it.'

'You're lying to me, Claudia. I can tell.'

He looked at her, and his gaze seemed to go right through her. The effort of meeting it made her briefly dizzy. She kept her mind blank and pushed back, and eventually he let go.

Twenty-eight

After her last visit to Jemima, Claudia needed to speak to Martin, Arnie and Davina. The knowledge was too much to bear on her own. If long-term survival in the Dome was impossible, then there was no point trying to change things, whatever that meant. There was no golden future inside. Their only hope lay Outside.

What were the subversives planning? Did they know what she now knew?

Sending a message to meet up through the open system seemed too risky. Instead, she went to the D-Sector Youth League node, thinking they might still be meeting there.

Not seeing them, she headed through the crowds to the service passage. She had no clear plan of how she was going to find them, but she couldn't stay alone with what she knew.

The emergency exit was fitted with a new swipe reader.

Stupidly, she stared at it.

'The toilet's this way,' someone called behind her.

Maybe he thought she was drunk. He disappeared into the male toilets and she didn't see his face, although his voice sounded familiar.

Out in the common area, she saw two troopers standing by the far wall, and another two near the door.

'You're Arnie's friend, aren't you?' Someone was standing behind her, a man, speaking in low tones, hardly audible over the usual background beats. 'Citizen, if you want a credit card, you've picked the wrong night. The MT are all over us.'

'Has something happened?'

'Nothing I know of. Arnie's keeping a low profile. You won't find him here. Best not to look for him.'

'What about Davina and Martin?'

'Haven't seen them. If you want to avoid the wrong sort of attention, you should get back to your own sector.'

She turned, but he had already moved away, his back to her.

Leaving the node, she headed back across the square to the Transit station. Beyond it lay the Ring, dark and empty as usual. Without thinking, Claudia kept walking. None of her decisions were rational. She was acting on new compulsions she didn't understand.

Away from the lights of D-Sector, she looked up. It was night Outside; there was no moon and the Dome vault was too thick for starlight. There was nothing overhead, and nothing around her. With her back to the lights, she could have been falling through space.

When she heard the hum of a powerbike behind her, she kept walking. The bike overtook her and pulled to a stop.

'What the freed are you doing out here?' said Tia.

'I don't know,' said Claudia. 'I just needed some space. How did you find me?'

'I picked up a location anomaly. There's a watch on you. You're under observation, you should be in place.' Tia gave her a searching look. 'Are you feeling OK? I heard you've had a couple of special interrogations. They can really mess with your head.'

'To be honest, I don't know what OK feels like anymore,' said Claudia.

'I can see that,' said Tia. 'I'll give you a ride home.'

She took the Ring run more slowly than Luke on that first ride, not quite flying, or perhaps Claudia was getting used to powerbikes.

Dropping Claudia off at the B-Sector entrance, Tia checked her screen.

'I can see another interrogation scheduled.' Reading on, she grimaced but didn't elaborate, instead folding her screen and putting it away. 'Claudia, whatever you're hiding, you shouldn't keep resisting. You might think you're getting the better of them, but you're not. They'll just break you. Luke's very good at interrogations. Some people have a talent for it. Don't waste yourself.'

Tia's concern seemed genuine, and Claudia had a very brief, mad moment of wanting to tell her everything because it was all too much to bear on her own.

A message came through on Tia's comms device.

'That's me,' she said. 'Got to go. Take care of yourself.'

As she snapped down her visor, Claudia noticed, for the first time, the Grade VII insignia on Tia's jacket. She was always aware of people's Ideo grade, and sub-lieutenants were usually only Grade VI at most.

If Claudia's fleeting shock had registered with Tia, she gave nothing away, her own face now hidden.

* * *

The results of the Senior Trials were going to be announced the following week. A social alert came over the system that graduating officers were meeting up in the C-Sector Youth League node for a pre-emptive celebration.

Claudia had just got out of the shower when the door buzzer sounded.

'Coming!' She quickly pulled on her clothes. If Luke had sent troopers to arrest her, she wasn't going down naked.

She wasn't thinking straight. She hadn't been sleeping very well, and when she did sleep, she fell into nightmares that cast a shadow across her waking life. Sometimes the two seemed to overlap, and she had flashbacks to things she'd only dreamed or seen on the Party Machine. This blurring was a known side effect of jenny use. Tia was right, and so was Pierce: they were messing with her head.

'Hi! I haven't seen you around for ages,' said Ally. 'I figured you'd be at the party tonight, and I thought we could go together. Like old times.'

'Yeah, sure.' Claudia stepped aside to let her in. She'd been feeling so weird and disconnected lately that the innocuous presence of Ally felt like a hug. 'Good to see you. What's up? I haven't seen anyone lately.'

The normal chit-chat came easily. Maybe she'd just been on her own too much since her mother had died, and it was nothing to do with the jennies.

She rubbed her hair dry by the ventilator outlet while Ally chattered on. 'Juanita's doing really well in the Barracks. She loves it there, says it feels like home. She'll get her blacks fairly soon. Pierce has already been promoted to full, so we'll see him in his uniform tonight.'

Claudia did not mention that she'd already seen Pierce in

full blacks. There was so much she hadn't told Ally since Martin's party.

'I think I did OK,' Ally went on. 'I mean, I never expected to go any further than Grade III, and I'm going to be assigned to Food Production, no surprise there. I might get something with the local Citizens' Brigade as my civic duty. My Game rank is strictly recreational, but that's fine. Juanita's in the MT top league, did you hear?'

'No, I didn't.' Claudia felt guilty. She hadn't seen much of Juanita lately.

'What about you? Haven't you heard anything? Have you had the tap on the shoulder?'

Ally didn't know. Nobody had told her about the special interrogations.

'Nothing yet,' said Claudia. 'But I'm pretty sure I've topped out at Grade V. My med training is ongoing. After what happened at the semi-finals, I might not even be let onto a pitch again.'

'Yeah, that was weird, Clau. But your mum had just died. Maybe they'll overlook it. You have such a good record.'

You have no freeding idea, thought Claudia, and she felt sad that there was so little she could share with Ally anymore.

The C-Sector Youth League node was already crowded when Claudia and Ally arrived. It was identical to the D-Sector node but for its reputation, furnished with table games, long benches, and low chairs and divans. Several key Ideo quotes were inscribed on the walls, alongside posters for the 30th Anniversary celebrations and the recent Senior Trials. The speakers were set to the party channel, a low but insistent background beat that matched the festive atmosphere and the quantity of visibly available synthanol. The lead-up to

Senior Trials had been long and stressful, and there was a sense of release that ramped up as more people came in, as if they were all feeding off each other, even without jennies.

'Adult citizens!' Martin waved from across the room and they went over to join him.

Arnie and Davina were there too. Claudia's heart jumped a little. If she could shake off Ally, this was her chance to talk to them. Nobody would be monitoring them amid the crush.

'Don't bother with the waste-water, have some real alcohol,' said Arnie, passing them cannies.

It was so strong that Claudia felt a glow after the first swig.

'Where did this come from?' she asked. 'This isn't the stuff you were drinking in D-Sector last time.'

'Yeah, this is the shit. He was promoted to the MT and he's running their brewhouse,' said Davina and laughed hoarsely. Claudia realised she was already drunk.

Arnie winked. 'Don't ask.'

'Pierce will probably bring some official brew as well,' said Martin. 'Whoa, I feel drunk already just thinking about how much we're all going to drink.'

Ally started to bounce up and down in time to the beats, the usual sign that she was in party mode and wanted them all to dance. Claudia figured, hazily, that after a few dances, she could draw the other three away for a discreet chat. This seemed like a reasonable plan.

A few cannies later, they were still dancing. Juanita and Mickey had joined them, along with other friends. The beats changed subtly, ramping up the mood. Claudia was aware of a dissonance in her own mood: the usual alcoholic group euphoria was undercut by something else, a dark current that pulled her down as hard as she fought to remain buoyant.

Flinging her head back as she danced, she briefly thought she saw stars on the low ceiling.

When Arnie went to fetch more drinks, she followed him. One out of three would have to do. And she wanted another drink.

'Arnie, we need to talk.'

She leaned into his ear to say this; nobody else could possibly hear, but Arnie pulled away as if she'd bitten him and shook his head.

It all came out in a garbled rush. She was even drunker than she'd thought.

'I know you're planning something. Martin hasn't told me anything, so don't worry, I don't know anything.' She grabbed his arm as he tried, again, to move away. 'The only way we can be free is to leave the Dome. We can't survive indefinitely. There's no such thing as 99%. It's a lie.'

He recoiled as if she'd kicked him in the groin. 'Clau, I know you're in a weird place right now, but you are freeding insane! What have they done to you? That's the most warped thing I've ever heard, and I've heard some weird shit.' He forcefully detached her hand, peeling back her fingers and pushing her away. 'You've lost the freeding plot.'

Nursing her fingers, Claudia leaned against the wall and watched as he rejoined the group on the dance floor. She saw Martin glance in her direction; Arnie said something in his ear and Martin's eyes went wide.

It was Ally who came and fetched her. 'Why are you all alone there? Come on, come back and join us.'

Then Pierce appeared, in his blacks, with a few other troopers. They brought some more drinks and the tempo picked up again.

'Are you on duty or are you allowed to party?' said Claudia.

'I'm not on duty,' he said.

Ally squealed and hugged him. 'You look great in your uniform! We're all so proud of you.'

At that moment, Claudia wanted to punch her.

The party deepened. Some people moved to the low couches or stood against the wall together or simply disappeared. Claudia put her arms around Pierce. She could barely stand up. He'd been drinking as well, more than usual.

'Come home with me,' she said.

He turned his face away before she could kiss him and her lips connected with his jaw.

'You're drunk.'

'So are you.'

She tried to kiss him again, but he took her by the shoulders and held her back.

'Not like this.'

It wasn't clear what happened next. She was slumped for a while on a couch next to a couple who were either getting off or not quite managing it but making all the right noises. Then she was standing in the desert again, but it was daytime and her throat was parched. Above, the sky was a pitiless blue, the sun scorching. Going Outside was freeding insane; it served her right that she was going to die.

When she finally woke up, she was on the couch in Martin's unit. Arnie and Martin were standing in the kitchenette, drinking water and talking in low voices.

With difficulty she sat up, clutching her head.

'How did I get here?'

'Special transport operation,' said Arnie. 'Just as well it wasn't far. You were completely nuked.'

The memory of Pierce pushing her away shattered through her mind.

'Where are the others? Where's Pierce?'

Martin and Arnie exchanged awkward glances.

'Sorry, Clau,' said Martin. 'He and Ally went off together.'

She ran to the kitchen sink and puked, several times. Martin rubbed her back.

Twenty-nine

The pill took effect very quickly.

'What have you given me this time?' Claudia's lips felt thick, and it was hard to form the words.

'We've had to increase the dose because you keep resisting,' said Luke. 'Stop fighting us.'

There were no prompts from the Machine. She felt herself falling, the way she'd felt walking out onto the Ring when Tia found her. Of course Tia had logged the incident. There was a watch on her. Nothing she did was hidden.

She was staring, again, at the new swipe point in the D-Sector Youth League node. How long had that been there?

Why were you trying to get into the Underground?

Dizzyingly, Claudia felt herself going down all the stairs in double time, passing door after door. Seeing the emergency exit for the compost unit, she tried to grab it and pull herself sideways out of the spiral, into the blameless zone of medical training, but the door whipped out of sight and she was in the utter darkness beyond the last exit. Lucky's green eyes blazed out of the void and she started to run, because thinking about Lucky would lead to other places.

You can't run away from your thoughts, Claudia.

She saw storage containers and modular units, all with

MNT Group painted on the side.

Lisowski's ideas on extreme and survival governance were popular with neofascists and the people who wrote the Ideology.

Jemima's voice was very clear, but her face was still hidden.

We know who wrote the Ideology, and it sure as hell wasn't God.

Claudia yanked her thoughts in the opposite direction.

Make the sheeple think.

She needed to get out of the Underground.

The narrow stairs in the backup reactor chamber went on forever and seemed to get narrower and narrower, while the space around the reactors became an abyss.

What's the Bible?

The memory of Ally's voice set off a wave of rage, pain and jealousy. She couldn't stop it. The Machine flared up under their hands.

What happened the night of the party? What's going on with you and Pierce?

She was in the Senior Youth League hall, kissing Pierce. All those feelings rushed back, overwhelming her. She couldn't hide them. And it felt so real, as if the Machine somehow had recorded that night and was playing it back to her: the smell of his sweat, the softness and taste of his mouth, the faint roughness of his jaw and cheeks, the slickness of the skin on his back as she slipped her hands under his t-shirt. Every cell in her body seemed to combust.

Except she was kissing Luke. She had her arms around his neck, and he was holding her tight against him.

* * *

'Was the dose supposed to be that high?' A man's voice, unfamiliar.

'She's put up a lot of resistance.' This was Luke. His voice sounded distant, as if he was speaking from the other end of a long corridor. 'Kate wants to keep upping the dose until she cracks, but I think we've reached the limit.'

'I agree. We don't want to damage her. She's a valuable resource.' The voice paused. 'How are you doing, Commander?'

'I had to give myself a downer,' said Luke. 'I'm feeling OK now, but I'm going to need some time out.'

'I'll tell Kate to back off. Her zeal is commendable, but she needs to respect the limits of her authority.'

When Claudia came round again, she smelled antiseptic and felt the sting of an injection in the crook of one arm. She was lying on a narrow bunk and Luke was sitting beside her. Vaguely, she thought that his technique was pretty good for a non-medic.

'It's part of the training in drugs administration,' he said.

Even in her dazed state, Claudia was sure that she hadn't spoken this aloud.

'That will wear off, don't worry,' he said. 'A temporary side effect of drug-assisted deep interrogation.'

Luke dropped the needle into a sharps waste container and held an absorbent pad over the tiny pearl of blood that welled out of her vein. He was close enough that she could smell his sweat.

The memory of the kiss blazed up. From his sudden, perturbed expression, she could tell that he was remembering too.

'Are we finished? Can I go now?' She tried to get up.

'Not in this state.' His hand on her shoulder, holding her

down, set off a shiver.

He fetched a cup of water. 'Drink.'

She drank.

'That was quite a trip, citizen,' he said, watching her. 'There's a lot you've not been telling me.'

'Are you going to send me to Re-Ed?'

'As much as Kate would like to chemically rearrange your brain for the greater good, no. That would be a waste.'

'You're protecting me from her. Why?'

His face registered a flash of anger before closing down.

'Don't try to read my mind, Claudia. I'm a lot better at this than you are.'

She met his gaze, but the quicksilver connection was gone, and it was like staring at a wall.

'You're trained to do this,' she said. 'You can block it.'

'Correct. The question is, how did you learn to do that?'

When he looked at her, she had the familiar feeling of transparency, that he was somehow looking past her eyes and into her mind. Instinctively, she parried, and felt immediately dizzy and a little ill. She fell back and put her hands over her face as if she could stop her head spinning by holding it still.

Luke took her wrist and felt her pulse. His hand was warm and firm.

'There's still a lot of jenny in your system,' he said. 'The shot should've neutralised it by now.'

Claudia opened her eyes when she heard another voice. An Oldie, a woman in medical scrubs, was standing by the bunk.

'This is Bertie,' said Luke. 'You're going to spend a night under supervision. Bertie will be keeping an eye on you.'

'Hello, kid.' Bertie looked at Claudia as if she were an interesting problem to be solved. 'Another interrogation gone wrong, oh dear me. Some very gung-ho dosing. Well, let's get you up. If you can walk, that's a good sign. Come on, Luke, you can help. I'm not putting my back out again.'

Claudia was so shocked by Bertie's casual tone that she was hardly aware of Luke lifting her to her feet. Bertie took hold of one of her arms. She was taller than Claudia, and she felt strong and solid, for an Oldie.

'Not going to fall over on me?' said Bertie.

'I'll try not to,' said Claudia faintly.

Bertie wasn't impressed. 'Luke, this is a two-person job.'

Claudia had the strangest sense that Luke was submitting to the authority of an old woman. The only insignia on Bertie's scrubs was an Ideo ranking: XX. Claudia had no idea that such a rank existed.

'Let's take the private route,' said Bertie.

Between the two of them, they half-carried Claudia to a lift at the end of the corridor. Bertie swiped and the lift went down without stopping.

Thirty

Claudia was in what seemed to be a small medical unit. There was only one other patient, a young man groaning away in a corner bed, in a foetal position.

'Don't mind him,' said Bertie. 'I call him Object Lesson. He used to be my assistant. Moral of the story: don't play around with drugs you don't understand. He's a waste of resources now, but I haven't the heart to pull the plug and I occasionally use him as a lab rat.'

Various sensors were attached to Claudia's head and chest. Her bulky frame perched on a wheeled stool, Bertie rolled herself between various machines, waving up displays and scrolling through them with brisk hand movements.

'God, I miss an old-fashioned MRI machine. The bioplastic version here is pretty good but I'd love a proper ten-tonne clanger, full of real magnets. I'd swear the image was clearer on the old model, but that's probably just sentimentality. Don't move, now, you'll bugger my picture.'

Claudia had minimal desire to move. She almost slipped into unconsciousness, but a sharp prick in one arm pulled her awake. Bertie was taking some blood and her hypodermic technique was less gentle than Luke's.

Claudia's gaze settled on the silvery insignia on Bertie's

scrubs.

'What's Level XX?' she asked groggily. 'I didn't think Ideo went up that high.'

'It means I know everything, and I'm not going to tell you anything,' said Bertie. 'Now pipe down and let's see what they've done to you. With any luck, it won't be permanent.'

'You're old to be in the MT,' said Claudia, or perhaps she just thought this; she couldn't be sure.

Bertie grinned. 'Sweetheart, I'm not in the Mentargh. I'm just useful to them. In another life, I was a doctor and a neuroscientist. Thanks to the MT, I get to continue my research, although facilities here are pretty limited.'

Neil's voice: *The shit they make here is evil.* And Jemima's: *All sorts of off-the-books research, dangerous directions.*

'So much interesting research, in the old days,' said Bertie. 'We were at a pivotal point, on the brink of an evolutionary breakthrough. Some ethical problems, lots of pushback, half-arsed attempts to regulate, except politicians didn't have a bloody clue, and the ones who had half a clue wanted in. There were plenty of governments and corporations who were more than happy to provide research and deep-cover labs for no-limits research. Mind you, a certain type of neuro-anarchist wouldn't take the money. They wanted freedom from the power, unchained human possibility, yada yada. High-minded nonsense. Went off-grid, did their own thing, backyard experiments, for fuck's sake. Me, I liked big shiny machines and state-of-the-art labs, didn't give a damn about the power; it's all the same to me. I took the money and ran with it. Lost quite a few friends that way. Hey ho.'

Claudia had no idea of where she was in the cycle when she woke up again. There was a strong smell of food. Nearby,

Bertie was eating a large portion of scrambled egg and bacon in front of several screens. The food allowance for Oldies was decreased as they aged, in line with their lower metabolic requirements, and they were usually very slight, like Jemima. Bertie was eating the serve of a man Luke's age, or even Elliot. That would explain her bulk.

'Feeling more the thing?' she said, without looking around. 'I ordered you Bertie's special breakfast. Lab-bacon was pretty well perfected back in the 2020s, but they never got eggs right. They really only work as scrambled. Eat up! You need the salt. I'll give you some supplements before I eject you.'

Claudia didn't usually like bacon, but she found herself craving more. At her screens, Bertie was sucking on the rinds until the salty, greasy essence was completely leached out. Absently, Claudia reached for the rinds on her own tray, then pulled her hand back, revolted.

Along with the supplements, Bertie gave her a special comms code to use if she had any after-effects.

'This comes straight through to me. But don't you dare ping me wanting party drugs or sleeping pills or sex pills. I'm not your dealer.'

Claudia was mystified.

'Christ, a complete innocent,' said Bertie. 'OK, forget I said that. I don't want to see you again in Bertie's private mind-lab. Now bugger off. Your ride will be here in a minute.'

She turned back to her bank of machines, as if she had found another, more interesting problem to work on.

The lift door opened. Claudia felt a surge of anticipation, but it was Tia, not Luke, who had come to take her home.

Tia didn't speak until they were out of the building.

'You look rough.' Tia's tone was entirely factual, but Claudia sensed what seemed to be concern, even criticism.

'Kate set the dose too high.'

'So I gathered.'

All Claudia's usual boundaries were down. 'What do you know about Bertie's mind-lab?'

'You need to forget about Bertie. Officially, she doesn't exist.'

Claudia stumbled slightly, and Tia grabbed her by the shoulders.

'Claudia!' Pierce ran towards her from across the quadrangle, pushing past other people. In his full blacks, he looked like any other Mentargh.

'What's he done to you? Claudia, are you alright?'

She hadn't seen him since the night of the party at the node when he had gone off with Ally.

He reached out to her, but the hurt and fury in her face pulled him up short and he stepped back.

With Tia holding her steady, she walked past him and towards the swipe gates.

Thirty-one

The beat party to celebrate the results of the Senior Trials was held in the SYL stadium. This time, Claudia went alone.

'No drugs for you tonight, that's bad luck,' said the trooper who swiped her in. There were various reasons for being designated off-drug. 'You'll have to make do with hardbrew. Get in fast before it all goes.'

She danced with Juanita and Mickey, and then with some people from her Game squad and her med cohort. Without the drugs, the music didn't have the same effect. Everyone else was going on the journey without her, and the hardbrew didn't take her to the same place. Surrounded by people, Claudia was lonelier than she'd ever felt in a crowd. She was on the outside, looking in.

She went to get another drink. Nearby, Elliot had one arm around Ally's shoulders while he talked and laughed with other troopers. Claudia caught Ally's eye, and her old friend detached herself and danced over.

'Pierce isn't here tonight. He's on duty,' she said. 'Anyway, he's all yours. We only did it once. He was thinking of you the entire time. I could tell.'

She was smiling and gyrating as she said this, but Claudia felt her bitterness, an emotional radiation that poisoned the space between them.

'Have fun with Elliot. He's more your type,' she said and went back onto the floor with a fresh drink.

She saw Martin dancing with Arnie and Davina and went to join them. Arnie immediately moved away and merged into the crowd.

'You freaked him out last time,' Davina shouted in her ear. 'He won't tell us what you said, but it must have been seriously perverse.'

Was Arnie afraid she could read his mind? Claudia remembered how he had prised her fingers away at the last party. She could feel wariness and suspicion rise off Davina and Martin even while they danced with her. They were obviously pretending that everything was normal between them, although they weren't feeling it. These negative emotions clashed with the party drugs, and she could understand why they also edged away from her. It was like moving to avoid a bad smell. Juanita was dancing nearby with Mickey, their energy completely focused on each other.

The music changed up and a different energy, more hectic, spread through the crowd. Claudia was going through the motions, but she wasn't feeling any of it, as much as she tried. The hardbrew blunted her feelings and sapped her energy. *This is a good time*, she told herself. *This is a great party, a ten-megaton blast. We are all having fun.*

Around her, the dancing suddenly seemed like pointless rhythmic jerking, as if everyone were being shocked by the same electric current, passing through them in time with the music.

Now the Senior Selection Trials were over, there was nothing more to aim for. Her peers would fulfil their assigned occupations and take part in prescribed community activities, perhaps have one or two children, if they met the genetic criteria. They would live in identical res units, wear the same clothes, and eat the same food.

Bertie's voice: *They never got eggs right.* Claudia's generation would never know the difference.

At the very end, a dutiful citizen would make the ultimate contribution: their composted remains would be recycled into the community's common resources.

They were lucky to be alive at all. This truth had been impressed upon Claudia from the very first day of Basic and to doubt it was like turning herself inside out, but another, troubling, truth had settled in: that without all the drugs and the choreographed communal events and engineered togetherness, their life in the Dome was as dead and empty as the world outside.

If it was still dead and empty.

Jemima's voice, from that first visit, as clear as if the Oldie were speaking right in Claudia's ear: *Humanity is going to die out from boredom.*

She needed to drink more, to quash these pointless thoughts. Is that why her mother had turned to roughbrew, as the only way to numb this knowledge? Had Faye chosen roughbrew over the drugs because she didn't want to unknow the truth? She had chosen to live with reality and it had been too much for her, in the end.

The thought of another drink was suddenly nauseating. The alcohol felt like lead inside her, dulling her mind and making her limbs heavy. Dancing became an effort.

A guy from her medical cohort caught her eye and danced closer. They'd done team projects together and been in the same revision cell for finals. She'd known Nic for years; he'd always been there, but always at the edge of her awareness, a friendly presence, almost brotherly in his familiarity.

All the same, she wasn't surprised when he bent down and kissed her. Accepting the kiss, she moved into his embrace.

It felt good, for a moment, and then it didn't: he was too tall and knobbly, and he tasted wrong.

'Sorry, Nic. I'm really sorry.' Claudia pulled away and headed for the exit, swimming through the crowd.

Nobody tried to make her stay. She was an alien object and the system was rejecting her, a healthy reaction, like a body vomiting up bad food.

A few troopers were standing by the exit.

'Going already?' said one.

'Too much hardbrew. I need to get home,' she said.

The trooper who had swiped her in waved her through.

'It's not the same without the jenny, is it?' he said. 'Try not to puke in a public area.'

The stadium and the surrounding buildings cast long, eerie shadows, a sign that it was a full moon Outside. Approaching the Transit station, Claudia saw two figures waiting behind a pylon. One of them was Arnie.

He saw her, and she stopped dead. Whatever he was going to do, it was better she didn't know.

With the tiniest nod, she walked on, straight to the Transit entrance, as if she'd seen nothing. From the corner of her eye, she thought she saw Arnie give one of his sly grins and wave before disappearing into the shadows.

Thirty-two

Pierce was waiting for her under the tower tree when she came out of the Med Block.

'Are you officially surveilling me?' she said.

'You're flagged in the system but no, I'm not on your case,' he said. 'Claudia, we need to talk.'

'About Ally? I heard that only lasted one round. She went off with Elliot at the beat party, so just as well you didn't have your face rearranged defending her the last time.'

She didn't intend to say any of this, but it all just came out, mean and sour, like a drink someone had spat in.

'No. Not about Ally.' Pierce looked at his feet and then over Claudia's head. 'That shouldn't have happened. I was drunk too, just not as drunk as you. Ally was all over me … that's not an excuse, and I feel bad for her as well.'

'She's made a quick recovery, so don't bother.'

He leaned in, almost as if he was going to kiss her, and spoke right in her ear.

'It's about Arnie. We need to go to a dead spot. Follow me.'

She remembered the screens in Luke's office, the tireless scanning of crowds, the tracking of faces. The Dome was one vast monitoring device, producing more visual, audio, environmental and physiological data than any human brain could process. Under the direction of humans, DOMUS learned what was important. It had been learning for thirty years.

'Is this part of your training?' she said. 'Knowing how to avoid surveillance?'

He didn't reply until they were standing by the side wall of the Science Block, which formed a narrow and deserted lane with the neighbouring annex. 'We can tell if people are avoiding being surveilled. Clear patterns emerge. Arnie was a pretty good dodger.'

'Was?'

Pierce put his hands on her arms as if to brace her. 'Claudia, he's been arrested.'

Her knees wobbled beneath her.

'I saw him at the party,' she said. 'He was leaving at the same time as me. Pierce, what's happened?'

He kept his voice low. 'He was found in the Underground with someone else. That's all I know. I wasn't involved in the operation, and I don't have the clearance to find out, but it was pretty serious. They weren't just taking a walk downstairs or brewing contraband, although he was up to his neck in that. People get up to all sorts of things in the Underground, and a lot of it is tolerated, as long as it's contained. A bunch of Oldies meeting for a chat rather than going to their community hub, not really a problem, not worth the resources. People Arnie's age, with his free-spirit profile and bad attitude, that's a problem.'

'What'll happen to him?'

'Interrogation, re-education, redeployment. If we ever see him again, he might not recognise us.'

Their cheeky, funny, defiant friend, reduced to submissive

drone-labour. It was unthinkable.

'They really do that?' Claudia whispered. It had only ever been a rumour, and she'd never actually seen any drone-labour.

'You've had a taste of it. Arnie's interrogation won't be half as gentle as yours.'

The sudden bitterness in Pierce's voice shocked her.

'They almost rewired my brain with the last dose! Luke had to call in some weird Oldie with an Ideo rank of twenty for brain first-aid.'

'There's no such thing!' Pierce's grip on her arms tightened so much that it hurt. She didn't care.

'Apparently there is.' She returned his stare. For once, she knew more than he did.

'Claudia, what happened up there? When I saw Tia bringing you down the other day ...'

He pulled her into a sudden, tight embrace. Of its own accord, her body relaxed into his as if they were designed to fit together. She felt safe. She could almost forgive him Ally.

She waited for him to kiss her, but he seemed to be crying, very low and controlled.

'Arnie's gone, the freeding idiot. I've always been afraid something like this would happen. I've warned him, so many times, stepped well over the line myself, but he never listened. He wanted to make his own choices, wherever they led. I hated that, but I had to respect it. And now you're on the line as well and there's freeding nothing I can do to help you.'

He pressed his face into her hair and held her so close that for a moment she could hardly breathe. 'What's happening with you and Luke? I know how these sessions go. There are no limits. They'll get in any way they can find.'

The memory of the kiss burst through her. She was glad Pierce couldn't see her face.

'Nothing's happened.' As she said this, she was aware of not being fully honest, with Pierce or herself. 'He's seen fragments, but I managed to block him. Anyway, I had no idea what Arnie and the others were planning.'

Pierce's hold softened. 'If they did think you were involved, you wouldn't be standing here.'

'What about Martin and Davina? Martin said he didn't know anything.'

'They're known associates, they'll be kept under surveillance. At this stage, they might not even know Arnie's been arrested. He'll just disappear. It's never announced. Claudia, you can't tell them anything. It's better that you avoid them.'

He stood back and looked her in the face. His eyes were completely dry.

'They've been avoiding me, so that won't be a problem.'

It seemed to her that Pierce resembled his brother more as he got older, even as their differences became more defined.

Whatever might have happened in that moment was crudely interrupted.

'Pierce! Cutting in on your brother in a dead spot! Bold move! I won't tell.'

Two troopers were standing on the corner. One was Byrne, the same trooper who'd been on patrol with Pierce the night of the Re-Ed centre escape. The one who had spoken was Finn, a younger version of Elliot.

Claudia and Pierce quickly moved apart.

'Freeding arseholes,' muttered Pierce.

'I should get to my afternoon shift,' said Claudia.

She walked past the two troopers, ignoring Finn's leer and

closing her face to Byrne's scrutiny. He knew she and Pierce were complicit in something, that they weren't just stealing a dead-spot moment, and this latest encounter was being added to a larger picture. Finn was merely gross; Byrne was dangerous.

Thirty-three

At the end of her session that same afternoon, Claudia went to C-Sector. Entering Building 4 of Res Block G, she walked past Martin's door without hesitation.

The door to Jemima's unit was sealed. Two diagonal strips of official tape and a further horizontal one across the door frame and a digital padlock on the keypad so it couldn't be hacked.

Claudia stared, trying to take in this new fact. Had Jemima been arrested? For what? Talking to her? Did the Mentargh interrogate old women? Or had she come to the wrong door? Without thinking, Claudia raised her hand to the buzzer, as if pressing it would summon Jemima as usual: the sound of shuffling, the click of the lock being released on the other side and the careful opening of the door, just a crack at first, a habit of suspicion formed in the Aftermath years.

'Looking for someone?'

At the far end of the corridor, she saw Elliot and another trooper. It was as if they'd been waiting.

'What's happened to Jemima?' she said as they approached, with a boldness she didn't feel.

'You'll need to ask the Commander,' said Elliot.

They walked on either side of her, all the way down to

where their powerbikes were parked, not quite touching but close enough that she was aware of their physical bulk and that she had no choice.

'Get on,' said Elliot.

His torso felt like one of the massive columns in the reactor chamber. Claudia suppressed a disturbing image of Ally lying, naked, beneath his weight.

The way to Luke's office was familiar now: the process of swiping in at the main gates, crossing the quadrangle and swiping in again at the Admin Block. This time, between Elliot and the other trooper, she felt conspicuous. As a civilian, there were only a few reasons for her to be here, and being under escort narrowed those options. People looked at her as if taking mental notes and adding her to their private watchlists. From being a blameless, dutiful Level V junior citizen with a clean record, Claudia had graduated into being a suspect adult citizen. After a certain stage, the only way back was through intensive re-education.

Seeing Luke again, Claudia was burned by the memory of the kiss.

Had it been a shared drug-dream, summoned by the pills, or had they kissed for real? She had no idea.

Maybe she'd wanted to kiss him, and the drug had dissolved all layers of self-protection, forcing her mind wide open and revealing what she hadn't even acknowledged to herself.

Had he sensed a weakness and taken advantage?

They'll do anything it takes to get in.

Claudia braced herself and got in first.

'What's happened to Jemima? What have you done to her?' she demanded.

'Citizen-Survivor Jemima Winston is dead.'

Claudia reeled.

'Did you kill her?'

She shouted without realising.

Luke seemed genuinely taken aback. 'Why would we kill her? She was ready to go any moment. She was an Oldie. Very old, actually. Over eighty. I don't think we have many left that old. She died naturally. We picked up cessation of life on the system. I went around with a special team to clear her unit. She had quite a collection. It's all been deposited in the Archives.'

Tears began to flow down Claudia's face, although she wasn't aware of crying.

'Sit down.'

Luke propelled her towards the table, where all the previous interrogations had taken place. Obediently, she sat.

'It seems she made quite an impression on you.'

Sitting next to her, he laid out the photographs on the table: the young Jemima and her husband in the rainforest; the group picture from the Chinese university; Jemima in her pink rain jacket; the two sisters at the beach. Several fat tears slid off Claudia's cheek and fell into the sea.

'You knew about all her books and pictures and you didn't do anything?' she said.

'Of course we knew about her. Professor Winston was a special case. We had orders from the very top to leave her alone. And that animal.'

'What happened to Lucky?'

'It ran away. Elliot got quite a scratch trying to catch it.'

'Good.'

Luke may have smiled; she wasn't looking. He picked up the beach photo and carefully shook off her tears.

'How did you come to talk to her?'

Was there any point trying to hide? Claudia felt herself surrender.

'At Martin's party,' she said dully. 'Jemima came to ask Martin for some milk, for Lucky. I went with her to her unit, to save her the trip back.'

'Just before we came around with the Machine?'

She nodded.

'That begins to explain things. How long did you talk to her?'

'Not long.'

'What did you talk about?'

'I saw the photographs, and I asked if things were really so bad Before.'

'And what did she say?'

'She said that we were only told half the story and that the human race was going to die out from boredom.'

Luke's face was unreadable, but she could feel a pulse of something powerful from him. Shock? Or understanding? It was as if the interrogations, especially the last one, had created a permanent connection between them.

'And you went back later, despite being Level V and knowing the dangers?'

'I was just curious ...'

'But you're told all you need to know in Ideo. Why did you want to know more? Pure individualistic curiosity?' Luke's tone was suddenly harsh. 'Kate was aware of this tendency, and she'd helped you with it, directing it in socially useful ways, but this time, you deliberately withheld information from her, putting yourself in even more danger and making yourself potentially dangerous.'

Claudia felt cold all over. Their connection was merely chemical; he was a Mentargh commander, a trained special interrogator, and all her efforts to hide had been futile. Her presumption that she'd been able to resist was pathetic. He'd been manipulating her the whole time.

Tia was right: Luke was very good at what he did.

'There was so much I wanted to ask her.' Her voice trembled. 'And now it's too late.'

'If you hadn't resisted interrogation, I could've helped you.'

She sat defeated. Vaguely, she thought of all that wasted effort training for the Senior Trials and her exams.

'What happens now? Are you going to send me off to the Re-Ed centre, like Arnie, and turn me into drone-labour?' She was so tired, she hardly cared anymore. Was this how her mother had felt before jumping off the Hydroponics roof terrace?

'How do you know what happened to Arnie?' he said quietly.

'Pierce told me.'

'Pierce should know better. And he's only a junior trooper; there's a lot he doesn't know about how things really work.'

'He didn't know about Level XX Ideo,' said Claudia. 'If you're going to send me to Re-Ed, you may as well tell me while I can still think. Before my individualistic curiosity is cured once and for all. How do things really work, Commander?'

She expected him to react to this empty bravado, but he said nothing. His expression was contained yet intense, his eyes fixed on hers.

'Do you really want to know?' he said, eventually.

'It's not as if I'll remember.' She took a jagged breath. 'How did you know about Arnie? Is it my fault? What did you see? I tried so hard to block you.'

'You did. But it's not that simple.' Luke seemed briefly pitying. 'We already knew that you and Arnie and the others, including Pierce, went down into the Underground that night. We know that you, Martin and Arnie went back. You only went two more times, but they kept going.'

'You've known the whole time?' Claudia felt as if her head were being squeezed very tightly between a pair of large, invisible hands.

'Did you really think anything is secret in this place? We've been watching Davina for a long time now, although she has protection in high places, and she knows exactly how to stay on the right side of the line. Arnie took risks. He crossed the line.'

'If you knew already, why did you interrogate me?' Claudia whispered.

'Because you were on the line. Something was going on with you that we didn't know about, and you were withholding. Kate took that quite personally.'

Claudia began to cry properly, so hard that her breath came in gasps.

Next to her, Luke was watching, waiting. Finally, he said, his voice softer, 'Stop. Claudia, stop.'

She couldn't. There was so much sadness inside her, suddenly forcing its way out.

He put one arm around her, and then the other, holding her close. She was aware of making damp spots on his t-shirt. He was big and warm, and she could feel the strong thud of his heart against her cheek.

Eventually, she cried herself out.

'Claudia, you need to trust me,' said Luke. He was still holding her and she couldn't see his face. 'I realise this might not make any sense right now, but it's part of the process. You're almost there.'

She had no idea what he meant. 'You're not going to arrest me and nuke my brain?'

He sighed and she felt his breath in her hair. 'No. That would be a waste. I'm going to consult the Commodore. It's his decision, but I'm pretty sure he's not going to nuke your brain, or whatever you think happens in Re-Ed.'

He held her for just a little longer before releasing her and then called up a junior trooper to escort her out.

Thirty-four

The summons to present herself at the Barracks at the request of Commodore Lloyd came the next morning. She wondered, briefly, what would happen if she didn't respond but simply waited in the unit, the way Faye used to go to ground when summoned by her workplace disciplinary committee. Faye had had the dubious advantage of being a roughbrew addict, which enabled her to check out of reality and ignore the passing of time. Claudia was all too aware that there was no avoiding whatever Commodore Lloyd had decided.

He was the highest visible authority in the Mentargh. Beyond that was the Directorate, formed out of the original Survival Committee. Claudia had no mental image or idea of who they were; they upheld the Ideology and entrusted the Mentargh with its enforcement.

She swiped in to the Barracks and ignored all the stares as she walked, yet again, across the quadrangle to the Admin Block. The Commodore's suite was on the top floor, and a special code was required for the lift. The lieutenant on entry duty double-checked the instructions that came up on his screen.

'I've never been to the top floor,' he said, and it seemed to Claudia that he was impressed that she'd done something to merit such an honour.

When she came out of the lift, she was surprised to see Tia waiting for her.

'What are you doing here?' she blurted.

'The Commodore is waiting.' Tia's expression was neutral, but Claudia felt strangely reassured.

Lloyd's office was claustrophobic and dim, illuminated only by shafts of light from the low ceiling. He had his back to the door as Claudia entered, his attention on several screens. In the gloom, in his Mentargh blacks, he was almost invisible.

She waited. The screens were angled so that she couldn't see whatever he was monitoring. More subversive activity? The interrogation of Arnie? Who else had been with him, whatever he was doing?

When Lloyd finally spoke, his voice seemed very loud in the silence. It was the voice she'd heard in Luke's office at the time of the overdose.

'Citizen Claudia X69-398. You're an interesting individual.'

Individual was not a compliment. Claudia stiffened.

He turned to face her. He was older than she expected, well into his thirties. Her mother's age.

'I've been looking at your record.' He picked up a tablet and swiped. 'A quiet, conscientious student … Claudia works well, but is more thoughtful than necessary … special mention must be made of her unusual grasp of the fundamental aspects of Ideology … introverted nature with individualistic tendencies … performs adequately in the Game although shows lack of genuine enthusiasm … unhealthy inclination to request more information in historical education sessions … tendency to question and even attempt to interpret elements of Ideology.' He continued to swipe. 'And then a report by Commander

Luke about a bad trip on the Party Machine, very strong reaction. That doesn't happen very often. After that, a report from Lieutenant Kate. Claudia is suspected of withholding information from her mentor, allowing aberrations to develop unchecked. Increased interaction with Junior Citizen Davina, a known free spirit. This is where the rot sets in, eh?'

He looked up, unsmiling. Claudia returned his gaze, her expression blank and submissive. There was nothing to say.

'Kate waited quite a while for you to come clean, but you didn't. There are several reports of erratic behaviour, including an unexplained out-of-place encounter with Commander Luke in D-Sector. You had no history of going to D-Sector, and suddenly, there you were. Had Citizen Davina been so influential? But you're too intelligent to be easily led. Maybe you've always had free-spirit potential and only needed to meet the wrong people to bring it out. Did Kate underestimate you? She's a skilled mentor, but perhaps it went too deep for her. And then, your mother's regrettable death.

'I knew your mother, briefly.' Lloyd's tone became almost chatty. 'We came to the Dome at around the same time. New arrivals had to go through a process of decontamination, medical checks, debriefing. Some people were too compromised to be allowed in. Faye didn't want to be chipped. I remember how she kicked and screamed. The old couple who'd brought her begged and pleaded. Eventually the medical officer had to sedate her. Even then, at seven years old, I thought, not everyone will like living here. Not everyone will fit. I was determined to survive. After what I'd seen Outside, I was ready to make any adjustment, follow any rule. To be honest, I didn't expect Faye to last as long as she did.'

He said this in a genial but impersonal way. Claudia's heart was beating very fast and she felt a little sick. She had no sense of this man at all; he was completely unreadable and he had total power over what would happen to her.

'But you're not like Faye,' he said. 'She was broken, very early. You're stronger. You've had the benefit of security and predictability. People are damaged by chaos and deprivation. That's why the efficient functioning of society is so important. You understand that, don't you, Claudia? I'd expect nothing less from an Ideo student of your calibre.'

'Yes, sir.'

'People like your friend Arnie have had the luxury of underestimating the value of security and predictability, the absence of chaos. Even people who had lived through the chaos of the Aftermath, like Jemima Winston, could still romanticise anarchy. Do you really believe that humanity will die out from boredom, Claudia?'

The question was almost sarcastic. Her tongue was glued to the roof of her mouth.

'There are worse ways to go, believe me,' Lloyd went on. 'As Professor Winston knew, very well. But old people have a different perspective on life, because they have so little of it left. It's a shame she chose not to help us. She had so much knowledge that she wouldn't share.'

'But she made all those recordings. For the Archives.' Claudia's voice was low and husky.

'She didn't tell us everything,' said Lloyd. 'Not by a long shot. She had remarkable empathic skills, which she'd developed in the years before the Event. There were networks of people all over the world, seeking a secure means of communication, an unmediated mutual understanding that reached across borders and languages. The digital universe, what people called the internet, had become completely corrupted. Parts of it were controlled by governments, corporations, political groups, data harvesters. Other parts were utterly anarchic, overrun by hackers, information pirates, criminals, terrorists of all kinds. Nobody trusted it. That's why we don't have an internet in the Dome.'

There was nothing in Level V Ideo about any of this. It didn't even sound like Ideo.

'I can see you're curious,' said Lloyd. 'Professor Winston saw that too, very quickly. She didn't need 2GenE to get into your head, and she did so much damage, just that first time. She was able to hide herself in your consciousness. Luke couldn't see her, and he's a very capable interrogator. But the Party Machine picked up the anomaly right away.'

Was Lloyd reading her mind too now? The ceiling seemed to get lower and the dimness intensified.

'Your sessions with Commander Luke were … very interesting. Even at the high dosage, you were able to resist. That's quite rare. It does show a very strong level of individual will. A shame that the dosage was … miscalculated. Otherwise we could have continued the process, gone deeper. We almost found Jemima Winston. The old images were very powerful, and their emotional impact, which she shared with you, was hard to conceal.'

'What's going to happen to me?' Even to ask seemed presumptuous, but she was already completely exposed.

'You're very intelligent, and it would be a shame not to harness that intelligence for the common good,' said Lloyd. He put the tablet down and came around the desk to stand in front of her. He wasn't an especially tall man, but he was heavyset, like Elliot, and his lack of expression made him all the more threatening.

'But there is the matter of your divergent thinking, your individual curiosity and will.' Lloyd let this hang for a few moments. 'You were assigned to the medical stream and you've done well in your training so far. I'm sure you'll be a conscientious and effective medical technician. But we could make better use of your abilities. How would you feel about that?'

'I will contribute to the efficient functioning of society in whatever way is required.'

Claudia directed her gaze over his shoulder to the blank screen behind. She had the sensation of balancing on the edge of something very high with nothing to stop her falling. Like Faye on the Hydroponics roof terrace, after she'd climbed over the barrier.

'Correct answer. That's exactly what I would expect from a Level V Ideo student. I know you're saying this because you think you have no choice. The fact is, you do.'

Claudia's eyes went involuntarily to his face. His skin was very pale and smooth. In the Old World, she had learned, people used to suffer premature ageing from sun damage.

'There, that got your attention. Ideology has its purpose, but sometimes we need to have a real conversation, especially at your level,' said Lloyd. 'You could continue your med training as a regular citizen, perhaps fighting against your curiosity and doubts—of course you have doubts, Luke felt your ambivalence very clearly—and probably falling in with a free-spirit crowd, now you know where to find them. As do we, by the way. Or you could pursue your individualistic curiosity in a more contained and socially useful way.'

She still didn't understand. The ground beneath her feet seemed to slip away.

'You see, Claudia,' he went on in a new, intimate tone, 'people of your age and level reach a critical stage. We refer to it as the crisis point, the crucial junction between giving in to subversion or overcoming one's doubts to become a loyal and valuable citizen. Subversion exerts a very potent and profound influence on young, malleable minds, as you have already learned. Professor Winston did us a favour, by providing that experience. Thanks to her, you'll have a unique advantage in studying the higher levels. One day, you could even be a very good interrogator.'

Claudia's disbelief was instant and irrepressible.

'You're going to promote me into the MT?'

He was watching her very closely.

'It would entail the strictest supervision and guidance, as well as hard work on your part, Claudia, but reaching the higher grades is always worth the effort. You'd have access to the Archives.'

'But ... the Selection Trials ...'

'Do you really think we hold the Trials to choose our Mentargh? Come on, now, Claudia,' said Lloyd. 'You're smarter than that. We need people with your insight in the MT, not outside it. We've always known about your divergency issues, and we knew you'd been down in the Underground. We needed to see how far you'd go. Your ambivalence, correctly harnessed, is an asset. You understand that Ideo is necessary for our survival, as the situation stands, but you can also think beyond it. Your friend Arnie and his companions simply wanted to undermine it, even destroy it. We wouldn't have survived the first year in the Dome without that level of control. Not even six months! Some people couldn't accept that, and authorities at that time had to let them go.'

'You mean, they were … ejected?'

'For the greater good,' said Lloyd. 'I know the Ideo says the Dome has been sealed since the Exodus, but the situation was actually quite fluid for the first year or so. This is the kind of delicate detail you'll learn at the higher grades. We're far less wasteful of our human resources these days. We certainly don't want to waste you.'

He seemed to be waiting, and then he said, 'I take it that's a yes?'

He fitted something tightly around her left arm. It was a black armband.

'You'll continue your med training, as Tia has done, alongside MT training and higher Ideo, which is all done within the Barracks. Two of your cohort are already with us—Pierce, Juanita—so you won't be on your own. Not that anybody is ever on their own in the Dome, certainly not in the Barracks.'

Claudia was too stunned to reply.

Lloyd stepped back. 'Citizen Claudia, I hereby invest you as a prospective Mentargh cadet-trooper.'

It took her a moment to return his salute.

'I'll inform Commander Luke,' he said. 'He's been waiting to hear my decision, with some impatience, I believe. You'll be serving under him, but you'll report to Sub-Lieutenant Tia. She'll be your mentor now. I think the relationship with Kate has run its course, don't you?'

As she left, he said, his back already turned, 'By the way, Ideo only goes up to Level XVIII. Bertie likes to think she's cleverer than everyone else, so we indulged her.'

Thirty-five

Tia was waiting to escort her down.

'Congratulations, Prospective Cadet-Trooper!' she said. 'I don't think you were expecting that.'

How much did Tia know?

'Aren't you working with Ash anymore?' Claudia asked.

'That was a kind of probation,' said Tia, shrugging. 'Ash has found his natural level. I haven't. And neither have you.'

There was so much more Claudia wanted to ask.

'We can talk more later,' said Tia. 'First, we're going to move you out of that grim little res unit and into the Barracks. You'll be in the same res block as one of your cohort, Juanita.'

Dazed and disoriented, Claudia hardly took in what Tia was saying. She waited as Tia adjusted her permissions at one of the consoles in the Admin Block lobby and entered requisitions for new bedding and clothing packs.

'You now have access to the gym, the canteen, the rec hall, the study block, all the basics. Most levels of the Admin Block are still off-limits, and other places,' said Tia. 'I'll send the training timetable through to you. You won't have a problem with Basic. Most people on it are only Grade IV.'

Tia accompanied her to the distro for a bedding and clothing pack, and then across the quadrangle to one of the

MT residential blocks.

'The junior units are on the small side, but there's a common area on each floor. You'll be a lot less isolated,' she said.

The unit was a single-person pod, with a bunk, a tiny kitchenette, a shower, toilet and a small table. It was otherwise bare, with no sign of any previous occupant. The ventilation was on full, and there was a very faint smell of disinfectant.

One window looked out on the quadrangle. The shift-change had just sounded and Claudia could see figures in black and grey moving between the buildings.

'It feels strange at first, I know,' said Tia, following her gaze. 'But you're better off in here, believe me. Leaving you in the family unit after your mother died wasn't one of Kate's better decisions, and she's made some bad ones lately, I hear.'

'I haven't seen her for ages,' said Claudia.

'She was taken off your case a while back,' said Tia. 'Anyway, I'll do your full induction in two days' time. Go over to your old unit, get your stuff and come home. Why don't you try out the gym tomorrow? There's also an MT Game on in the afternoon, an inside match, although I know you're not a massive fan.' She grinned briefly. 'Neither am I, to be honest, but it's all for the greater good and the smooth functioning of society.'

Was she making a joke? Claudia wanted to trust her, but she was too confused.

* * *

Getting off the Transit at the B-Sector stop, Claudia couldn't decipher her own feelings. She'd lived in B-Sector with Faye all her life, in the same unit, with its fluctuating chaos and reek of roughbrew. The wall by her bunk was discoloured by the press of her body over the years; the drinking water outlet in the kitchenette dripped and had defied all attempts to fix it. This had been her home.

She didn't have much to take away. Some people displayed printed victory tokens from the Game. Juanita had a whole collection. Very rarely, people had personal items or mementoes from Before. Things brought in from Outside during the Exodus had often contained dangerous levels of contaminants and had been destroyed, or they'd been confiscated and stored in the Archives. Materially, every citizen of the Dome was equal and imbalances were not permitted.

Claudia still didn't understand how her superior MT-issue trainers fitted in to this basic ideological precept. But it didn't matter anymore: in the Barracks, everyone would have the same ones.

A Sanitation Team would remove and recycle the bedding and kitchenware, do a full decontamination and carry out any repairs. *Good luck to them fixing the tap*, thought Claudia.

Her athswear, base layers, personal hygiene kit, Ed tablet and remaining dry snack rations took up all the space in her backpack, but there was nothing else to take. Unlike Lisa, she didn't have fifty pairs of shoes.

Lisa would not have taken part in whatever Arnie had planned on the night of the Senior Trials beat party. Did the MT know about her? Had they even cared that she baked unauthorised biscuits on the side and met other Oldies in the Underground? No such meetings would take place for a while, at least not down there.

Claudia had no idea where in the Dome Lisa lived and worked. She hoped she was safe, and still making biscuits.

The door buzzed. Was it the local Citizens' Brigade leader, come to congratulate her on her promotion? Claudia's main dealings with her neighbours had been to apologise when Faye tried to bash her way into the wrong unit at odd hours of the cycle or vomited in the common spaces.

Was it Luke?

'Tia told me the news,' said Pierce. 'She said I should come over and help you.'

'There's nothing to do,' said Claudia, gesturing to her pack, which was sitting on the table. 'I've never moved before. That's my whole life, in that bag.'

'Like the Exodus,' said Pierce.

'Do you think they'd let me into the Barracks if I turned up with a shopping trolley full of stuff?' said Claudia.

They both fell about laughing. A shopping trolley was inherently ridiculous: a large, wheeled basket used in the collection and purchase of consumer goods, which were then unloaded into motorised vehicles and conveyed back to residential units. Large cold units and lots of storage space were required to house all the food and durables that people used to acquire and then throw away.

Many of the refugees who found their way to the Dome in the Aftermath had arrived with shopping trolleys laden with belongings. Many of these items were useless and merely sentimental, but people had been so attached to material possessions Before that they had been unable to give up what pathetic remnants they had left.

When Claudia and Pierce had first learned about the Exodus in Basic, the very simple version taught to children, the idea of a shopping trolley, the mere sound of the words, had made them so hysterical that their instructor had banished them to separate quiet spaces to calm down. They were usually very good students, but that afternoon they'd been out of control.

Years later, the words *shopping trolley* were still hilarious.

'Imagine their faces at the swipe gates!' said Pierce.

Claudia mimed pushing a shopping trolley, or what she thought this would look like.

Pierce put his arms around her, his body still clenching with laughter.

'Clau! I've been so worried about you. It was bad enough that you were hanging out in D-Sector with Davina and the others, and when Faye died, you went into self-destruct mode. And then you were called into those interrogations. Luke wouldn't tell me anything. I wanted to freeding punch him.'

And then they were kissing, hard, and they were back where they'd left off the night of the Junior Trials party. She tried to pull off his t-shirt at the same time as he was pulling off hers, and they almost got tangled, and then the t-shirts were underfoot and she was pressing herself against his bare torso as he undid her trousers and she stepped out of them.

The only male bodies she'd seen naked were patients, sick or injured men submitting to inspection by trainees like herself as they underwent treatment. If she glimpsed a penis, it was shrunken and soft, a harmless appendage, especially if it was attached to an Oldie.

When Pierce took off his shorts, his penis sprang out, hard and upright, curving slightly to one side.

'Well, hello,' she said, suddenly shy.

'Hello.' He grinned and pulled her in close again. His penis poked against her stomach as he kissed her.

They stumbled, locked together, to her little bunk. In their impatience, he almost fell on her, banging one knee on the side of the bunk. He took his weight on his elbows as she adjusted herself beneath him. Then he was inside her.

The shock and joy of it made her cry out.

'Am I hurting you?'

'No! Don't stop.'

She held his face as he cried out. Up so close, his dark eyes were as opaque as ever, but she could see flecks of brown.

They lay fitted together, one body. She felt a little raw. When she put her hand between her legs, there was some blood, but only a little, much less than if she was starting her period. She wondered if Ally had bled much, and if Pierce had been her first time, and then quickly dismissed those thoughts.

Pierce reached out and touched the blood on her fingers. All physical boundaries between them had dissolved.

'Everyone in the Barracks just assumed that Luke's been doing it with you,' he said. 'Freeding arseholes like Finn, giving me crap the whole time about special interrogations. I couldn't bear it. But I'd been such a dick, and then I'd gone off with Ally, so it would've served me right.'

'Luke's jealous of you,' said Claudia. The knowledge came to her suddenly. 'That's what I felt from him, especially in the last interrogation. He's jealous of our friendship, that we can trust each other. Does he even have any friends?'

'He and Kate had a thing for a while, but I wouldn't call them friends,' said Pierce. 'That's too warm and cosy for either of them. Maybe one day they'll hatch Mentargh babies and deposit them in a childcare hub. They're not really the family type. Commodore Lloyd would have to order them to reproduce, for the common good. Luke isn't close to anyone. I should know.'

'That's sad.'

As she said this, Claudia realised that all her sessions with Luke had created attachment as well as insight. She was aware of his loneliness, and she felt sorry for him. How long would it take to wear off? That was not something she could ask Pierce.

He fell asleep, quite suddenly, his breath soft against her cheek. One of his arms lay, very heavy, across her chest. How could an arm be so heavy?

Claudia's mind and body were thrumming. She felt abandoned.

'The Sanitation Team is coming around later.' She shook him. 'Wake up! If we don't move on, we'll be put out for recycling as well.'

After disentangling herself, she went into the kitchen and drank some water. He came up behind her, his feet padding on the floor. She felt his hot, bare body pressed against her back as he reached for the cup, drank deeply, and passed it back to her.

He put his arms around her and kissed her shoulders and neck.

'I'm awake now.'

He lasted a bit longer this time. She shuddered and melted inside. He collapsed against her, bracing himself against the wall. She pressed her face against his chest, inhaling him.

If the people next door were at home, they probably heard, Claudia thought, but she was never going to see them again.

'We really need to go,' she said, her face muffled against his chest. 'The Sannies could come any minute.'

They tried to get dressed, but they kept touching and kissing, and eventually they gave up and fell onto the divan together.

****

Pierce had come across on a powerbike. When he rode back through the Barracks vehicular entry, the boom gate lifted automatically to let them pass. Claudia was on the system; she belonged in the Barracks now.

The garage area had vehicles she'd never seen: four-wheeled buggies and closed-in transports with tiny windows and big tyres.

Pierce found a space for the bike and plugged it in to recharge.

'You'll have to learn to ride now. That's one fun perk of being in the Mentargh,' he said.

They stood kissing by the helmet rack until some other troopers came by and jeered and made rude comments and gestures.

'Not so fun: the dickheads who live here,' said Pierce.

This was his world, which had been hidden from Claudia all the years she'd known him. And now she was part of it too.

'Show me your new place,' said Pierce, and they held hands as they walked across to the res blocks, not caring who saw them.

Thirty-six

After the strange, lonely lull around the Trials, Faye's death and her interrogations, Cadet-Trooper Claudia-398 began a new, busy and regimented life that took up where Senior Youth League had left off.

Her days were divided between Mentargh basic training, her ongoing medical studies and Grade VI Ideo sessions, along with physical training and participation in one of the lower-ranked MT Junior Game teams. She built up an image of herself as a studious, inconspicuous cadet. Her aptitude for Ideo, if not the Game, earned her a certain respect. Whatever the rumours—and the Barracks was a hothouse of rumours— about her former free-spirit connections, the fact of the special interrogations by Commander Luke and personal promotion by Commodore Lloyd put her in a different category to obvious recruits like Juanita.

Claudia was still the same person, with the same ambivalence, the same individualistic curiosity, but the Mentargh, an organisation she had feared for most of her life, had absorbed her regardless, for its own purposes, and she wasn't sure what this said about her. She was uncomfortably aware of the ease with which, as a one-time individualist and divergent thinker, she now fitted in to the Mentargh, adopting its habits and lingo, absorbed into its military camaraderie, but she didn't have the time to ponder this too deeply.

And there was Pierce. Claudia had never been aware of being unhappy before, but now she was happy, a simple, almost stupid contentment that minimised everything else. The truth about the Dome's future was a distant fact, and she lived entirely in the present. Every morning she woke up in his bunk, or he woke up in hers, unless he had an overnight shift, and they had breakfast together before going their separate ways, and then they met again in the evening, during training or afterwards, and went to the canteen to eat or to the junior common room and ended the day together.

While she was assigned to Luke's command, he had no involvement in the day-to-day activities of a mere cadet-trooper. She sometimes saw him across the quadrangle or in the bike hangar or in the gym, and he would acknowledge her with the faintest nod, but there was no reason for him to speak to her and he didn't. Often, she was with Pierce, a fact Luke always seemed to note, although his expression never changed. She never saw the brothers interact. Luke was a commander and Pierce was only a junior trooper; they had lived in the Barracks all their lives and their respective ranks seemed to have superseded their blood relationship. Claudia had no relations left, and the very notion of siblings was alien to her.

Before Pierce, her closest relationship had been with her cohort and perhaps with Kate. She'd only seen Kate once since moving into the Barracks, in the canteen queue, and Kate had smiled and asked how she liked being in the MT and said how proud she was of Claudia. The conversation had been so horribly fake that Claudia felt stupid for ever trusting

Kate at all.

She didn't see much of Juanita, who was in a different stream and was already going out on regular patrols. Juanita was genuinely pleased by Claudia's promotion but also confused.

'I never thought of you as a Mentargh type,' she said. They were in the gym change rooms together, where everyone wore the same trainers. 'I mean, you're super-smart and good at Ideo, but you were also a bit of a free spirit.'

By Juanita's standards, being a free spirit could mean having less than the required enthusiasm for the Game.

'I was pretty surprised as well,' said Claudia. 'But I guess they know what they want.'

'I suppose you're not friends with that weirdo Davina anymore. She was really down on the Mentargh.'

Claudia had glimpsed Davina and Martin going in and out of the Science Block a few times. Davina's expression, on seeing her black band, had been one of shock, followed by pure venom. Martin's was simply shock. Did they blame her for Arnie's capture?

'No, we're not friends anymore,' said Claudia. 'Did you hear about Arnie?'

Juanita looked troubled, as if thinking about Arnie was too difficult.

'I heard that he was arrested. That's all. I know he was a free spirit, that he was involved in some dodgy stuff and hung around with the wrong people, the D-Sector crowd. But he's not a bad person. I'm sure there were good reasons for arresting him. They'll sort him out with some Re-Ed, and we'll see him around again, same as ever, maybe just a bit quieter.'

She did not sound entirely convinced.

'I hope so,' said Claudia.

'And that Davina made things worse. I wish Martin had never invited her to his party. I blame her. We were all doing fine before she came along. I'm keeping an eye on her. She's mine,' said Juanita.

Saying this, she sounded exactly like some of Claudia's new peers, the kind she liked least, the fanatical ones who revelled in their new status, swaggering about in their grey or black uniforms and seeing subversion everywhere. Suspects and possible suspects were chattily discussed during coffee breaks and rec periods. Even old friends were kept under scrutiny, suddenly acquiring subversive traits as the recruits acquired new theory.

Juanita was unlikely to progress beyond Level IV or V, but she didn't need new theory to know something was not right about Davina.

Claudia only spoke to Ally once. She was sitting alone in the MT canteen, looking glum. It was not unusual to see civilian girls around the Barracks, ones who'd been taken up—'special recruits'—by older guys in the Mentargh. They appeared at the swipe gates at certain shift-changes and headed straight for the res blocks. To go anywhere else in the Barracks, they had to be accompanied.

'Has Elliot abandoned you?' This came out in a way Claudia didn't intend.

'Something came up and he was called out.'

Claudia saw a large tray of half-eaten food in the space next to Ally. Elliot's calorific requirements were impressive.

'I can show you out. When you're ready. If you want.'

'Thanks.' Ally smiled wanly.

Claudia softened. She sat down next to Ally with her cup of coffee.

'How are things with you and Pierce?' Ally asked. 'I never really expected that anything would happen between me and him. It's always been you two, but it took you freeding ages to get it together.'

'Well. Yeah. I know.' Telling Ally that she was deliriously happy seemed cruel. 'Things are pretty good.'

Ally nodded and poked at her own breakfast. She wasn't eating much.

'How are things with you and Elliot?' said Claudia. 'I mean, it wasn't an obvious thing, and he's always seemed a bit of a … thug. But maybe he's different when you get to know him.'

Ally took a few moments before speaking, as if getting her words in order first.

'Is it supposed to hurt when you do it?'

'Uh, maybe a little the first time, but not generally. Why?'

'It didn't hurt when I did it with Pierce, but that was only the once. Maybe there's something wrong with me. You're a med tech, should I get checked out?'

Claudia winced. In the old days, she and Ally used to share this kind of detail. She would've told Ally about the cystitis she'd developed within a week of moving into the Barracks. She'd asked Tia for meds rather than going to the clinic.

Tia had grinned. 'I know you and Pierce are making up for lost time, but you need to take a few days off.'

Claudia's face burned just remembering.

Her eyes shifted from Ally's uneaten breakfast to the bruises on Ally's wrists. Ally quickly pushed her sleeves down as far as they would go, which wasn't very far. Clothing was printed according to individual specs and came with very little extra fabric.

'What happened, Ally?'

Ally wouldn't look at her. 'He can be a bit … rough sometimes. He doesn't always realise his own strength.'

'Ally, that's awful!'

'I like him. He makes me feel safe.'

'From what?'

'I don't want any more of this.' Ally pushed her tray away. 'Can you show me out now?'

After that, when she saw Ally around the Barracks, her old friend avoided her.

* * *

Even as life in the Barracks and the working of the Mentargh became normal to her, Claudia learned new things that still had the power to disturb her. One was combat training. This took place in a dedicated hall in the gym building. As a recruit with a civilian profession, Claudia was taught only basic self-defence and control and restraint techniques, not the full operational skillset. She wasn't destined for regular patrols and front-line duty. Full-timers like Pierce and Juanita did more intensive physical training. Pierce often had bruises all over his body and Juanita appeared one lunchtime in the canteen with a monstrous black eye, which earned her a round of applause.

Sometimes Claudia saw this training in action, on the far side of the combat hall. She was used to seeing physical clashes as part of the Game, but the concentrated, precise violence of hand-to-hand combat unnerved and even horrified her. The training included the use of tactical batons, which she'd only ever seen hanging off Mentargh belts. One time, she witnessed a recruit called Bee, a girl not much bigger than Claudia, setting about the trainer, who was wearing a padded suit.

'C'mon, little girl, I can hardly feel it. Stop tickling me!' he taunted her.

By the end, Bee was thrashing him as if fighting for her life, the sweat streaming off her.

'That's more like it, good girl.'

Claudia was watching from the sidelines. When he finished the session and took off the protective suit, she could see the red marks up and down his arms. Her shock seemed to please him in some obscure way.

'Don't fancy a round yourself?' he said. 'I could do this all day.'

Some MT full-timers regarded parallels like Claudia as not quite the real thing.

She hated seeing the bruises on Pierce's body.

'It doesn't hurt at the time,' he told her. 'They give us meds to block the pain.'

They were lying together in his bunk. She gently traced the outline of a large yellow and purple bruise on one of his thighs.

'That's horrible. Who are you training to fight, anyway? The average citizen is pretty placid. I mean, the drugs are very efficient.'

Sometimes, now that she was a Mentargh herself, she was appalled by the words that came out of her own mouth.

'There are always exceptions,' said Pierce. 'Some people

resist the drugs. This is classified, but we think people are trying to make counter-drugs. A while back, a patrol picked up a guy who was out of control. He was berserk. The meds thought he'd had too much roughbrew, but when they ran tests, it turned out that he'd taken something that was supposed to counter the usual civic dose but had sent him crazy instead. Stimulated or blocked the wrong receptors or something. It's way over my head. Trying to develop that kind of highly sophisticated drug without the proper equipment or knowledge is like doing brain surgery with a spoon.'

They'd taken him to Bertie's mind-lab, thought Claudia. She could imagine, very clearly, the Oldie's pleasure at being presented with such an interesting problem. She did not mention to Pierce that she had managed to resist the drugs herself.

'And what kind of person volunteers—if he even volunteered—to be a lab rat for a homebrew drug?' Pierce went on. 'There are some scary people out there, Claudia.'

They never referred directly to Davina and her friends in the Underground, even when they were alone together, but there was no need.

'What happened to him?'

'I don't know.' Pierce held her closer, despite all his bruises. 'Maybe they had to just wipe and recycle. They had to use critical force against him, so maybe there wasn't much to work with anyway.'

Had Arnie been involved with such experiments? Was Davina?

Claudia's heart froze. 'It wasn't Arnie, was it?'

'No. No, it wasn't. I couldn't have—I wouldn't have said anything if it was. Claudia, I shouldn't be telling you this stuff.

You're not cleared for it yet. You need to forget it.'

What else did he know that he didn't tell her?

She hadn't told him about Jemima Winston. Their conversations were locked away in a separate part of her mind, along with the terrifying knowledge that their golden future inside the Dome was a dead end, and the equally shocking possibility of life Outside.

If there was nothing to be done, she would've been better off not knowing, like everyone else, and living in drug-assisted contentment. Her own presumptuous curiosity had led her astray. It served her right for wanting to know the unknowable.

If she shared such heresy with Pierce, would he report her? Claudia didn't want to know the answer.

How much had Luke seen? What did he know?

'Don't think about it. I can feel you thinking.'

Pierce started to kiss her.

* * *

Martin and Davina were standing near the entrance to the Central Zone Transit station, by one of the pylons. As usual, Davina glared at her and then right through her.

Instead of walking by, Claudia stopped.

'Hello, citizens.'

'Do you want to swipe us, Cadet-Trooper?' Davina held out her wrist.

'I'm a med tech. I don't do swipe checks. Anyway, you're in place.'

She found herself enjoying the effect of this language on Davina, but not on Martin.

'You're one of them now, Claudia.' He looked at her as if he no longer recognised her.

'I'm still me. And I didn't know anything about Arnie.'

Their position by that particular pylon was a dead spot. Claudia had learned to be aware of citizens who repeatedly loitered in dead spots.

'You really expect us to believe that?' sneered Davina. 'All those special sessions with Luke. Horizontal interrogation by Pierce's big brother. I suppose Pierce had to go along with that, for the greater good.'

Davina's crudity was more hurtful than the insinuations that still crept around the Barracks, having superseded the rumours about Ash and the new trainers.

'It wasn't like that! They almost wiped me,' said Claudia.

'I don't believe you betrayed Arnie,' said Martin. 'You didn't know anything. But I can't believe you're in the freeding Mentargh, Clau! Even with your Ideo rank, I never thought of you as one of them. Not like Pierce and Juanita.'

'I don't know that I am one of them,' she said. 'It's not like I had a choice.'

Davina scoffed. 'The MT don't recruit free spirits.'

'My old mentor, Kate, used to be a free spirit,' Claudia retorted.

'And now she's hardcore,' said Davina. 'They turned her. That's how it works. My granddad warned me about that. Never trust an MT, especially anyone who tries to convince you that they're still the same, that there's a subversive network inside the MT. It's all crap. They're just out to trap you.'

'A subversive network in the MT? That's the first I've heard,' said Claudia. Of all her new peers and colleagues, there was not a single person whose loyalty was in doubt, including Pierce. 'That's insane.'

'Yeah, well that's one thing we can agree on,' said Davina. 'Anyway, you can't change the system from within. You need to break it from outside.'

'Break it?'

'Claudia, you're smart, you're curious, don't you want to know the truth?' For a moment, it seemed that Davina was speaking to her properly, without the intervening static of distrust and hatred. 'Don't you want to be free?'

'What does that even mean?'

'To not have every aspect of our lives monitored and controlled! To be able to access the Archives and learn about Before, to ask questions, to find out what really happened, not the freeding mental goo-stew they feed us. To make choices about your own life. Imagine not having to play the freeding Game to prove you're a good citizen! Imagine not having a freeding implant rammed up you at age sixteen, regardless of what you want to do with your body.'

Claudia's heart was beating so fast that anyone monitoring her body stats at that moment surely would've noted the anomaly, since she wasn't scheduled for training.

'But as long as we live in the Dome, we need this level of control,' she said. 'It's an extreme finite, restricted area, and the slightest imbalance in the equilibrium could cause the whole artificial biosystem to collapse. There's no margin for individual divergence.'

'Thanks for the lecture on Level I Ideo, but I did pass Basic,' said Davina, her voice scornful again.

'The Ideo system is the only way of life possible within the Dome. To survive, society requires a high degree of organisation and control. To replace the system with something similar to the free-anarchy societies of the Old World would be disastrous. What I'm trying to get through to you'—Claudia glared back at Davina—'is that we can't have what you call freedom inside the Dome. And even if we did, and somehow maintained the equilibrium, we'd still be eating lab-food designed for outer space and wearing the same clothes and living the same drab, minimalist kind of existence.' She didn't even know where the words *drab* and *minimalist* came from. 'Yeah, I'd love not to play the freeding Game ever again, and maybe I'd like more than two pairs of shoes at a time, but as long as we live in the Dome, I can't have that.'

'Did you just say what I think you're saying, Clau?' Martin gave her an almost scared, sideways look. 'That night at the node party, whatever you said to Arnie totally freaked him out. He said you'd lost the plot. He said you'd gone crazy, like old Jemima down the hall.'

'Did you know she died?' said Claudia.

'For real? I haven't seen her around for ages, but I didn't think—' Martin seemed ashamed.

'She wasn't crazy. Not at all. She used to be a climate scientist. We had some pretty interesting conversations. Actually, there's a chance it's not completely dead Outside. That's what I was trying to tell Arnie.'

Martin and Davina recoiled visibly, as if Claudia had a highly infectious and deadly disease.

'That's as freeding crazy as it gets!' said Davina.

'You think you're such a subversive, but you're as stuck in

the Ideology as the rest of us! You're trapped in Dome-think and you can't think outside that!' It took all Claudia's self-control not to shout. Instead, she hissed. The look of horror on Davina's face was almost worth the mad risk of sharing this terrifying knowledge.

'So what do you suggest, Cadet-Trooper?' Davina's tone was acid. 'That we leave the Dome? Is this an MT plan to get rid of free spirits—lure them out for a look? Quite a few people were kicked out the door in the early days. My granddad was almost one of them.'

Claudia looked at her levelly. 'The Dome's capacity to regenerate is finite. Ask Neil. We only have a generation left. At some point, we'll need to take a look Outside.'

'And they let you into the MT? Holy freeding hyper-fuck.' Was there a brief glint of admiration in Davina's eyes, or did Claudia imagine it? 'And how are we meant to do that? Rock up to Commodore Lloyd and ask for the back door code? Hey, Lloyd, mate, we just want to pop outside for a breath of fresh radioactive air and get instant skin cancer? If we're not fried on the spot.'

'Clau, what did they do to you?' said Martin in a low voice. 'Whatever Luke did to your brain in those interrogations, you've lost it. Pierce wouldn't tell me, but I know something bad happened to you in the last session. You looked like hell. He thought you were gone.'

'Life's a bit boring in here, but I don't want to die just yet,' said Davina witheringly. 'At least if I get wiped and recycled trying to make things better inside, it won't be for nothing. Walking out into a radioactive wasteland isn't going to solve anything, except ridding the Mentargh of antisocial elements, and I'm not going to do them the favour.'

'Whatever you have planned isn't going to solve anything either, except giving them a reason to tighten up to Control Level Six,' said Claudia. 'Yeah, this is the stuff I learn now. We're only at Level Two now, cruising along. We'll go up to Level Four around the time of the Anniversary, just to be on the safe side. Existential threats justify Level Six. That's pretty tight. No moving out of place, no biscuits in the Underground, no free-brewing. Life would be more *boring* than you can even imagine.'

She hated the way they both looked at her now, and she hated the sense of power that came with being able to frighten them.

'Freed, Claudia,' said Martin. 'You sound like one of them.'

'She always was,' said Davina. 'Jim was stupid to trust her. I never did. Luma was right.'

'Luma is the crazy one! She tried to kill me in the change rooms!'

'Yeah, I heard about that. Too bad Juanita got in the way.'

Did Davina really mean it?

'Whatever you're planning, it's going to fail,' said Claudia. 'What you think they know, it's only a pixel of the whole picture. Do you want to end up wherever Arnie has ended up? I don't know, but it's not good. I don't want that to happen to you.'

'Yeah, that's what Pierce kept telling us,' said Martin. His voice hardened. 'You *are* one of them now.'

'What does Mentargh Boy think about all this?' said Davina. 'Can't be good for his career, snuggling up to these sorts of wacko ideas.'

Claudia was silent.

'You haven't told him, have you?' said Martin.

She almost felt she'd won his trust again, and then Davina spoke.

'Don't be sucked in, Martin. She's manipulating us. Who knows what she really told Arnie, or Luke, or anyone? Pierce's probably in on it, and big brother too, really cosy, all in the family. Come on, let's go, before she tries any more mind-games. Anyway, being seen with a Barracks scrubber, a freeding MT *special recruit*, is bad for my reputation in D-Sector.'

This final insult was too much for Claudia.

'It's fine for you to play at being a subversive, when your granddad's old mates are still looking out for you!' she spat. 'Arnie didn't have that protection! If it's anyone's fault he's gone, it's yours! You got him into it!'

'What the fuck are you talking about?' Davina went white and stepped right up to Claudia.

'Go on, then, have a go. Finish what Luma started.' Claudia braced herself. Even with her recent combat training, she wasn't confident that she could defend herself against Davina's superior bulk, but she didn't care.

'Don't you freeding dare talk about my grandfather!'

Claudia could feel Davina's moist, slightly rancid breath on her face.

'What deal did he make to keep you safe all this time? What did he tell them before he croaked?' This possibility voiced itself even as Claudia thought it.

'Davina, leave it.' That was Martin. He put a hand on her shoulder and pulled her back, and she let him, her eyes still fixed on Claudia.

'We're done, Trooper,' she said, her voice cold and dead. 'I don't know you. From now on, we're strangers.'

She shook off Martin's hand and walked away, leaving Martin and Claudia facing each other.

'I thought she was going to kill you for a moment there,' he said.

'Would you have let her? I'm a Barracks scrubber, I deserve it.' She spoke in the same dead tone as Davina.

'Stop it! Freed, Claudia, what's happening to us? I hate it.'

'But do you believe me, just a bit?'

Martin closed his eyes briefly before replying. 'I wish I could trust you, Clau, but I can't. I don't think you're out to get us. They've nuked your brain. Old Jemima was crazy, and now so are you. I'm losing everyone I care about, and I don't know what to believe anymore. I feel like I'm going crazy too.'

As she watched him walk away, she saw that she was being watched too: Byrne was standing by the entry to the Transit station with another trooper, doing swipe checks. Meeting his gaze, she saluted him coolly. After the merest pause, he saluted back.

* * *

One evening when Pierce was on a night shift and she was sitting on her bunk, reviewing the day's Ideo on her new, superior MT-issue tablet, someone buzzed at the door.

'Come in!' called Claudia, wondering if it was one of her classmates. She and Pierce were known to be inseparable, so people didn't generally drop by. Also, people who wanted company hung out in one of the junior staff nodes, the gym or the canteen. Res quarters were for sleeping and down-time, and socialising in private spaces, while not forbidden, was generally discouraged. Also, junior quarters in particular were extremely compact.

It was Luke.

'Cadet-Trooper. We haven't spoken in a while and I thought I'd check in on you.'

Claudia leapt off the bunk and saluted, aware of being only in her undershorts and t-shirt. She'd showered after coming in from training and had no reason to get properly dressed again.

'At ease.' Luke looked around the unit. There wasn't much to see. 'I used to bunk with Pierce when we were kids, so I've never lived in a junior single.'

'It's better than living with Faye. Sir.'

'Tia says you're doing well.'

The last time they'd spoken, he'd told her Jemima was dead. The memory of that encounter set off a cascade of unsettling feelings. He looked at her, and she could tell that he was feeling the same.

'When will it wear off?' she asked. There was no need to explain.

'Maybe never,' he said. 'Do you want it to?'

She didn't know what to say, and he didn't seem to expect a reply.

'Claudia. One day, not too far off, Commodore Lloyd will summon you again. He'll ask you to do something that you'll hardly believe, something that goes against everything you've been taught. It's part of the reason you've been recruited, because you understand, and you can be trusted to do what is necessary. I saw this in you the night of Martin's party, and in interrogations. I saw more than you knew. I can't tell you anything more than that.'

She stared at him, utterly confused and a little scared.

'I might not see you again after that,' he said.

She wasn't completely surprised when he kissed her.

It felt just as it had during the final interrogation.

'Goodnight, Claudia,' he said, and left her.

It was a long time before she could get to sleep, and she was still asleep when Pierce came in, very early, at the end of his shift and slipped in beside her.

Thirty-seven

Pierce and Claudia were out riding on the Ring.

There hadn't been much time for riding lately, with the preparations for the 30th Anniversary and all the extra security detail. The opening ceremony was to be held in the Central Zone, in the main stadium, the following day, followed by a week of events, including top-level Games, and performances, matches and parades by the Junior and Senior League and Citizens' Brigades, as well as activities organised by Mentargh public relations units.

The Mentargh were deployed everywhere in the Dome on strict schedules. There had even been special training in positive citizen interaction, known as PCI or 'peacing', because some troopers had developed an unhelpfully antagonistic attitude towards civilians and needed reminding that their duty was, at least officially, to serve. Active repression only came into play in the rare cases of citizen defiance and resistance.

Claudia had learned how to ride a powerbike not long after her promotion. Since she'd been upgraded to her greys, she was allowed to take a bike out under the supervision of a full trooper. At quiet times, she and Pierce went out together. There was no surveillance on the Ring, and the only other people were MT units on regular patrols. It still felt odd for Claudia to see an MT patrol and get a nod and a wave instead of feeling guilty and fearful.

They'd ridden out as far as the A-Sector perimeter. Behind the residential blocks was the Recycling and Regeneration Depot, where sabotage had supposedly occurred all those months ago, and where Arnie had been due to start work as a trainee, quite possibly under the supervision of Neil.

If it wasn't for yours truly, that bloody Recycling Depot would've broken down a long time ago.

Where was Arnie now? Claudia's eyes moistened and she blinked hard, even though her visor was down, hiding her face.

Did Pierce ever think of Arnie? Since he'd told her about Arnie's arrest, in the blind spot by the Ed blocks, the subject had been closed between them. Some things couldn't be talked about, even in private. Protecting people from distressing or even dangerous information was a form of care, and Pierce cared about her.

A Transit shuttle pulled into the station and then moved out. A few people came down the stairs and filtered into the res area. Many people would be working through the opening ceremony, which would be relayed to workplace screens, as appropriate. The Dome would continue the myriad, mostly silent functions that ensured their survival. While much of this was automated and monitored by DOMUS, some human attendance was necessary throughout the cycle.

Everything seemed peaceful. Behind them, across the Ring, the lights of the Central Zone seemed brighter than usual.

Pierce flipped up his visor.

'I heard the Directorate authorised extra power usage as

part of the celebrations,' he said.

'It's an improvement,' said Claudia, putting up hers. 'From a distance.'

Up close, the increased lighting made the Dome look drabber.

As they looked across at the familiar landmarks, they both became aware of a sudden absence. In place of the red Power Station lights in D-Sector was an ominous chunk of darkness. It was as if a section of the sky was missing.

'What the freed?' said Pierce.

Their comms went off at the same time, an urgent summons to return to base.

'Is it them?' said Pierce. He stared at her, almost accusingly. 'Is this what they were planning all that time? This is freeding madness. They'll kill us all.'

'If I knew what they'd been planning, Luke would've seen it,' she said, her voice sharp. 'He went in deep enough.'

She snapped down her visor, restarted her bike and headed back towards the Central Zone without waiting for Pierce.

The last time she'd gone so fast, she'd been on the back of Luke's bike. But for the sweep of the headlight on the ground, the bike could have been flying through space. Pierce quickly caught up and rode parallel.

As they approached the Barracks entry, other riders flowed in around them. Instead of the usual banter, the atmosphere was tight and hard.

'What the freed's going on? Has there been an accident?' someone shouted.

'It has to be sabotage. There are procedures for breakdowns, they wouldn't call us all in,' said someone else, a lieutenant. 'Get your arses to the briefing hall, pronto. This is not a fucking drill.'

The Barracks was on full alert, the usual neutral lighting replaced by an eerie red glow. The briefing room was already overcrowded and people had to stand in the adjoining common room, their eyes fixed on the screens suspended from the ceiling. More troopers were arriving all the time. Every so often, the crowd parted to make way for another stern senior officer, some wearing insignia Claudia did not recognise. There were even some civilians, older people, in black rig, some consulting large tablets as they walked. One was a grey-haired man, an Oldie, although not the kind Claudia had ever seen before, in peak health and exuding a quiet, menacing authority, an authority she had always associated with Luke.

She hadn't seen any of these people before.

'It's the fucking Directorate,' someone said, and a shiver of fear, anticipation and excitement ran through the entire common room, like the shared buzz at a beat party when the music hit a certain phrase and geared up another level.

The Oldie's gaze lifted from his screen for the briefest moment. It landed on Claudia. A pair of startlingly blue eyes, almost transparent, fixed on hers. She felt as if her skull were made of glass. Instinctively, she pushed back and closed down, as she'd done with Luke.

The blue eyes narrowed. She looked away, and the Oldie was gone, ushered through the crowd by an escort of black-suited senior Mentargh officers.

Conjecture was flying about in the crowd.

'I heard there are subversives involved, a whole nest of them down in the basement,' said someone near Claudia and Pierce.

'Yeah, remember the two we caught a couple of months

back? The weird old guy with the brain-light and the kid with attitude, in the backup sector? Well, this is strictly off the record'—the speaker paused and lowered his voice, although everyone was now listening—'but they were trying to disable the emergency reactors.'

Arnie and Neil. If Claudia hadn't been held up on all sides by the press of people, she might've slid to the floor. She didn't dare look at Pierce.

People made exclamations of horror and outrage.

'But that's insane! Why the freed would they do that?'

'Why do subversives do anything? Because they're antisocial psychotic misfits.'

There were derisive murmurs of agreement.

'What I think,' continued the speaker importantly, 'is that they were connected to this lot. They weren't just carrying out random vandalism and sabotage, it was the first part of a plan. I reckon there's an organised group behind this trying to shut down the Dome's power.'

'For what? If they don't want to survive anymore, fair enough, free up resources for the rest of us, but don't take us with you.'

The screens all came alive and the room was suddenly silent.

Commodore Lloyd appeared, flanked by three other commodores. As the head of the MT, he had operational command.

In the background, just visible, was the Oldie with ice-blue eyes. It seemed to Claudia that he was really the one in charge.

'Troopers!' Lloyd saluted, and hundreds of hands went up in response. 'We are in an unprecedented situation, one that has not arisen in the thirty years we've lived in the Dome. A subversive cell has taken control of the Power

Station. A previous attempt to disable the emergency reactors was foiled and we have enough power capacity to continue in maintenance mode. All res sectors and non-essential functions have been put on minimum power. Citizens have been ordered to stay in place. The Transit is offline and comms have been shut down, except for the emergency civic messaging system. The MT system, of course, is separate.

'Teams have been in place around the Power Station since we were aware of the situation. The subversives have made certain demands, which, naturally, we will refuse, although we are going along with negotiations for the time being. Select teams will be deployed to force entry and regain control of the facility. In this state of emergency it is vital to prevent any kind of mass panic and unrest, and teams will be deployed throughout the Dome to contain the situation as it develops. The appropriate adjustments are being made to the water and air supply to ensure that the public mood remains optimised.

'The interception teams Alpha, Delta and Gamma are to report to muster point A immediately. Everyone else, your assignments will be up very shortly. Remember, survival is a team effort. I expect you all to do your best.'

With a brisk salute, Lloyd dismissed them.

People began to surge out as their unit numbers and muster points scrolled up.

Standing beside Claudia was Sal, a fellow second-class cadet. They'd done MT Basic together.

'This is our first biggie, hey?' she said, elbowing Claudia playfully. 'I'm really nervous, but it's also sort of exciting.'

Claudia thought of Martin and Davina and the others—Jim? Luma? Debs?—barricaded in the Power Station, awaiting the inevitable confrontation. Were they excited too, or were they afraid, perhaps already regretting what they had done, realising that nothing could change and that they would disappear anonymously like Arnie and Neil, expunged from society as cleanly and efficiently as bodies sent for composting?

'Hey, what's up? What's the matter?' Sal was keen, but she was also kind.

Claudia's response was as honest as she dared. 'It's just that … before I joined the MT, I used to know people, some free-spirit types. We were in Basic together, and the Senior League. They changed a lot. I tried to talk sense into them, but they just got angry with me. They were completely contaminated. It could even be them in the Power Station. If it is, I know they have to be neutralised as a threat to the efficient functioning of society, that it's all for the common good, but it still makes me sad. They weren't bad people. They used to be my friends.'

Sal squeezed her shoulder. 'I know how it is. Contamination is a tragedy, and it happens to the nicest, the most useful people. You can't always save them, however hard you try. Some people just won't be reached, even with the best mind-opening drugs, and it makes you want to cry.'

Sal was being trained as a counsellor-mentor, and her work already distressed her.

'You'll be alright,' said an older trooper, another woman, standing on the other side of Sal, a Level VI sub-lieutenant. 'Once you get out there and you find them, you know what you have to do, and you do it. But the first time's always hard, when they're your friends. That's when you know you're really a Mentargh.'

Claudia realised that she didn't know yet, and that she dreaded finding out.

Pierce was called up first. His unit was supporting the Gamma team.

His face was hard, a look she hadn't seen before. Martin had, she remembered. A dead-eyed stare. If he came face to face with Martin, he'd make the necessary choice.

'That's me,' he said. He gave her a quick, hard kiss, his focus elsewhere, and went off without looking back.

'He has to be like that,' said the sub-lieutenant, following her gaze. 'I see it all the time. Don't take it personally.'

'Oh, that's me,' said Sal, looking up at the board. She gave Claudia a brief hug. 'Good luck. Take care! See you for a drink later.'

'Good luck,' said Claudia, without knowing what she even meant by it.

Her unit was one of the last to be called up. They were assigned to the B-Sector Transit station. Unlike Pierce and Juanita, Claudia was marginal to the repressive apparatus of the Mentargh.

Down in the muster area, she saw troopers being kitted up in gear she'd never seen before: body armour, helmets, night vision headsets. As her unit's medic, going to pick up her MedAssist pack, she saw a stack of body bags. The medic in front of her seemed to hesitate.

'Don't be coy, it's a maximum-force operation,' barked Commander Jane, the MT chief medic.

The medic took several. From the corner of her eye, Claudia saw her join a unit that was preparing to move off, all of them on powerbikes. Pierce was among them. She almost didn't recognise him in his helmet.

'Take at least one, Trooper,' said Commander Jane and winked. 'You never know, someone in your unit might get lucky.'

She took one. Heading back to her unit, she overheard one trooper asking another, 'What do these freeders even want?'

'I heard they're asking for democracy.'

'What the freed is that?'

'Fucked if I know. Some Old World shit?'

'Obviously it was a great idea that worked really, really well.'

Waves of powerbikes began to move out of the hangar. Claudia had no idea there were so many Mentargh. Where had they all come from?

Claudia's unit were ready to move out, and then their leader, a sub-lieutenant, was beeped on his commlink.

'What the freed?' He stared at Claudia as if seeing her properly for the first time. 'A summons, for you. Commodore Lloyd. In the briefing room.'

Everyone turned to look at Claudia with a new and disturbing curiosity.

'We're not going to wait for you. Catch up with us later.'

Claudia was still wearing her MedAssist pack as she returned to the main building.

What could Lloyd want from her at such a critical moment? Luke had seen everything.

The Commodore was sitting at the table at the far end. He was alone.

Claudia saluted and stood waiting. She hadn't seen Lloyd since her promotion. There had been no need.

He spoke slowly and deliberately.

'The people—the subversives—that we're going to flush out of the Power Station are people you know. I think you've already guessed that, Claudia.'

His use of her name without her rank seemed oddly

intimate.

'I didn't know what they were planning,' she said. 'They never shared it with me. They never trusted me.'

'I believe you, Claudia. We knew about them long before your sessions with Luke,' said Lloyd. 'I've been keeping an eye on my old friend Jim for years. We haven't spoken for a very long time. I believe he's taken up with a rather nice woman who bakes off-menu biscuits. In different circumstances, we could still be friends.'

Someone came up beside her. It was Pierce, still wearing his body armour but carrying his helmet. In combat rig, he looked bigger and not his usual self. He seemed bewildered and slightly truculent.

'I'm sorry to pull you out of the first major operation of your career,' said Lloyd. 'I'm aware how hard you've been training for this kind of thing, along with your colleagues. Thanks to the efficient functioning of society, our elite troopers don't often get a chance to put their skills to use.'

Claudia glanced at Pierce. He was staring at Lloyd.

'You said I was in the clear!'

'You were in the clear. But I've received further information that complicates the situation for you both. This information has come through Elliot, not Luke, which means I can't be seen to ignore it.'

'Elliot?' Pierce was incredulous. 'That … drone?'

'You should've been nicer to Ally,' said Lloyd. 'Both of you. Innocuous little Ally! I know friendships can change a lot at your age, and in different circumstances, you could've drifted apart, found your own level, without repercussions. You both should have been wiser, considering what she knew. She kept it all to herself for almost a year. If it had got out another way, she'd have been a suspect herself, for not reporting your little expedition and encounter immediately.'

'But why did she tell Elliot, and why now?' Pierce demanded. 'That kind of thing should go straight to Luke.'

'If she'd gone to Luke, we wouldn't have a problem,' said Lloyd. 'Pillow talk, I assume. An encounter with Claudia in the canteen was the final humiliation, it seems. She was very upset.'

'He leaves bruises on her!' said Claudia. She was struggling to decipher what Lloyd was saying about Luke. 'I told her she shouldn't put up with it.'

'Well, it's not as if she could have what she really wanted, is it?' Lloyd raised an eyebrow. 'And we have a further problem. Pierce, your second, Byrne, has proved more observant than required, in your case. You knew that Claudia, Martin and Arnie were regularly visiting the Underground and associating with the subversives after that first expedition. You warned them not to, but you did not report them. He also witnessed your interaction with Claudia in a known dead spot.'

'Maybe we were having a private moment,' said Pierce heatedly.

'A private moment! Really, Trooper. There's no such thing. You should know better. Byrne also recently witnessed Claudia having a long and apparently intense conversation with Martin and Davina in another dead spot.'

'I didn't know about that,' said Pierce. He shot an angry glance at Claudia.

'Davina reacted badly to my promotion,' said Claudia. 'Martin stopped her from killing me. We also had some words about her grandfather.'

Lloyd raised his hand. 'I believe you. The substance of your conversation is not the issue. The problem is that Byrne and Ally have both connected you with the group involved in the current emergency. You are both implicated. I've been put in a difficult position. I can't silo this information any longer without drawing doubts upon myself. The situation at the higher administrative levels has become … unsettled.'

'You're going to arrest us? On the basis of that?' said Pierce.

Claudia's knees almost gave way. She'd thought she was finally safe, inside the Mentargh.

'Once the subversives are contained and interrogated fully, your connection will become clear in any case,' said Lloyd. His gaze became disconcertingly intense. 'Tell me, do you believe in what your old friends are doing in the Power Station?'

'They're trying to kill us! Of course not,' said Pierce.

'They want to abolish the Ideo and change things,' said Claudia. 'They want less control, the freedom for everyone to make their own choices. But we can't have that. Even if you did what they wanted, which I know you won't, all they'd achieve would be to jeopardise the equilibrium. We need the Ideo to survive in the Dome.'

'Answered like a good Ideo student. As I expected,' said Lloyd. 'They're demanding democracy and the free play of creativity, which, they declare, is vital to human survival.'

'That's true,' said Claudia, or perhaps Jemima was still inside her head. 'But it's not enough.'

Pierce looked at her, shocked.

Lloyd seemed strangely sympathetic. 'You came to that conclusion even sooner than I expected, Claudia. Well done. But you did have some help.'

'From who? You never said anything,' said Pierce.

'I told Arnie, and he was horrified,' said Claudia. 'He was almost scared of me. Davina and Martin thought I was crazy.'

'Even subversives are horrified by the truth. That's how well we've been indoctrinated. I had nightmares when I first realised,' said Lloyd.

'Realised what?' There was a violent edge to Pierce's voice.

'Tell him, Claudia. I know what Jemima Winston told you, and so does Luke.'

She turned to Pierce, who was staring at her as if she were a stranger.

'As long as we stay in the Dome, we have to abide by the Ideo to survive. But even that's finite. The 99% renewability is a lie. The Dome is not fully sustainable. Eventually we'll need external input.'

'And?' prompted Lloyd.

'It means that we'll need to go Outside.' Claudia said this calmly. She no longer cared about consequences.

'What the fuck?' Pierce almost screamed. 'A crazy old woman said we have to go Outside?'

'Some members of the Directorate, who knew the professor, believed, as she did, that there was a chance that there were habitable zones Outside, or even that the planet had begun to regenerate. At the very least, we could refresh our environment. The Dome has done us very well, possibly better than its builders could have imagined, without external repairs or supplies, for three decades. It's getting old and tired. It can't go on forever.

'These ideas were not popular, and those who held them were, shall we say, neutralised,' said Lloyd. 'But others kept coming to the same conclusion and became better at concealing themselves.'

'You're telling me you're a subversive? But you're the Mentargh commodore!' Pierce seemed suddenly lost, as if his whole life had been exposed as a lie.

'No need to shout,' said Lloyd, with a tiny smile, although the briefing room was completely soundproof and secure. 'If you want to put it that way, although I don't think I have much in common with your old friends in the Power Station. Democracy sounds all very nice in theory, but in practice it was so often a mess, and very corruptible. Creativity is another matter. It'll be a shame if we have to wipe Neil. The old bugger is quite the genius, and we need more of that. A pity he wouldn't work with us.'

'What are you going to do with us?' said Claudia. She had no more secrets to share. Perhaps Lloyd had no further use for her.

'But I do have a use for you,' he said. 'It's not just the Power Station that's down. Neil has also compromised the DOMUS surveillance network. That's how they got into the Power Station to begin with. We've been keeping track of things through the MT web, but it's not the same. That information has been kept locked down, for obvious reasons.'

All those screens she'd seen in Luke's office, the massive data drawn from millions of cameras and sensors—it was all offline.

'So that's why the entire MT is deployed all over the Dome,' said Pierce. 'You're almost working blind. If something went wrong, you could lose control entirely.'

Lloyd nodded. 'Of course, our best teams are working flat-out to restore it. So we need to hurry, to take the opportunity while it lasts.'

'You want us to … take a look?' said Claudia. 'Outside?'

'The approach to the exit is heavily monitored, in usual circumstances, and nobody can get anywhere near it,' said Lloyd. 'For the moment, the way is clear. Attention will be on the Power Station. Nobody will notice two troopers taking up a new position, and once you're down there, you'll be on your own, until DOMUS is live again, and the system will send out an automatic alert for your arrest, because you have no authorisation to approach the Barrier Zone. Breaking the seal is the ultimate crime against the Dome. Perhaps you were part of the plan all along. A shame, two such promising young troopers.'

'And what if it's dead out there, and we're fried in an instant?' said Pierce.

'We'll reseal the door with you on the Outside and that'll be that,' said Lloyd. 'The Dome will be as good as it gets, while it lasts. This is the golden future, already. Do you really want to live with that knowledge? Without any hope? Dying of boredom? The old girl was right about that.'

'I'll do it,' said Claudia.

'Do I have a choice?' said Pierce.

'Not really,' said Lloyd. 'Think of it as your last service to the Dome. You're doing your duty right to the end, a loyal citizen and trooper.'

He looked at his tablet. 'The Power Station is very secure, but they're making progress. You need to hurry.'

He gave them their instructions in the same clinical manner as he would've ordered the capture of Arnie and Neil.

'The vital thing is to open the main door. I'll be there with the first interception troops, who will be fully equipped to deal with a breach event. An elite squad, especially trained to protect the Dome's integrity, although we haven't had to deploy them for a long time. Pierce, you won't need your body armour or weapons. They'll only slow you down.'

The common room was completely empty now. Nobody saw them leave through the bike hangar. They moved quickly, not talking. Talk would only expand to fill the sudden chasm between them, draining all the energy they needed for what was to come. There was no time to share fear or grief, or even to realise such superfluous emotions. They moved with a quiet urgency, their thoughts dominated by a single object: to reach the final airlock door and open the seal. Beyond that, there was nothing.

The original entry point to the Dome was accessed through the Underground. The air became staler the further down they went. They had to use the stairs because there was no power for the lifts. Claudia was glad of Pierce's navigational sense and his memory for verbal instructions. After all, he was an elite MT trooper. She knew he was being fast-tracked, like Luke had been, but really, she'd had no idea.

Reaching the level for ground access, they came to a locked entryway, large enough for the vehicles Claudia had seen on her first visit to the Underground and in the bike hangar. She pressed in the code and the door slowly slid aside, moaning and squealing. The air that came out was fetid, and they both gagged.

'Freed, did they leave bodies down here?' said Pierce, coughing. 'Do we need the masks?'

Lloyd had told them to take oxygen masks on the way out. Claudia checked her air-quality meter.

'No, it's fine at the moment, but I'll keep checking.'

This was the way to the surface. Faye and Lloyd had come this way as children; Neil, Lisa, Jim, Lily and Jemima Winston as adults. Nobody had been here for thirty years. Claudia was momentarily overcome remembering the noise, the stink, the crying, the fear: not her memories but Jemima's.

She shook herself back to the present and closed the door behind them.

The passage sloped up gradually. Claudia had lost track of how long they'd been walking, in silence, when the lights suddenly came on, two parallel lines of narrow tubes that reached all the way back to the previous door.

'We won't have much time now, if the power's back on,' said Pierce.

They broke into a jog, coming to another door, and into a large antechamber. Piles of stuff were heaped around: ragged textiles that used to be clothes, portable storage units with broken handles and tiny wheels, various receptacles, two-wheeled contraptions hung with circles of perished rubber, small plastic or fabric figurines representing people or now-extinct animals.

'For freed's sake. Claudia, look.'

Even among all the discarded junk of the Exodus, it was clearly recognisable: a wire basket with four small wheels.

'A freeding shopping trolley!'

And there were others. There were old shopping trolleys parked everywhere.

Claudia began to laugh and cry at the same time. Pierce reached out and squeezed her hand.

'Come on, we're almost there,' he said, sounding like himself again.

Together they approached the final airlock door, a massive circular contraption. Bolted to the wall were two plastic-framed notices: *Airlock Procedure* and *Quarantine Regulations:*

NovaGaia Biodome Authority/SRAE Corporation. Both were dated January 2048.

Claudia was working the keypad when the passage behind them was suddenly filled with shouting.

'Claudia, hurry!' Pierce was ready to turn the wheel.

There was a whine and a loud click as the first airlock door released.

'We're through,' said Claudia, almost disbelieving, and Pierce gave her a fierce, final kiss.

In front of them the second airlock door was slowly opening. A red light began to flash and a klaxon went off, signalling that the other door had not been closed.

The shouts became shrieks.

Holding hands, they waited to see what lay Outside.

The light. The brilliant, blinding light. Dazzled by its glare, they stood half-frightened, half-hypnotised, feeling its alien warmth on their cold faces. Air currents rushed around them, buffeting their bodies and filling them with a strange exhilaration. With childlike wonder they reached out, oblivious to the voices and the sound of running feet behind them.

The Archives Project

Book Two of *The Survivor Covenant*

The shocking events of the Thirtieth Anniversary have challenged the equilibrium of the Dome. Alone and haunted by a past she can't remember, Claudia is relegated to the top-secret Archives Project. Her new friends are other system rejects who, like her, have been wiped and recycled.

To regain her memories and learn what really happened on the Anniversary, Claudia has to trust someone she's always feared.

For the Dome community to survive, things have to change, but the system has to change too, and forces in the powerful Directorate are pushing back.

But change is coming all the same. Betrayed and angry, what price will Claudia pay to know the full truth?

Available at Amazon and other online retailers: https://book s2read.com/jilldobsonthearchivesproject

For updates on *The Survivor Covenant* series and my writing, please sign up for my newsletter at http://tinyurl.com/jilldobsonwriter

*

If you enjoyed *The Inheritors*, please leave an online review so that other readers can find it.

Also by Jill Dobson

Time to Go (1988) (YA coming of age)

Danny, flamboyant and fragile, is a promising ballet dancer. Her stoical friend Laura is a talented musician. Two very different girls on the verge of adulthood dream of escaping 1980s country-town Australia.

A Journey to Distant Mountains (2001) (YA fantasy)

Inspired by old stories, Princess Atlanta rejects an arranged marriage and runs away in search of adventure. She befriends the mysterious traveller Orrin and discovers a world beset by portents, on the brink of chaos.

These are currently out of print. Information on new editions will be posted on jilldobsonwriter.com.

Acknowledgements

Heartfelt thanks to my beta readers Caroline Baptie, Sarah Bos, Chris Harding and Michael Nest for their comments. Thanks also to members of the Alliance of Independent Authors (ALLi) for their advice to a first-time indie author.

And thank you to my first editor, the late Barbara Ker Wilson, who pulled the original (typewritten) manuscript of *The Inheritors* from the slush pile back in 1986 and published it as one of the early titles on the University of Queensland's Young Adult Fiction list.

Author photo by Julie Broadfoot.

About the Author

Born in Yorkshire, Jill Dobson grew up in country Australia and now lives in Glasgow, after stints in Melbourne, London, Moscow, Edinburgh and Tokyo. *The Inheritors*, her first novel, was written during her last years of school. It was originally published by the University of Queensland Press in 1988, followed by *Time To Go* (1991) and *A Journey to Distant Mountains* (2001). This new edition of *The Inheritors* is the first in a five-part series, *The Survivor Covenant*.

You can find me online at https://jilldobsonwriter.com

For updates on my writing, please subscribe to my newsletter: http://tinyurl.com/jilldobsonwriter.